Deep Dark Secrets

Joy Ann Ribar

Ten16 Press
ten16press.com - Waukesha, WI

Deep Dark Secrets
Copyrighted © 2019 Joy Ann Ribar
ISBN 978-1-64538-034-4
Library of Congress Control Number: 2019940144
First Edition

Deep Dark Secrets
by Joy Ann Ribar

For information, please contact:

Ten16 Press
ten16press.com
Waukesha, WI

Edited by Kaitlyn Hein
Cover design by Tom Heffron

For Mom - Delilas, who taught me that once you're a mother, you're a mother forever. Who showed me what devotion looks like through her love. Who taught me gritty perseverance amid the storms of life. You have inspired my best decisions, and always will.

Chapter 1

"Nothing is as tedious as the limping days,
When snowdrifts yearly cover all the ways,
And ennui, sour fruit of incurious gloom,
Assumes control of fate's immortal loom"
– Charles Baudelaire, Paris Spleen

Frankie loaded the last few boxes of donations for the Valentine Jubilee into her salt-stained blue SUV. She wondered when the frigid temperatures might break so she could stop by the Wonder Wash and get the much-needed washing her SUV craved. January in Deep Lakes had thus far been a grim affair with temperatures in the single digits and below zero wind chills blowing from the town's three lakes. On days when the sun came out, generating sparkles off the white snows and icy pine boughs, it gave the impression of warmth, but looks were deceiving - temps hadn't been above 15 degrees for weeks. Oh well, another Wisconsin winter - typical, Frankie thought. Still, she gave a disappointing look at her SUV, trying to remember what color it was under the salty grime as she climbed in and headed down Granite Street. She passed her shop, Bubble and Bake, with a quick wave to Carmen, her dear friend and co-worker, who was finishing the weekly shopping list before heading down to Madison, where most of Frankie's suppliers were located. Bubble and Bake was a cleverly combined business - bakery by day and wine bar by night. It was hard for Frankie to believe she had been in business almost five years now. Since it was Monday, the shop was closed to reset for the week ahead. With the Christmas holidays over, January was the time to log inventory and come up with new ideas to bring in customers when the town came back to life in spring. Inventory - that's what Frankie was supposed to be focused on this week and maybe now she could, after boxing up items she could live without and donate to a community event.

Heading East on Highway 76, she turned right on Pine Tree Avenue, mentally checking today's To Do List in her head as she slowed down for the driveway into the First Congregational Church. Frankie was a self-proclaimed champion list-maker, figuring she had to have something to keep her busy life organized since she couldn't afford a personal assistant. The thought of having a personal assistant made her laugh out loud and shake her bobbed mop of red-brown hair. At 40-something, Frankie Champagne was wildly independent, having raised two daughters by herself after her husband, Rick Davidson, bailed and disappeared for over a year. Rick, a long-haul trucker, eventually returned to Deep Lakes with divorce papers so he could follow a different dream (her name was Mary Sue, a horse woman from Wyoming). Frankie had already adapted to the life of a single mother long before Rick left her, as long-haul trucking didn't leave a lot of time for family. Still, Frankie hated the idea that the father of her children left all of them - not just her - and she did everything in her power to be both parents to the girls. Only now did she realize that was never possible as she worked two, sometimes three, jobs to keep them fed, clothed, and sheltered. So, hiring a personal assistant was something someone with a lot more wealth and a lot less resourcefulness would do.

As Frankie entered the First Congregational Church driveway, she passed a black sedan speeding out the other side. She recognized the driver as Nan Kilpatrick, who had a less-than-happy countenance. I wonder what's up with Nan and why she's in such a hurry, Frankie thought. The Kilpatricks were members of Frankie's Catholic church, St. Anthony's, further down Pine Tree Avenue, but the Deep Lakes citizens joined forces for multiple community events, regardless of one's denomination, or lack-thereof. Maybe Nan had been dropping off items for the Jubilee raffle, as Frankie did every year, even before she owned her business. A little goodwill goes a long way in any small community and besides, it made Frankie feel good. She received support from many community members as a single mom and it felt satisfying to give something back.

The First Congregational Church building was a

one-level building with brick trim that had been built about 20 years earlier when Pastor Johnson, the long serving minister, had built up the congregation to over 300 members. When Pastor Johnson passed away three years ago, the whole community felt the loss. He was well-liked, a man with a big heart and an easy laugh. An avid storyteller, he filled every room he walked into with his larger-than-life presence. The church council moved quickly to fill the Pastor's vacancy in hopes of healing the broken hearts of the congregation. The new minister was Pastor Bradford Rawlins, in his mid-30's, who lacked the fatherly personality of Pastor Johnson and ran the church more like a business than a family operation. Granted, filling Pastor Johnson's shoes was a daunting task, but still, you'd have to look far and wide to find two men who were more different. Many of the members decided to leave, choosing from the several other churches Deep Lakes offered, or going to another town, anywhere from 10 to 20 miles in any direction.

Rumors circulated for months that the church was having trouble meeting its financial obligations. Whether those rumors were true or not, Frankie didn't know and didn't care all that much. However, when the church decided to relaunch the Valentine Jubilee with a fancy-dress dinner and dance, many members of the community thought it was a wonderful idea to combat the cold winter blahs that settle into town after the holidays end. Part of the Jubilee included a raffle, so the church advertised in the local newspaper, inviting anyone to contribute items worth raffling. Frankie put together three baskets of leftover items from her eclectic merchandise that didn't sell before the new year, added a bottle of her own crafted wine to each basket (she hoped that was okay with the Congregationalists, after all, her church didn't frown on alcohol), and was dropping them off today before January got away from her. The Jubilee was February 10th, just before Valentine's Day, and she knew the church volunteers would have a lot to organize to be ready on time.

The parking lot was empty except for one lone car, which she assumed belonged to Patsy Long, the church secretary. Monday is always a slow day for any church, and she assumed Patsy was only there today because the Jubilee was just a couple of weeks away. Frankie parked under the carport for easy unloading, left her SUV running, and popped the hatch. She could only carry one box at a time since each basket of donated items was already dolled up with colorful shredded curly papers and a raffia bow. She grabbed the first box, opened one of the double doors and stepped inside the foyer. She could hear a woman's voice on the phone from the front office and quietly stepped over the threshold of the open office door in time to hear Patsy Long's disbelieving tone, "Why, that just can't be true! Oh no!" Following a few muffled words possibly mixed with tears, "Well, who should I call? What do you think I should do? Okay. Alright Officer, I'll see you in a little while then." Patsy's red cheeks and teary eyes looked up at Frankie.

"I'm so sorry to intrude. Is everything okay?", Frankie asked. Patsy was clearly in shock and though she didn't know Frankie well, Frankie was the first person to whom she could share the grim news.

"That was the police," Patsy said. "Pastor Rawlins is dead. They found him . . . I mean, oh my gosh, I don't know what to do."

Frankie patted Patsy's hand. "Why don't you sit down, and we'll figure out what to do next," she offered. "Who's the head of the church council? I think you should call him or her." Patsy nodded slowly but didn't stop staring straight ahead. Frankie sprang into action, looking beyond Patsy's desk to the Pastor's office. One might say Frankie was nosy, but she would argue that she was just extraordinarily observant. She spied the pastor's rolodex on his desk, picked it up and brought it out to Patsy. "How many members are on the council? I can help you call them," Frankie offered.

"Yes," Patsy said, "that would be very nice of you. Thank you." Patsy rifled through the rolodex with shaking fingers, located the names of the seven members and handed three of them to Frankie.

"Is it alright if I use the phone in the pastor's office?" Frankie asked. The idea that the office would no longer be used by Pastor Rawlins started a stream of tears from Patsy that turned into shocked body-shaking sobs.

Frankie was at a loss. "Here, Patsy. I'll take the names and numbers. Why don't you take a break? Maybe use the restroom or make yourself some tea. Or just rest. I can fix you some tea after I make the calls."

Frankie walked into Pastor Rawlins' office and began the unpleasant business of notifying the council members their pastor of less than two years was dead. She had no details to offer any of them but asked them to come to the church to help their secretary, who was not handling the situation well at all. Frankie's calls were met with disbelief - at least from the five members she was able to reach. She had work numbers for the other two but didn't want to deliver that kind of news at a workplace, so opted to let the other council members pick up the task later. The council President, Dave Kilpatrick, was a respected businessman in Deep Lakes and would surely be the one to take charge of the situation - Frankie was glad she had found him at home.

Now it was time to attend to Patsy, whom she found sitting on a high-back stool in the church kitchen at the counter, still staring off in the distance and wringing her hands. Frankie patted her shoulder and busied herself making some chamomile tea, which she located in one of the cupboards. Patsy began to calm a little so Frankie ventured, "What happened, Patsy?" Patsy didn't know except that Pastor Rawlins was ice fishing on the lake and there had been an accident. The police were coming to the church to speak to her and the council members.

So many questions ran through Frankie's curious brain. What kind of accident could it be? With the extreme cold temperatures, the ice on all three lakes was frozen thick. Frankie had seen several shanties set up the past three weeks and most of the seasoned fishermen had driven their vehicles out on the ice as well. It couldn't be a case of falling through the ice, could it? She assumed Pastor Rawlins was in church Sunday so, unless he went out fishing after church, death from exposure didn't seem likely. Patsy called it an accident and exposure didn't seem to qualify as accidental. Maybe he got hit by a vehicle driving on the ice? That would be weird and unlikely. There probably wouldn't be anyone out fishing today. The lakes were loaded with people on the weekends, but Mondays were slow days for recreation and the temp today was still hovering at a biting 6 degrees. Why go out fishing today, she wondered? But of course, Monday is a weekend day for a pastor. Then another thought - was Pastor Rawlins alone? Who found him?

Frankie needed an excuse to hang around the church a little longer, so she could hear more when the police arrived. Her focus returned to Patsy, a woman she barely knew. Assessing her current condition, Frankie suspected Patsy was slowly coming back to reality. She had regained a little pink in her flat cheeks, but her light-colored eyes were bloodshot and still lost. Patsy must be in her early 30's, Frankie guessed, fitting into the generation between Frankie's and her own daughters'. Patsy had a mousy appearance, downcast eyes, a pancake-flat face with a short stub of a nose and straight light brown hair, parted in the center, hanging over her shoulders. Even though the church office was technically closed, Patsy wore a mid-knee length plaid skirt with a black cable-knit bulky sweater. If Frankie had to use one word to describe Patsy, she'd say "dutiful". Suddenly, she remembered her SUV was still running in the carport and she had only brought in one box for the raffle. Here was the perfect diversion. "Patsy, you don't need to do anything, but can you tell me where to put the raffle items? I want to finish unloading my car if that's ok with you."

Patsy nodded and took Frankie down a hallway past the church kitchen to a door near the back exit of the church. "This is the storage room where all the raffle donations are for now. You can bring them back here if you don't mind," Patsy smiled weakly. First, Frankie decided to move her car in case the police wanted to park in the carport area, so she parked next to Patsy then made a slow process of bringing in the boxes and placing them in the storage area. As she finished up, she heard multiple voices in the foyer.

The council members had arrived and were all talking at once. Frankie knew them, at least by name or face. Deep Lakes had a population of about 10,000, but eventually everyone had pretty much bumped into everyone at some time or place. Since Frankie ran in several social circles, she had a large collection of acquaintances. She recognized Wade Benson as one of her regular customers at Bubble and Bake - he was a sourdough bread and semi-sweet red wine man - and beyond his bakery and wine preferences, he was the Vice President of the Deep Lakes Savings and Loan Bank. Wade Benson looked dour and stern today, his round face and balding head accentuated by frowning, perplexed wrinkles - not a man thinking about sourdough and red wine. Karen Kurtz, a younger woman, had volunteered at the local library summer program with Frankie last August. She had two little boys who were rascals to corral but had endeared themselves to Frankie by gobbling up the baked goodies Frankie brought to story time. Karen, her long blonde hair in an untidy ponytail popped up on top of her head with a pink hair tie, looked tired and Frankie wondered who was watching the little boys if she was here, or maybe they were in Kindergarten? The third member was a tall elderly man stooped from age, or maybe from long-term physical labor. Frankie didn't know him, but he was dressed in overalls and smelled distinctly of farm life - not vile by any means, but earthy all the same. Mr. Overalls sat down on one of the chairs in the foyer and Frankie noticed he wore work boots that had seen some field muck.

Dave Kilpatrick was there as well and gave Frankie a quizzical look, and if Frankie had to qualify the look, she would say Dave was not pleased she was there. Well, Frankie was an outsider after all and this occasion called for a members-only discussion. Frankie didn't know Dave well, although his parents, Nan and Roger, were members of her church St. Anthony's. But Dave had married Glenda six or so years ago, and she was a life-long Congregationalist, not from Deep Lakes; Dave had converted to her religion. Frankie remembered that Glenda and Dave were no longer together, she had left town just a few - was it weeks or months ago? Nobody seemed to know the real story, and most people were too polite to ask questions, preferring to speculate or garner bits and pieces from local gossips. Dave was talking in quiet conversation with Milton Conway, another council member and Deep Lakes businessman. Milton owned Conway Quality Printing, just outside of town on Highway 5 and, if memory served, Frankie recalled Glenda Kilpatrick being an employee there. The two businessmen were turned away from the others, speaking too low to be heard, but Frankie noticed that Milton Conway was visibly shaken by the news, whereas Dave was the face of calm seriousness.

The others were all talking at once, mostly asking questions, and Patsy returned to her former state of tearful shock and helplessness. Frankie knew she either had to leave or say something - she opted for the latter, something that often got her in hot water. "Hello. Sorry to intrude, but I was here dropping off raffle items when Patsy got the phone call from the police." They all stared at her as if she just sprouted a unicorn horn in the middle of her head. So, what? Frankie read their minds - what further business do you have here now? None she knew of so she better go.

Karen processed her words first. "Oh, how awful, Francine." This was Frankie's more formal name used by those who didn't know her well, or by her mother when she was out of her good graces. "It's good you were here with Patsy though." Patsy gave a tearful nod which at least confirmed that Frankie had provided some comfort to her.

Mr. Overalls looked up impatiently, "Well, when are the cops gettin' here anyway?" Dave Kilpatrick threw Mr. O a dirty look in return but didn't have time to add any thoughts to that look as the door opened, and Officer Baxter of the Whitman County Sheriff's Department walked in and surveyed the scene. Officer Baxter was a new recruit and didn't know anyone in Deep Lakes too well yet. After the briefest of introductions, Baxter ushered the five Congregationalists toward the cafeteria to provide what information he could. Frankie didn't know what to do next. She clearly wasn't a council member, or even a congregation member, and had no business parading to the cafeteria with the others. Instead, she walked halfway down the hall with them to more suspicious looks from Dave Kilpatrick and the officer, then ducked into the ladies' restroom where she stood looking in the mirror. Could she hear any of their conversation from in here? Not likely with the automatic fan going. She decided to turn the light off and see if she could catch any information at all in the next minute or two. Then she'd have no choice but to leave. Baxter was speaking softly (darn him anyway) but thankfully, Karen and Patsy both reacted to the details Baxter provided. "An ice auger? But how?" That was Patsy's stunned voice.

More muffled conversation, then Karen wailed, "He bled to death? How awful! My God!"

That was Frankie's cue to slip out of the bathroom as quickly and quietly as possible. She sped into the foyer and noticed the rolodex still on Patsy's desk. "Better put this back where it was in case the police need to search Pastor Rawlins' office," she thought. Grabbing the rolodex, Frankie set it back in its place when she noticed a torn scrap of paper from the Pastor's desk calendar. On it was today's date with a partial name "patrick, 8 a.m., important" - underlined twice. Frankie knew better than to take the calendar page, but she snapped a picture of it with her cell phone and ran out the double doors, her mind still racing. An ice auger and bled to death - was Pastor Rawlins murdered or was this just an accident? She knew at least two ways to begin finding out.

Cruising back into the business district, Frankie surveyed the quietness of a Wisconsin winter day in her community, known for bustling tourism during the warmer weather. Autumn still attracted tourists to Deep Lakes, thanks to luscious fall foliage of yellows, oranges, and reds from surrounding Birch, Oak, Maple, and

Tamarack trees. The city made the most of the season, sponsoring pumpkin patch festivals and Halloween fun fare, progressing to November's deer hunting season with Chili Suppers for hunters and craft fairs for the hunters' widows, and wrapping up the year with Christmas events of multiple varieties. At this time of the year, the city turned into a Brigadoon of sorts, as if surrounded by a peaceful slumber, covered in a cloak of gray and white.

Most of the businesses remained opened during winter, many with shortened hours of operation, managing to eke out a living until spring arrived. The smarter ones followed the examples of squirrels in the fall, stashing away anything extra earned during the busy season to stay afloat during the sparse winter months. Frankie was one of the smarter ones, having the wise guidance of her successful oldest brother, James, who had a vested interest in her financial well-being having loaned money to Frankie for her ventures.

Turning back onto the long stretch of the main drag, Meriwether Street, Frankie noticed several locals parked at Dixie's Diner, a breakfast mainstay in town, and a hotbed of local gossip. Frankie was sure that Dixie's would be the first place to hear about Pastor Rawlins' death and begin kindling all kinds of rumors about it. A few buildings further, Frankie spotted Henrietta Munroe, setting out a sign in front of her salon, Henrietta's House of Hair, advertising discounts on tanning packages. Any locals planning winter vacations somewhere sunny were likely to get a little tan on their milky white hides before heading South. Henrietta looked like she could use a suntan herself, Frankie thought, taking in the tower of platinum blonde curls, piled like a wedding cake atop her head. Henrietta's fair face, decorated with bright cherry red lipstick, false black eyelashes resembling hairbrush bristles, and vibrant blue eyeshadow up to her brows, was like a movie marquee announcing a sleazy feature film. To think Frankie's mother still went to Henrietta to have her hair done was beyond Frankie, who favored a younger, subtler hairdresser, Janie Wheeler, owner of Mane Tamers on Jefferson. Henrietta's saving grace was that she listened to Frankie's mother when it came to her preferences, or Peggy Champagne would no longer be a customer there.

The rest of downtown was all but empty, nobody on the streets and few businesses opened on Monday to entice customers. Nearing the intersection of Granite Street, where Bubble and Bake presented the other half of its face, Frankie saw lights on at Karlsens' Wisconsin Specialty store, a local and tourist favorite for all things Wisconsin - the best cheeses, savory sausage sticks, bratwurst, local honey and jams, maple syrup from nearby sugarbushes and, nine months out of the year, creamy custard ice creams. Frankie saw Lew and Julia Karlsen taking down a leftover Christmas display, probably working on inventory as she should be doing herself.

Everything looked so normal and undisturbed, as it

should, Frankie thought, except that nothing was normal now. A violent death, or so Frankie surmised, would soon awaken her hibernating town, dirtying the whiteness of winter, lighting up Deep Lakes with fiery rumors - changing the peaceful landscape.

Chapter 2

"Blow, blow, thou winter wind.
Thou art not so unkind, as man's ingratitude."
– William Shakespeare

It was almost 10 o'clock by now and Frankie surmised that many townspeople already knew about the death on the lake. Because she didn't know which of the three lakes Pastor Rawlins was fishing on, she couldn't just go cruising down Lake Road hoping to find the right spot. Deep Lakes included three lakes in a long chain - Lake Hope on the south end, Lake Joy on the north end, and smack dab in the middle - Lake Loki. Frankie assumed the long-bearded fur trappers of the area must have had a sense of humor to place Loki, the Norse demon trickster and god-stalker, between Hope and Joy but figured it was actually quite logical. Wasn't life just like that - hope and joy as bookends with sorrow, suffering, twists and turns in between? She set aside her musing to turn left onto LaFollette Street and travel to the end of the block where the ugly concrete structure that housed *The Whitman Daily Watch* was located.

Maybe Frankie was biased about the "ugly" description

of the building. Formerly, the county newspaper was located downtown on the main drag - at the corner of Granite and Jefferson Streets, where it made its home for over 100 years. The old paper, named *The Whitman Warbler*, gave Frankie her first professional job. After finally earning her Communications degree from UW-Madison, Frankie's then husband Rick wanted to move back to their hometown, away from the larger city of Madison and away from the higher cost of living. Frankie was already pregnant with Sophie but wanted to make use of her degree in some way. The *Warbler's* owners, Howard and Helen Waters, hired Frankie part-time to work at the front desk answering the phone and collecting ads, photos, and articles dropped off by area residents, not at all what Frankie had in mind when she thought of journalism. Frankie worked there five years under the old-fashioned conservative ways of Howard and Helen, who shied away from any controversy or conflict. The newspaper was more like a newsletter, comprised mostly of scrapbook-worthy items such as school events, and community festivities. Of course, the paper provided plenty of space for social whatnot: *Mr. and Mrs. Spurgeon held a dinner party with guests from Milwaukee and Chicago last week.*

Frankie was serious about journalism. She had studied its rich and sometimes tawdry history at college and possessed a strong fondness for Edward R. Murrow - a pioneer broadcaster who brought truth to America through his groundbreaking series on McCarthyism, which helped bring the Red Scare to an end. Frankie could be an idealist about certain things. She saw journalism as a necessity in society, keeping a fragile democracy in balance through objective reporting, even when that reporting might topple the mighty. She too wanted to use her Comm Degree to make a difference, but when she tried to do some "down and dirty" investigative reporting, her articles were always edited, chopped to pieces, then left out altogether with the excuse of there not being enough space this issue. She privately and jokingly referred to the entire paper as "watered" down by the Waters. Frankie was grateful for one thing though - her small writings gained the attention of Dickens and Probst, a law firm in Gibson, where she was offered a full-time job with benefits, writing legal correspondence of all kinds. It wasn't journalism, but it paid the bills. And after Rick disappeared, she needed the money to support her household and her girls.

Anyway, when Howard suffered a massive heart attack and passed away three years ago, Helen sold the newspaper in 6 months and moved to Florida to live with her sister. Frankie always knew that Helen wasn't interested in the importance of the newspaper as a community fixture, but only her partnership with her husband, so she wasn't surprised at the quick sale. The paper was purchased by a real journalist who wanted to make it more than just community picnics and school photos. Abe Arnold had been an editor in both Green

Bay and LaCrosse, but wanted to own his own daily. He closed up the small office downtown and moved the paper to the old jail building on LaFollette. He renamed the *Warbler* something more serious and fitting and hired two part-time male reporters to cover the whole of Whitman County. Well, in Frankie's opinion, the so-called reporters were Abe Arnold's lapdogs, hired because they were easily controlled by Abe. Anytime Frankie saw them in action, covering a meeting or community event, she observed a fumbling awkwardness. Rance Musgrove, whom Frankie jokingly referred to as Rancid Muskrat, due to allergies that always left him squinting and sniffing, like a rat nosing around trash, was incapable of making eye contact with anyone. Few people treated him with much respect; it didn't help much that he looked like he was still in puberty with a boyish 1950's haircut, high thin nasal voice, and 5' 4" stature. Topping it off, Musgrove had the demeanor of a hyper chihuahua, making it impossible for him to conduct interviews with any comportment. Not that he'd have the chance to take on any gritty assignments - Abe did all the serious work himself. Frankie decided the other reporter, Barty Gouge bore the appearance of a Shar-Pei. Encased in puffy cheeks, his eyes were barely visible, yet a high forehead advertised bushy eyebrows much darker than the rest of his comb-over. Completing the Shar-Pei look, his neck was overlapped with several folds of chin. He must have fooled many a carnival con-artist in the "Guess Your Age" booth;

Gouge could have been 25 or 45: nobody knew for certain.

In the *Warbler's* days, Howard and Helen covered the county by themselves, relying on local officials to bring in articles about school board, county board, and city council meetings. Frankie knew this did not represent real journalism, but the county politicians supported the paper whole-heartedly, since they controlled its content in full. One can only imagine the flack Abe Arnold took in transforming the *Warbler* into the *Watch*. All meetings were now covered by his trained lapdogs, who took copious notes and who didn't sift through the facts to make them palatable to the politicians or business owners. Real issues and concerns were brought into the light and Abe Arnold had made some enemies, but a number of other citizens, Frankie included, welcomed the change, believing an honest paper made the community stronger.

Frankie introduced herself to Abe shortly after the paper changed hands and shared her journalism background with him, stating she would like to be considered for any extra reporting assignments. But despite being on cordial enough terms with the owner, she concluded she lacked the male parts needed to get into his club. Abe was a man's man - old fashioned and in his late 50's, part of a tradition where men did hard reporting and women submitted gardening articles and recipes. Still, Frankie submitted a few feature pieces here and there about raising grapes and crafting wine - this was good business after all. Eventually, she answered an ad from the *Point Press*, a bigger city daily, who hired her as an "occasional" reporter. Larger newspapers couldn't cover every small town in Wisconsin so they relied on "stringers", who could submit articles on the chance they might get published. Since stringers were paid by the published article, the newspaper wasn't out much money. Frankie figured it was better than nothing and satisfied her craving to write whenever possible. With all the irons she had in her fire, possible was not often.

Frankie wasn't sure if Abe would be willing to share much information with her about the pastor's death, but she was hoping she could just get an exact location for starters. Luckily, the paper's front desk receptionist, Chelsey Mathis, informed Frankie that Abe wasn't in. He was out covering a story. Frankie knew Chelsey most of her life as Sophie's best friend who spent many days and nights at Frankie's house. She was like another daughter to Frankie in many ways and she knew she could use their familiarity to get information if she needed to (even though Frankie didn't like to use manipulation on anyone she truly cared for).

"Can I help you with anything, Ms. Champagne," Chelsey offered with the same friendly perkiness she always showed.

Frankie hesitated. "Well, I suppose you heard about Pastor Rawlins…" Frankie began. Chesley didn't even let Frankie finish.

"Yes, it's terrible, isn't it? That's where Mr. Arnold is

right now, at the scene to get the scoop," Chelsey had an eager look in her eyes. Frankie was thinking that Chelsey might make a good reporter someday; she had the fiery attitude for it, but she was going to have to learn how to be discreet.

"Can you tell me where the scene is, Chelsey? I'd like to see for myself," Frankie was being truthful.

"We-elll," Chelsey stammered. She must have been told she wasn't supposed to give out that information. Abe liked to sell newspapers and didn't want anybody getting in his way when he was working a story.

"I'm just going to drive by," Frankie said. "Mr. Arnold won't even know I'm there." Frankie wasn't sure if the truth had just taken a left turn or not - she honestly didn't know what her plan was.

"Ok, I guess. It's on Lake Loki, just a little past Dane's Landing. Please don't tell anyone you heard this from me." Frankie assured Chelsey her lips were sealed but didn't think it would matter much anyway. Bad news travels fast in a small town and with the many folks who owned police scanners, she was sure half the town probably knew already.

Onward. Frankie tooled to the end of LaFollette and back toward the main drag of town, but veered off to the Lake Road - a lovely pastoral drive any time of the year, lined with pines and hardwood trees on the left side, and sparkling miles of lake views on the right. Lake Road attracted tourists and locals alike with its miles of bike and walking trails, wildlife sanctuaries, glorious sunsets, and lucent navy-blue waters. The three lakes, along with the two rivers, were the lifeblood of the community, especially in the spring, summer and autumn, when resorts and campgrounds were open, expanding the city's population ten-fold. For visitors and residents alike, the attraction to the beauty of water was fierce. But today, that attraction was deadly and Frankie sobered thinking about Pastor Rawlins. Even though he was a transplant, he obviously mattered to many of her fellow Deep Lakers and she wanted to learn what she could about his demise.

After passing Lake Joy, she continued south, watching for the small brown sign that pointed out "Dane's Landing". Named after Hogar Dane, the original surveyor of Lake Loki in the late 1800's, the landing was one of the many spots along Lake Road where eager water babies could launch boats of all kinds. She began to slow as she passed the large blue sign announcing Lake Loki. With the lakeshore in its winter bareness, Frankie was able to spot what she imagined was the accident scene as parked cars lined the shoulder ahead and the lake area below was a hubbub of activity. Choosing a safe spot on the shoulder, Frankie parked and pulled out the pair of extra winter boots she kept on the floor of the backseat for a good six months out of the year. Taking winter weather seriously is part of life in Wisconsin, and every smart traveler needs an emergency stash in their vehicle. Frankie's included extra boots, snowmobile mittens, a heavy wool-lined sleeping bag that had been her father's from Boy Scout days, a first-aid kit, jumper cables, a heavy-duty flashlight, and of course, emergency chocolate bars! She even had a flare gun because you just never know - she didn't want to be at the mercy of a stranger if she didn't have to. Her black boots had ice traction spikes and she made a quick change from her insufficient gym shoes, so she could navigate the short but rocky descent to the lake.

The day was cold - a booger day indeed. Frankie smiled inside at the childhood memory of naming all days cold enough to instantly freeze the inside of one's nose "booger days". The air was sharp enough but there was little to no wind, maybe that's why a few of the hardier breed ventured out to fish today. An ambulance was on the ice along with two county squad cars and a gray F250 pick-up belonging to the coroner. People at the scene were congregated by one ice shanty wrapped in a brown-poly tarp, although there were several other similar-looking shanties in the area. Frankie spotted Abe Arnold talking with one of the officers and she was grateful to see Sheriff Alonzo Goodman, separate from the others, speaking with the coroner. A long line of tell-tale yellow police tape wrapped around a couple of poles marked off the scene. She dodged the left-side of the shanty where Abe was taking notes and made her way to the right where the sheriff was standing. Frankie knew the ambulance lights were only on as a safety beacon so other fishermen and the nosy onlookers would keep their distance. She imagined Pastor Rawlins' body was loaded in the ambulance to take a short trip to the County morgue; in fact, it appeared the coroner was wrapping up his conversation and heading to his truck.

Garrett Iverson was coroner for all of Whitman County, but this was hardly a full-time position; he did electrical work on the side. Not a bad combination - both jobs required digging around in dark places with precision, dexterity, and caution. Garrett turned toward Frankie, giving her a disarming smile. "How's it going today, Miss Francine? What brings you out here on this brutal day?" Frankie didn't know Garrett Iverson well. He had been coroner for maybe 3 years and their paths had crossed a few times professionally and socially at some community events. She knew he was from Green Bay and had a good reputation both as coroner and electrician. He was handsome in an unobvious way, a little on the rugged side with over-the-collar dark hair sporting a few silver streaks. His brown eyes reminded her of melted caramel, which was his most noticeable feature, mesmerizing Frankie into a dreamworld. Oh my, could she actually be attracted to this man? Garrett was friendly, but that didn't mean he was flirting, or was he? Frankie wasn't batting above average in the opposite sex department - there had been no man in her life for years. Well, it couldn't hurt to be nice to this man, could it?

"Hi Mr. Iverson. I'm trying to get some information about the accident, um for the newspaper." When Garrett pointed his head in the direction of Abe Arnold, Frankie quickly added, "Oh, the Point Press paper, not our local one."

Garrett raised one eyebrow, "I see. First off, please call me Garrett. Mr. Iverson is my dad and I may not be a youngster anymore, but I don't fancy myself an oldster either."

Frankie laughed at his comment. "Okay, Garrett it is then. What can you tell me?"

Garrett looked at the frowning face of Sheriff Goodman and decided, "Not much, I'm afraid. You'll have to talk to the sheriff." Frankie wasn't surprised - Alonzo ran a tight ship and he was in an elected position.

"Well, okay, bye then," Frankie said, but seemed to be rooted to the spot, unable to shift her gaze from those warm brown eyes. How lame was she, unable to come up with anything clever to say to Garrett to continue their conversation or to follow up her question with something that would gain her some fact to walk away with. Geesh, she felt like a girl.

She turned back toward the shanty and Alonzo Goodman, getting the wind's full force right in her face. Nothing like a wintry wind on a frozen lake to keep a person alert. He met her halfway, clearly maneuvering her away from the yellow taped off scene. "Hey Lon," Frankie gave him a little wave. They had been friends since high school and had an easy relationship. She had mentored Lon through many attempts at starting romances with girls, but none seemed to work out the way he wanted them to and the poor guy had remained a bachelor to this day. But then Frankie's track record wasn't any better. Lon had been the best man in her wedding, but he chose sides after Frankie and Rick split and Rick never spoke to him again.

"Frankie, what in Sam Hill are you doing here?" Lon was all sheriff today. This wasn't going to be easy after all.

"Come on, Lon. I'm covering for the *Point Press*. Just looking for some information to report," Frankie was trying to sound professional yet informal at the same time. Alonzo looked down at her at least a full foot, took off his ranger hat, thumped it against his leg and ran his fingers through his cropped hair. He was clearly stressed out and uncomfortable, and now Frankie wanted to know exactly why that was. "Come on, Sheriff. I'm not going to step on your toes. But please let me do my job," Frankie coaxed.

Frankie used the Notes app on her phone to tap down the facts. The time of death was uncertain until the autopsy report came back. So, there would be an autopsy? Frankie wondered if this was standard procedure in a freak accident. The pastor was discovered by the Larson brothers, Tim and Troy, on the way out to their shanty about 50 feet from the pastor's. The shanty door was open, and they saw the body on the ice inside and a lot of blood. Tim called 911 while Troy, a volunteer fireman, checked vital signs. What time was this? Around 8:15. Cause of death?

Alonzo hesitated. "Ok... and this is not for publication, Frankie. Unofficially, he bled out from the main artery in his left leg, after it was pierced by the ice auger."

Frankie shuddered a little. "How can an ice auger do that? I mean, isn't there a safety feature or something to shut it off if it starts jerking around when it's not drilling ice?"

Alonzo looked at the ice under his feet. "Can't answer that until we look at this particular auger."

Frankie pressed on: "Any witnesses?"

Alonzo was getting annoyed now. "You're cheesing me off, Francine. We just started investigating for Pete's sake. Of course, we're looking for witnesses."

Frankie took it down a notch. "Sorry, Lon. You know you're good at what you do. Would it be ok if I looked inside the shanty?" The irritation rose from Alonzo's collar up his neck.

"Why?" he wanted to know.

"I just want a photo," she blurted quickly, "I'm not going to print it until I get your permission." Not a good enough explanation for the sheriff today. Alonzo told her she could take a photo from this side of the yellow tape.

"My people are trying to gather evidence, Frankie. You should understand this." Frankie expressed a fast thanks and walked over to the tape, as close as she could get with the best view of the shanty's interior. It was hard to imagine so much blood but there was nowhere for it to go except down the fishing holes inside the shanty, and

with today's frosty temperatures, the blood was sticking
to the ice surfaces.

Surveying all she could, she snapped a few photos
with her phone but knew that the bright outside light
and the darker interior of the shanty wouldn't produce
anything with much detail. The blowing wind didn't
help either as she struggled to keep her long scarf out
of the camera lens. She reopened her phone notes and
jotted down what she saw. The newly built ice-shanty was
crafted from plywood that still looked unweathered with
a bench on each side, and bare ice down the middle where
two holes had been drilled out. The holes looked wide
enough and ready for fishing. On the benches she saw a
portable coffee mug and thermos, a brown paper lunch
bag, a small tackle box with jigs, line, swivel heads, a fish
bucket, a small container (possibly minnows), a ladle, and
two poles ready to go. Since the shanty was likely 4 by
8 feet, the ice floor was a narrow space, just big enough
for a couple holes and the dead body of Pastor Rawlins.
Not to mention the blood that looked like someone had
tipped over a gallon or more of cherry slurpy. Frankie
shuddered, envisioning the Pastor's body lying askew
there. She wished she could get a closer look inside. Her
gaze shifted to the outside. Nothing special to see - a
narrow door with a window and the brown poly tarp -
both looked new. A small snow shovel leaned against the
outside wall of the shanty and right next to it was…huh?
Frankie saw what looked like a large blood smear on the

ice. How could that be when Pastor Rawlins was inside the shanty?

Continuing to gawk at the smear and trying to get an angle with her phone that would capture a clear image, she saw a shadow cross in front of her. "Can I help you, Ma'am?" Questioned the irritating voice of the new hot-shot officer Pflug, Frankie's adversary for reasons she wasn't quite clear about.

"Good morning, Officer Pflug," Frankie attempted to sound amiable but the officer's name coming out of her mouth made it seem like she needed to cough up some phlegm. Pflug wasn't in the amiable mood.

"There's an investigation going on here and you're in the way, Mrs. Champagne." Frankie was not a *Mrs. anything* – Champagne was her maiden name, the name she reclaimed following her divorce. Pflug had been on the force for just a few months, though, so maybe he didn't know better. However, the two already had a couple memorable encounters. "Sheriff Goodman said I could take photos of the shanty as long as I stay behind the tape," Frankie used her most "I told you so" voice. Pflug didn't budge and clearly didn't agree with his boss's decision.

"Take one more photo and move on, Ma'am," Pflug uttered sternly as he crossed under the yellow tape toward Officer Shirley Lazaar (a part-timer who came out of retirement from the Chicago PD after working on the force for 30 years). Shirley was inside the shanty, putting items into plastic evidence bags as Pflug appeared to be looking over her shoulder to make sure she did it correctly.

"What a pompous jerk," Frankie mumbled. This was her third confrontation with Donovan Pflug in the few months he had been on the county force. Due to budget cuts in Deep Lakes, the city staffed a skeleton police crew, consisting of a chief and two patrolmen. The city opted instead to contract with the county to handle most police matters and since Deep Lakes was the county seat, Whitman officers usually got the calls. Her first meeting with Pflug occurred after one of the Bubble and Bake patrons had imbibed a little too much and fallen off the picnic table on the back balcony, where she had apparently been doing a little dance. She wasn't seriously injured, but had prompted a 911 call followed by a first responder and Officer Pflug to file a report. Pflug had made the accident out to be Frankie's fault for lack of supervision and/or possibly negligence in over-serving the woman. It happened on a summer Saturday night when the wine bar was filled with tourists and Frankie was understaffed after two servers had called in to say they wouldn't be there. If that wasn't enough, Pflug also insisted on an inspection of the back balcony for possible safety code violations. Thankfully, the balcony passed inspection and the woman's negligence outweighed Frankie's liability. Still, Frankie had to phone in a favor to her old bosses at Dickens and Probst in case of a lawsuit.

The second incident had happened just before Halloween when a large Rottweiler was running loose downtown and had tangled one paw in Frankie's garden fence behind Bubble and Bake. Busybody Bonnie Fleisner, who managed the Fleisner's hardware store around the corner from the wine bar, called the County Sheriff's department, complaining about "some beastly dog running amuck that was owned by Francine Champagne." How unfortunate that the responding officer was again Donovan Pflug. Frankie told Pflug she had never seen the dog around town until now and had no idea how it had become tangled up in her garden fence. Although, she suspected the Rott had been on a happy romp led by a neighborly black squirrel that often chowed down on Frankie's birdseed from the numerous feeders behind the shop. Pflug didn't seem to know how to handle the situation - he was clearly out of his element and afraid of the Rottweiler. Frankie sympathized - strange dogs were unpredictable, and this one was afraid and unhappy, not a safe combination. It was Frankie who suggested calling the local shelter/animal rescue unit, that sent one of its volunteers who had a way with dogs. Nearly an hour later, the Rottweiler was muzzled and freed from the fence, loaded into the rescue van and hopefully on its way to its owner or some other happy home.

Instead of being grateful for Frankie's assistance and cooperation, Pflug began a stream of demanding questions about why Mrs. Fleisner would have stated the dog belonged to Frankie. Pushing Frankie too hard was like pushing a bull - eventually the perpetrator is going to get the horns. Feeling backed up against a wall, Frankie, in her most assertive tone, suggested that Pflug "stop harassing me and go ask Bonnie Fleisner yourself." Next time Frankie saw Alonzo, she told him about Pflug and said she would appreciate it if some other officer could be sent for any future run-ins she might have with the law. Alonzo had laughed about it but knew full-well that Frankie could be a handful if crossed.

Now Frankie made a production out of packing up her phone in her shoulder bag, putting on her gloves and rewrapping her long woolen scarf under the hood of her parka. She watched as Pflug joined Alonzo, the EMT's, and a few fishing regulars some fifty feet away toward the middle of the lake. They were conversing easily, their words obliterated by the wind, but they had taken their attention from the scene. It was now or never, Frankie decided, as she moved as far left of the shanty toward the shoreline as possible and snuck under the police tape. She was right next to the blood smear - it didn't look like a footprint of any kind, just a distinct streaky smear, a couple of feet in length. How did it get here? Nobody in their right mind would believe the victim made that smear. She poked her head in the shanty. "Shirley Lazaar," Frankie knew Shirley as a customer at the wine shop. She loved bubbly - mostly Moscato, and pink was her favorite. She and her husband, Tony, a retired railroad worker in the Chicago rail yard, had moved to Deep Lakes for a quieter life. They had purchased tickets for Bubble and

Bake's upcoming Valentine's event, "Romantic Getaway" slated for February 17th. Shirley turned around.

"Oh, hello Francine. What do you need?" Shirley was a good officer, who had seen almost everything working in Chicago. She had to prove herself to earn an investigating officer's post, and that had made her gritty and efficient. Frankie knew better than to come into the shanty - from the amount of blood on the ice this was clearly where the action had taken place and there wasn't much room inside. The benches could seat four fishermen, but four people couldn't stand at the same time on the narrow ice floor. Shirley cleared her throat in Frankie's direction.

"Oh, well I'm putting together an article for the Point Press, so I just wanted to look at the shanty. I won't come in. Is that okay with you?" Frankie sounded her most professional.

"Suit yourself ,but you can't come in here and no photos of the inside. Got it?" Frankie noticed blood around both evenly drilled holes but no new details from her earlier view made from the other side of the tape. Except, she caught her breath sharply as she saw blood spatter across the ceiling. Shirley turned around, "You okay?" she asked. Frankie nodded absently and continued looking more closely at the benches and walls, as her eyes adjusted from the outer glare to the darker interior. Was that a streak of blood on the left bench? It certainly looked like it, but she wasn't going to bother asking a question she knew wouldn't be answered.

"What do you think happened here, Shirley?" Frankie ventured.

"Humph, not sure but it looks like it could be a messy business," Shirley commented. "Sorry, Frankie, call me in a few days when I can tell you more on the record."

Frankie backed away, scuttled back under the tape just in time to see both Pflug and Alonzo scowling in her direction. She turned her head toward shore, scrambled as quickly as the snowy rocks allowed her to, and started walking back to her SUV, grateful the wind was no longer a direct hit.

"Hey! Hey Francine Champagne!" It was Abe Arnold. Frankie turned to face him. "Are you trying to scoop me or what's going on here?" Abe asked. He seemed more amused than concerned. Frankie held onto her poker face.

"Just garnering some facts, Abe." She turned back toward the SUV, climbed in and headed back to the wine shop and home.

Chapter 3

"Conscience is a man's compass."
- Vincent Van Gogh

Still Monday and just past noon, but so much was running through Frankie's head from her tumultuous morning. Frankie's stomach was growling; how long had it been since breakfast? Too long, she decided, heading to the large refrigerator in the Bubble and Bake kitchen where the weekend leftovers could be found. Not much to be had since Frankie cut back on the menu in Winter to save money. She found some leftover Spinach Quiche though - not her favorite but it would due in a pinch. She grabbed a grapefruit, sectioned it after cutting it in half, then slid onto a chair in the kitchen, invisible from the outer world. Silently contemplating her options, Frankie still questioned why she felt the need to write an article about a dead pastor she didn't know. What was the angle here? The freak accident with the ice auger might be one of macabre human interest, or maybe a cautionary tale. Was it the piece of paper from the pastor's desk that bothered her? She already knew the answer to that. Something kept gnawing away at her about that note and she just convinced herself it was somehow connected. So, who was the "Patrick" Pastor Rawlins was supposed to meet at 8 a.m. today - the same day and time he happened to lose his life?

A thought occurred to Frankie and she hopped off the chair to head to the little office area behind the wine lounge in the shop. Crossing through the cozy seating area, she smiled at the lovely scent of cinnamon, balsam, pear and cloves - her chosen aromatherapy scent for the past few weeks. Frankie had read up on the art of hygge, a Danish practice of living cozy, and it influenced all aspects of ambience at the wine shop. Pleasing aromas were part of the hygge practice, but because she also served food items and was sensitive to individuals with allergies, Frankie only used the aroma diffusers during off hours. She grabbed the local phone book from the office shelf and returned to the kitchen when suddenly she remembered something else from the accident scene. A scent - vanilla and floral, and maybe citrus - she had smelled it clearly when she poked her head in the shanty door. Frankie was so surprised by this unexpected smell, she had looked around for the tell-tale cardboard tree announcing itself. Why would an ice shanty have an air freshener? She made a note to herself to ask Shirley Lazaar about that when she called her later in the week.

For now, Frankie busied herself looking up names in the local phonebook - names with "Patrick" in them. When she was finished, she had a small list of people she thought she could personally chat with. First there was Dave Kilpatrick - he was the church council president. He could provide a logical explanation about the calendar note - just a simple council matter he needed to discuss with Pastor Rawlins. Then Frankie remembered that Dave's mother, Nan Kilpatrick, was burning rubber out of the church parking lot that morning. Frankie should talk to her too. There were also the Fitzpatrick brothers, two residents she expected helped Pastor Rawlins set up the ice shanty and get him rigged for fishing.

Joe Fitzpatrick, an avid fisherman, was a long-time friend of Frankie's father, Charlie. In the summer, he ran a fishing guide service on all three lakes with his brother, Dan, who lives in Pike Junction, one town over to the north. Maybe the pastor was meeting one of the brothers that morning to help him set up the shanty and drill the fishing holes. Frankie knew she would be able to easily acquire that information. Joe had a soft spot for Charlie's daughter, and even at 40-something, Frankie would forever be viewed as the little girl Joe and Charlie took fishing. Frankie decided that was enough interviews for now. She still had a business to run and a Valentine event to prepare for. Her business cohort, Carmen, should be back in a couple of hours from shopping at the food suppliers, and Frankie needed to get her rear in gear and get some baking done or Carmen would wonder just what she had been doing all morning.

Not only was baking another form of therapy for

Frankie, it also filled the shop with more yummy smells that drew in customers. In the Winter months, most of the baking would be done on Thursday and Friday for the weekend when business was brisk. For a Tuesday, she would only need a few offerings for breakfast pick-up, along with any orders that needed to be filled. Luckily for tomorrow, there were no orders. She took out the pie crust dough she had made Saturday (she liked to rest her dough for a minimum of 24 hours) and began rolling out small circles for hand pies. Carmen would bring some kind of berries, if available, and they could make a second batch of hand pies later that week. Today she combined pears, apples and raisins with cinnamon, ginger, nutmeg, and anise for a hearty spicy fruit pie filling. After plopping big spoonfuls onto the circles, she crimped the edges together, applied an egg wash, and sprinkled the tops with coarse sugar. She then set them to bake on cookie sheets.

She cleaned up while they baked, thinking about what kind of cookies she wanted to make for the weekend, when the shop door swung open and Carmen flew into the kitchen, her arms full.

"Smells really good in here," Carmen said, then frowned a bit, as she noticed the empty counters, bereft of already-baked goods. "Slow start today, Frankie, or what?" Carmen tried to sound tough. The two had known each other practically their whole lives. Carmen and her large family lived one street over with the narrow Blackbird River flowing between them. Both girls had lived in the river during the summer months and often met in the water to play together, making up adventures, pretending to be Tom Sawyer and Huck Finn. Frankie had been invited many times to eat lunch at Carmen's house, which was always full to the brim with not only her eight siblings but countless aunts, uncles, and cousins, most of them speaking Spanish. Carmen's grandparents lived in Mexico and her parents had begun their adult life as migrant workers, following crops from Texas to the north, then south again as summer turned to autumn. Eventually, Carmen's father, Diego, was offered a manager's job at the commercial farm and canning factory outside Deep Lakes, which meant the family made the town their permanent home. Her parents were now retired and relocated to Texas to live near other family members. Most of Carmen's siblings lived in Texas and Florida but Carmen had fallen for a local, Ryan O'Connor; twenty years later, they were still happily married with teenage twin boys, Kyle and Carlos, a beautiful Irish-Mexican mix. Carmen had kept her maiden name "Martinez" to honor the parents and the heritage she loved so much. Frankie trusted Carmen implicitly and the two were straightforward in all matters, both personal and business.

"I'm sorry, Carmie," Frankie said. "This morning didn't quite turn out as planned." She frowned.

"Oh, oh," Carmen said. "I know that look Frankie Champagne. Spill it. Right now." Frankie sat back down in the kitchen chair, but Carmen shook one finger at her.

"Nope, you have to talk while we work," she said. "Help me unload the supplies, check off the inventory and then we can both bake together." Carmen was practical and knew that Frankie could get sidetracked. Today multi-tasking was essential. The details of the morning flowed as supplies were assessed. Carmen had scored some gleaming, fragrant strawberries from California, so it was decided a strawberry cream cheese coffee cake was in order, along with croissants for the Tuesday morning customers. Carmen crossed herself as Frankie told of Pastor Rawlins' sudden demise. "Dios mio," Carmen said, advising Frankie, "maybe you should stay out of this. You don't have anything at stake in this, Frankie. Could be trouble for you." Again, one floured Carmen finger pointed at Frankie's chest.

"Well, Carmen. I have the time right now to at least put a decent story together for the *Point Press*," Frankie was making excuses.

Carmen just shook her head. "You're going to do what you're going to do, as always," Carmen said, but smiled at Frankie all the same. The late afternoon shadows were closing in around the daylight and Carmen was ready to head home to help her husband with the evening chores on their sheep farm. "See you tomorrow morning. I'll be here at 6," she said.

"Good night, Carmen. Say hi to all your boys," Frankie called. She was so grateful to have Carmen as a business partner. Level-headed, frugal, creative - Carmen was someone Frankie could always count on. And of course, she might be right about not getting too far into the details of the pastor's death. But, Frankie dismissed that thought immediately, convincing herself this could be the journalism break she'd always longed for.

Frankie hung her baking apron on one kitchen hook then bent over to give some loving strokes to Brambles, the guest cat for the next few weeks at the shop. Frankie and Carmen had agreed to help the local vet, Dr. Sadie Chastain, by fostering stray cats that had been dumped at the vet clinic. Dr. Sadie would clean them up and one or two at a time, they became temporary wine shop greeters and snugglers, until someone adopted them permanently. Brambles, a young male cream and black-striped mixture, was both gallant and social. He had arrived right after the new year and Frankie didn't think he'd stay past Valentine's Day. "Somebody is going to love you for a Valentine's present," Frankie cooed. It was times like this she missed having someone special in her life. She was happy but knew, with two adult daughters who only needed her occasionally, there was a small empty space that advertised for an occupant. Her mind quickly switched gears from that melancholy thought. "I think I need to go back to that accident scene before dark," Frankie thought, knowing but pushing aside the idea that this could be the wrong move.

Back in the SUV, Frankie turned from Granite to Meriwether, out to Highway 76 and left onto Lake Road.

She arrived quickly, knowing there was limited daylight to guide her. The lake was all but empty now and the cold temperature was dropping rapidly, but thankfully the bitter wind had dissipated. She parked closer this time, right next to the landing and walked down the steps that led to the lake. The squad cars were gone but the yellow tape remained, although it seemed nobody was posted to keep people away. Was that fact going to justify Frankie's decision to go inside the shanty?

The little imaginary fireflies danced on Frankie's shoulder, constantly part of her daily self-examination. The one on the right had just spoken, urging her to get back into her vehicle and leave: she wore white, glimmered an angelic gold, and had the voice of her mother.

The one on her left dressed as a pirate, spoke like Antonio Banderas and Frankie found him irresistible much of the time. "Go on, Frankie. Get what you came for and go home," the pirate firefly said. Why they were fireflies instead of an angel and devil, Frankie would never know. She had been fascinated by fireflies from her first memory of watching them in the dark of a sultry summer night in her backyard. The fireflies were part of a childhood memory stew that included sparklers, pink lemonade, the scary game of "Ghost in the Graveyard" and an older cute neighborhood boy, a friend of her brother Nick.

Hesitation gone, she walked with conviction to the shanty, looking down at the ice to keep her footing. What blood remained had frozen in the frigid temperature but she sidestepped those areas anyway. She turned on the flashlight she remembered to bring from the SUV, so she could get a clearer look inside. All the items Frankie had listed were now gone - bagged as evidence she was sure. She beamed upward at the blood spatter, then over to the left at the blood mark on the bench. She inched closer, careful not to disturb anything that still might be evidence. She even had the wherewithal to tuck her hair inside the hood of her parka, pulled the hood tight and tied it with the drawstring so as not to leave a stray hair behind. Yes, she was pretty sure the mark on the bench was blood but why such a defined mark, she didn't know. Unless the pastor had stumbled after being stabbed by the auger. She shone the light up and down the ice floor, looking for marks from the auger. If the pastor was drilling and the auger went astray, wouldn't there be stab marks or gouges in the ice as he lost control of the drill? She didn't see any. She could still faintly smell the vanilla-something scent and found that odd, but scanning the walls and ceiling for any hanging air freshener was to no avail. As her beam scanned the floor again, she saw something bobbing in one of the ice holes. Carefully bending over, Frankie reached into the hole and picked it up with one gloved hand, thinking it was probably a jig and not wanting to get an unruly hook in her hand. When she brought it into the light beam, she saw it was a shiny silver cap from some kind of bottle. Still wearing her gloves, she stuck it in her coat pocket, as the mother firefly tsked her. She was just about to leave when her beam flashed on the corner of the doorframe. Something dark was sticking out of the corner , or maybe it was part of the tarp wrapping. She bent down and shined the flashlight. Tugging on the corner, she pulled out a dark blue business card with white and gold lettering. The card was from a Milwaukee law firm. She stuffed the card in her coat pocket. Now that she had stolen two items of possible evidence, it was definitely time to get out of here. Even the pirate firefly was urging her off the ice.

Enough for one very long Monday, Frankie headed home - the apartment above the wine shop beckoning her for a hot shower, pajamas, and maybe an old movie. Going through the shop's entrance, she bent over, picked up Brambles the purring furball, and headed up the apartment stairs, breaking her cardinal rule that guest cats never leave the shop. She needed some extra company tonight and Brambles would have to be just that.

Chapter 4

"Be like Curious George, start with a question
and look under the yellow hat to find what's there."
– James Collins

Despite Frankie's best efforts, sleep was not a long-term visitor, at 3:30 a.m. she surrendered. She climbed out of her warm bed and pulled on slippers, drawing a low meow from Brambles, who opened one wary eye and inquired what the heck she was up to, disturbing his deep slumber. "Sorry kitty," Frankie whispered. Padding down the steps to the shop, Frankie figured she might just as well get a head start on the order for the Library Board and Friends bi-monthly meeting. This month's order was for two dozen Butterhorns, half with nuts, and half without. Frankie would triple her batches, so she could sell some at the shop Wednesday. Butterhorns, with their yeasty dough and cinnamon sugar filling, were divine triangles of scrumptiousness rolled up and curled into crescents, then glazed and sprinkled with walnuts. They always sold out in a hurry when she made them for the shop, and since they were time-consuming to prepare, Frankie always tripled any order she got for them to make it worth her while. She snapped the light on in the kitchen and made a mental list of items to gather. But first, coffee. Call her a snob but Frankie insisted on having a professional coffee brewer for both regular and fancy coffees, even though she only sold the regular stuff from large carafes to her customers. She was a small business and didn't have time or money to hire another employee just to make lattes and cappuccinos, but that didn't mean she and her co-workers couldn't imbibe in some.

Latte in hand with an extra creamy meringue-like topping, Frankie thought about what she should do today after the customer surge was over by 9ish. She knew she had to give up the items she discovered at yesterday's unauthorized excursion to the ice shanty, deciding the best person to relinquish them to would be Shirley Lazaar, and not her buddy Alonzo. As a fill-in officer, Shirley had less to lose than Alonzo, whose every action could come under public scrutiny as well as the prying eyes of Donovan Pflug. It wasn't fair for Frankie to rely on Alonzo's friendship to keep her out of trouble when what she did was wrong, and probably illegal. Apparently, the mother/angel firefly couldn't sleep either and was now reprimanding Frankie.

By 5:30, the Butterhorns were in the oven with three more sheets waiting. Frankie made the filling and icing while the dough rose, then looked through her recipes for Wednesday's display case. Wednesday was usually muffin day, an easy day of baking for Frankie, especially since

Carmen worked a few hours so she could help Ryan out on the farm. Frankie decided she would call Shirley to see if she could arrange a private meeting, then she would pay a visit to Joe Fitzpatrick to see what he knew about the ice-fishing Pastor Rawlins. After that, if time permitted, she planned a stop at the Kilpatrick insurance agency on Meriwether Street, hoping for an outside chance that Dave would discuss the pastor.

The delightful aroma of baking sugar, cinnamon, and buttery dough permeated the shop as Carmen walked into the kitchen. "Wow, I'm impressed, Frankie. What time did you clock in this morning anyway?" Carmen asked. Frankie's smile was tired as she handed her friend a latte with a little vanilla sugar spun in.

"Couldn't sleep," she said. Brambles paraded into the kitchen like a prince, demanding in tiny but insistent meows that he needed some breakfast now. Carmen filled his bowl, poured fresh water into his dish, and asked Frankie what her plan was for the day.

When Frankie announced she would call the sheriff's office to turn in the possible evidence she'd purloined from the scene, Carmen huffed but gave her a thumbs up. "You better," she said.

Frankie didn't tell her the rest of her plans though. The next couple of hours flew by as the shop opened to waiting customers at 7, attended by Frankie while Carmen finished icing the Butterhorns and made a big batch of Cherry Almond muffins with some of the frozen

Door County cherries they always kept in stock. The two had decided to use local and regional products as much as possible in the shop, and both looked for a reason to visit the beautiful peninsula of Door County, which was like a piece of New England in Wisconsin. Cherry picking season was in July, and the short trees made for easy harvesting, but when they couldn't get there to pick, there were plenty of frozen and canned for the taking - well the buying - and they had a long shelf life in the freezer. By 9:15, the bakery case was all but empty and Carmen was mixing up some Banana Bread muffins to add to Wednesday's offerings.

"Did you call the sheriff's?" Carmen wanted to know.

"Yep," Frankie answered. "Shirley Lazaar agreed to meet me here. So, I'm going to need one of those Butterhorns to butter her up a little, get it?" Frankie thought she was clever, even if a bit corny. Carmen smirked, unimpressed. Frankie made a fresh latte for Shirley too, even though she had no idea if the officer even drank coffee. Oh well, the effort must count for something, right? Besides, every cop and detective on TV drank coffee all day long so she couldn't be wrong.

"Carmen, go home. I'll finish baking the muffins." Never one to leave a job unfinished, Carmen hesitated. She wanted to pull her weight as a full partner and her pride made her forget how often she had worked extra when Frankie needed time away.

"You sure?" she asked. Frankie nodded, and Carmen

was relieved. "Ryan needs more help when it's this cold. It takes a long time to clean the sheep barn in the winter. We have to take more breaks and the manure freezes, not so easy to dig out," Carmen grimaced. Frankie looked at the temperature on her phone: Minus 2 degrees. She was glad to be in a warm bakery kitchen instead of a sheep barn. "But, it smells better than on a hot summer day!" Carmen offered, adding, "See you tomorrow and stay out of trouble."

A few minutes later, the shop door opened to Shirley Lazaar in her county uniform. Shirley was a tall woman with short, snowy white hair and a muscular physique despite her advancing age. "Smells good in here, Francine," she said, taking a seat away from the window on one of the overstuffed chairs.

"Oh good," Frankie thought. Shirley appeared to be relaxed and settling in so explaining her decision to remove evidence from an investigation might be easier for Frankie than she let herself hope. "Here's some coffee and Butterhorns. I just finished baking them," Frankie said as she placed a cup in front of Shirley, and a large antique floral plate of pastries on the table. Frankie hoped this cozy corner would be just right for her confession. Shirley looked at the coffee and laughed, her voice a low suspicious rumble.

"Whad'ya call this stuff?" she asked, peering into the mug. "You must want some answers purty badly, huh?" Frankie decided that Shirley was not a person to be toyed with. She respected her and, for better or worse, she needed to come clean right now.

"It's even worse than that," Frankie said in a little voice. She placed the business card and silver cap on the table. "I found these at the scene yesterday.", she gulped, "in the shanty."

Shirley's face didn't offer a note of surprise or any other emotion for that matter. "That so," she said. "Better tell me where you found these." Frankie shared the information, just the facts, including that she had fished out the cap with her glove on, then wrapped it in a tissue as well as using a gloved hand to maneuver the business card from the shanty's corner. She certainly didn't want Shirley to think she had been careless with possible evidence. Looking a little surprised, Shirley took the sandwich bag containing the items and put them in her satchel. "Anything else you want to tell me, Francine?" Frankie shook her head and Shirley didn't ask for any further information. "Suppose you want something in return for these items…," Shirley quizzed.

Frankie shook her head again, then added, "Well, can you not tell the sheriff or Officer Pflug about this?" Frankie hated it that she sounded like a beggar.

Shirley gave Frankie an even and direct look: "So long as you don't give me a reason to tell them, I don't guess I need to." And with that said, Shirley helped herself to a second, then a third Butterhorn as the two talked about wine and the upcoming Valentine's event. As she got up to leave, Frankie asked if she could still call her later in the week after the autopsy. Shirley laughed that low rumbly laugh again, "You bet," she said and walked out the door. Frankie wasn't sure what to make of the exchange. She'd like to believe that Shirley admired Frankie's chutzpah, one female to another trying to do a traditional man's job, but Shirley could also consider Frankie's little venture as nothing more than amusing, a woman trying too hard, out of her league. If the second thought was correct, Frankie didn't think she could bear it. More than anything, she wanted to be taken seriously.

By 10:30, Frankie was pulling into Fitz's' Bait Shop and Guide Service off Highway 404. Both Joe and Dan answered to the nickname of Fitz, which could be confusing at times, but it had always been that way. Not much business this time of day as most fishermen head out early in the morning or late in the afternoon, hoping to catch fish at their most active times. With weather dipping into the minus column, most folks just stayed off the ice, period. She pulled on the steel door, setting off an overhead jingling bell that summoned Joe to the counter.

"Well, if it isn't Charlie's little gal!" Joe gave Frankie a toothy, warm grin. "What in the world brings you out here?" he asked. Joe may have been in his early 70's but he looked the same as Frankie had always remembered him: nearly bald head, large nose, rosy cheeks, five o'clock shadow no matter what time of day it was, and a papery chuckle that could make everyone around him laugh. Joe had spent his life fishing all three community lakes here along with the rivers, streams, creeks and other lakes in the area. Anyone who wanted fishing advice came to Joe. If they were smart and paying customers, they would book him or his brother as guides. Their reputations were known throughout the state, so booking the two of them was nearly impossible during the busy seasons.

"Oh, oh. You're looking mighty serious there, Frankie. I can tell you want something." Joe knew how to read people. He poured Frankie some coffee from the pot he always kept brewing on the counter, and offered her a seat on one of the high-back stools. He reached under the counter and produced a box of gas-station donuts.

"No thanks," Frankie tried not to shudder. "I just had breakfast." Poor Joe, buying boxed manufactured donuts. The golden firefly chastised Frankie for her poor manners, so Frankie quickly made a mental note to come with treats from her shop the next time she saw him.

From Joe, Frankie found out that he and Dan had built the ice shanty ordered by Pastor Rawlins. They had also sold him the ice auger and fishing equipment. "He sure was green when it came to ice fishin'," Joe said. "Of course, coming from the south, he'd never been ice fishin', so he didn't know the first thing, just knew he wanted to try it out. Dan and I met him on the lake Sunday afternoon, hauled the shanty there to find him a decent spot to set it. I was probably the last one to see him alive that morning," Joe went on, wondering if maybe he could have saved him if he'd been there.

"Wait a minute, Joe," Frankie stopped mid-sip, while this information sunk in. "What do you mean - you saw him yesterday morning?"

Joe nodded, "Uh huh. We told him he should get an early start and I'd meet him to drill the holes since he sure didn't know how to do it."

Joe seemed almost gloating about his fishing equipment expertise, but then sobered again as Frankie asked, "And what time was it when you met him? How long were you there? Did you see anyone else? Did the sheriff's department interview you?" Joe gave her a long look.

"Slow down, gal! What's got you all knotted up anyway?" Frankie admitted she was trying to piece together what happened and write a news article about it. Joe had met Pastor Rawlins at 6:15 a.m., drilled out the two holes, and rigged his poles for him with the minnows he'd brought along from the shop. The pastor was alone, and no, he didn't notice anyone else. "It's Monday and it was damn cold out there, Frankie, so not much action doin' on the lake," Joe finished.

Frankie had one more question. "What time did you leave him?"

"No later than 7 because I was at the diner for breakfast with the guys just after that."

Frankie jotted that information down in her phone

notes. "Did he say he was meeting someone out there?" she asked. Joe thought a second.

"He didn't say, and I didn't ask. Sorry." Frankie heaved a sigh, thinking for the first time that investigative work was slow, maybe too slow for her impatient mind. Joe slurped his coffee, studying her face. "What's got your hair in a curl, Gal?" Frankie grinned at the old-school expression; almost nobody was allowed to call her "gal" or "girl", but Joe was almost family so….

"Do you think the pastor's death was accidental?" she asked.

Joe shrugged. "Seen a lotta freak accidents in my time, Frankie. Could be accidental, but I can't figure what he was doin' with the auger. I mean, Dan and I had the holes drilled out clean. He didn't need to be touchin' the thing."

Frankie balanced on the chair rail, and gave Joe a friendly kiss on the cheek. "You are the best. Thanks for the information, Uncle Joe," Frankie switched from hot-shot reporter to the girl Joe remembered on fishing outings with Frankie's dad, Charlie.

Joe blushed, "Aw sweetie, you sure look good. Don't waste those looks on nothing - find yourself some nice man to take care of you."

Frankie switched to a more comfortable topic. "Speaking of nice men, how's Dan?" Joe's brother had lost his wife, Lois, just about a year ago. The couple spent a lot of time with Frankie's family as Dan's sons had been good friends with Frankie's brothers. She imagined Dan was quite lonely with two grown sons living out of state. Joe confessed Dan didn't see the boys too often.

"Ya know, Dan Jr. is a big-time advertising agent in Chicago now, and Michael moved to Detroit a couple a years ago to work on designs for Chrysler." Seeing the proud look on Joe's face made Frankie smile broadly.

"I think Dan's seeing someone," Joe said, rather abruptly. Frankie's surprise at the announcement made her think of her mother, wondering if she was used to being alone, her dad gone for five years already.

"Well, that's probably good for Dan. The company, I mean," Frankie tested the waters for Joe's reaction, but he held his poker face, looking down at a fishing magazine.

"S'pose so. Be good for your mum to have some company, too," Joe offered, giving Frankie an even look, which was lost on her. Before she had time to process the comment, he switched gears. "And by the way, you scooped the sheriff's office Gal, because nobody has talked to me about this but you." He looked at Frankie proudly, the way a dad would look at his daughter. Frankie smiled and headed back out into the cold.

Before she climbed into the SUV, a brown and white old Dodge pick-up rolled into the parking lot, spitting some loose gravel toward her. The two doors opened simultaneously to reveal the Larson brothers, Tim and Troy, the same Larson brothers that had discovered Pastor Rawlins' unconscious/dead body. Frankie went directly to high alert, the pirate firefly, nudging her into

action. Don't look a gift horse in the mouth - you need to
talk to these two. Frankie walked toward them, trying to
look official. She didn't really know the Larson brothers -
they were younger than Frankie's youngest brother, Will,
and older than her daughter, Sophie, so their paths hadn't
crossed much. "Hey, Tim and Troy Larson, right?" Frankie
began. They looked at each other, shrugged, then looked
at Frankie, trying to figure out what she might want.

Tim answered first, "Yep, that's us." Frankie went
right to work, telling them she was writing an article for
Point Press and had a few questions for them about the
accident on the lake.

Troy's turn to speak, "Yeah, well we were told not to
talk to anyone about it, you know, until the investigation
is finalized."

Frankie reassured them. "I already know you were
first on the scene and I just want to confirm what the
officers told me and maybe ask a few follow-ups." The
two thought that would be ok, maybe. They confirmed
they were walking out to their family shanty toward the
middle of the lake when they passed the new shanty.
Since they were curious, and the door was open, they
figured they would greet the newcomer and nose around
a bit, but then they saw the blood and the body. Frankie
asked what position the body was in and if they noticed
whether he had any other injuries - none they noticed.
Tim confirmed the time at about 8:15, that he had called
911 while Troy attempted to revive the man. "Did you

notice anything unusual? I mean, you two are pros when it comes to ice fishing, anything out of order, weird?" Frankie was using flattery now.

Troy shook his head, "Just thinking the guy didn't know what he was doing. How you get a hand auger stuck in your leg without trying is beyond me," Troy wondered.

Frankie's intake of breath was a little sharp. Hand auger? She assumed it was a power auger but then she didn't have a chance to look at it since it was already bagged and concealed in one of the squads.

Troy looked guiltily at Tim, he knew he might have said too much. "Don't print that," Troy said meaningfully.

"Oh, I won't. Not a problem." Geesh, what a wuss you are, Frankie. Get some professional backbone. "Well, thank you for the information. Can I have your number in case I have other questions after the police finish the investigation?" Frankie was being professional again.

"Ok," Tim said, "but I think we told you everything we know already." Frankie had seen enough cop shows to know that people frequently recalled little bits of information later on that didn't seem to matter at the time. She almost reached her vehicle when she remembered one more missing piece of information the Larsons might provide.

"Hey," she called back at them. "Did either of you leave a bloody footprint at the scene outside the shanty?"

Troy and Tim both shook their heads. "That footprint was there when I made the 911 call," Tim confirmed.

"So, did either of you see anyone around, on the lake or in the landing parking lot?"

Both men shook their heads in unison. "Pretty cold day to be out fishing. We just drove by 'cuz we had the day off, you know, sorta check out the lake, see if anyone was out," Troy shrugged the shoulders of his jacket up around his ears to keep the wind off, while Tim was already walking away from Frankie, figuring their business was concluded.

Frankie celebrated to herself as she started the SUV and jacked up the heat, even though it wouldn't even be lukewarm before she arrived at her next destination. She was feeling pretty good about the information she had gathered already, not to mention happy she wasn't on bad terms with the law for taking something from a potential crime scene. Every inch of Frankie now saw Pastor Rawlins' death as a murder, not an accident. The bloody smear outside the shanty all but confirmed someone else was there before the Larsons, but after the accident. The hand auger was looking more like a weapon now that Frankie knew it wasn't a power auger that got away from the pastor as he may have attempted to use or move it, accidentally turning it on. Troy Larson was right: even an inexperienced ice fisherman wouldn't stab the main artery in his upper thigh with a hand auger, not without trying. Unless he was trying to stow it and he slipped on the ice? That still doesn't explain the bloody smear. By now, Frankie was back downtown and parking the SUV next to Kilpatrick's Insurance Agency on Meriwether. She steeled her resolve, determined to ask pointed questions to Dave Kilpatrick, who just might be a suspect in this case.

Marjean Van Dyke looked up from the file she was reading at her front desk when Frankie walked through the door, ushering in a cold draft of January air. Located on Meriwether Street, the agency had once belonged to Marjean's late husband, Fred, who had probably sold insurance to nearly everyone in Deep Lakes and their future generations. Marjean had run the business side-by-side with Fred for nearly 40 years when he passed away after a painful battle with lung cancer. Frankie remembered the office always smelled of nasty cigar smoke under Fred's tenure. Some five years later, there was still a stale smoke smell present on certain days, maybe from the walls or the woodwork. When Dave bought the agency, he and his wife Glenda freshened up the office with new furniture, substituting attractive window blinds for the smelly drapes; the only remains from the Van Dyke agency were the stale cigar smoke, and Marjean. She had poured her heart and soul into the business and was a huge asset to Dave - she knew everyone in the area, and she knew the ins and outs of insurance. So, Dave kept her as office manager and receptionist.

Marjean looked up at Frankie, keeping one short but painted fingernail on the page she was reading. "Francine, is everything ok? Didn't have an accident or something

did you?" Marjean was already in claim mode, ready to
start gathering information. Frankie had both her auto
and business insurance with the agency, just as her parents
had for years before her.

"Oh no, nothing of the sort. I was wondering if I
could speak to Dave," it was a statement rather than a
query.

"Dave won't be in until later this afternoon," Marjean
said. "How can I help?" Marjean was used to answering
most questions in the agency. She was the authority on
insurance in Deep Lakes, and she knew it. Standing at
five feet two inches, Marjean was built like a concrete-
block wall and was tough as nails - she could give a
Marine sergeant heart palpitations. Frankie knew the key
to talking to Marjean was to stick to her soft spots: her
two sons, (rebellious, wild, and in constant need of bailing
out) Robby and Dougie, and her purse pet - a cute but
yappy Papillon dog, Monarch. Taking a seat across from
Marjean, she began with the first subject.

"How are Robby and Dougie doing these days? I
haven't seen them in a while," Frankie sincerely hoped she
hadn't stepped into anything by asking this, knowing the
two had served jail time in the past. Marjean brightened
immediately, reassuring Frankie. Robby was working
on his real-estate license and living in Vandenberg one
county over. "You know, where the police don't have it
out for him. A fresh start," Marjean said. Frankie nodded
while her head remarked that if Robby didn't give the

police a reason to be watching him, he wouldn't need to worry about that.

"Dougie's been having a run of poor luck, I'm afraid," Marjean continued. "He's not been at all feeling well, so hasn't been able to keep a job, what with being sick and so forth. He had to give up his apartment and move in with some friends in Madison for a bit," Marjean went on sadly. "I told him he could come back here and stay with me. Still have his old bedroom just the same as he left it, but you know, he didn't think that was a good idea," she finished. Frankie wondered if "not feeling well" was code for Dougie's return to a rehab facility. He had been busted for meth possession a couple years ago but went to rehab as part of a plea agreement. Marjean always defended the two boys no matter what they were into. Of course, the boys were now men in their 40's, but to Marjean, they were her precious babies.

Frankie wondered if now was a good time to ask some questions. Might as well give it a whirl. "What do you think about Pastor Rawlins's death? Must have been hard on Dave, huh?" Frankie began.

Marjean's face quickly shifted to a glare. "Humph, that one," she looked straight into Frankie's eyes, "some folks around here won't miss him."

"What do you mean by that Marjean?" Frankie asked.

"Well, I don't know anything for sure, but I have my suspicions about him. I think he did more harm than good in this town," she said sharply. Marjean's suspicions wouldn't go far in answering Frankie's questions so she tried a new direction.

"Did Dave have a meeting with the pastor yesterday morning?" Frankie inquired. Marjean looked a little offended at Frankie's question. Really, was it any of her business? But Marjean looked at her desk calendar that contained the office appointments and her boss's schedule.

"Don't think so, at least not on my calendar... why do you want to know?" Frankie had to give Marjean some sort of response, so she explained how she had been at the church when Patsy, the pastor's secretary, received the news, and that she made the phone calls to the council members, and thought she overheard some talk of Dave having a meeting with the pastor that morning. She had invented the third "fact", hoping it would confirm or deny the scrap of paper with the 8 a.m. appointment with "patrick" as being or not being with Dave.

Now Marjean paused to give the idea some thought, perusing the filing cabinet in her brain about the comings and goings of yesterday morning. Finally, she concluded, "Nope. Couldn't be. Dave was supposed to be at an insurance meeting in Madison at 10 a.m. He was probably getting ready to leave when you called him about the pastor's death," she said.

Frankie decided that was good enough for now, and rose to leave when she saw the file folder sticking out underneath the paper Marjean was reading. It had Bradford Rawlins' name on it - Pastor Bradford Rawlins.

Thinking quickly and deviously, Frankie noticed Monarch poking his feathery ears out of a basket in a sunny corner by a large, leafy Parlor Palm.

"Oh, there's that sweet doggie of yours, Marjean," Frankie said with extra syrup to her voice. "How is Monarch doing these days?" Frankie continued. Marjean brightened again as her attention shifted.

"Come here, Monarch and say hello to Francine," Marjean coaxed, doggie treat in hand. Monarch stepped regally from his cushy basket with a little yawn and paraded like a peacock to his mommy. When he saw the treat, he got up on two legs and did a circle dance, like a trained circus performer, then gobbled up the treat. Frankie clapped politely while Marjean gushed, "Isn't he a good boy?" Monarch was excitable, with large white feathery ears, and a smooth black and brown body. It was the ear "feathers" that gave the breed its name, French for "butterfly", and how he had acquired his name, "Monarch."

Marjean looked at the time, "I really better let Monarch out for his recess. Would you mind waiting for a few minutes and catching the phone if it rings for me?" Marjean asked. Looked like Fortune was smiling on Frankie today.

"Certainly. No problem," Frankie said. Marjean took her warm wool coat from the closet, a bright tomato red garment that nearly reached her ankles, pulled on her black gloves, then fastened a leash to Monarch's crystal-

studded collar, but not before wrestling him into a black
and red knit sweater. Wouldn't want her pumpkin to get
cold! Monarch's yapping and struggling clearly indicated
he cared less about the temperature than his dignity
being ruined by wearing such a stupid contraption.
Frankie almost offered her help to Marjean, but thought
Monarch might not appreciate her efforts, rewarding
Frankie with a sharp bite or poke from a spiky toenail.
Stifling a giggle, Frankie opted to just watch the spectacle
of Marjean in her restrictive long wool coat, looking like
a giant red beachball, stuffing a whirling furry Tasmanian
Devil into a mitten! Finally, the chore was completed,
and they trotted down the hallway and out the back door
to the alley.

Frankie wasted no time at all. Picking up a pencil
from the desk, she used the eraser end to slide out the
Rawlins folder and flicked it open. She assumed the
pastor had life insurance and the folder had been pulled
out for contacting the beneficiary. To her stunned surprise,
Frankie saw a declaration sheet, not for life insurance, but
for a personal liability policy in the amount of a million
dollars! Why would a pastor need a personal liability
policy? Maybe that was normal, maybe not. She forced her
thoughts to pause mode while she flipped up the page to
see what else the file contained. Underneath was nothing
notable, just the pastor's completed information for the
application, then a yellow legal pad piece of paper with
some scribbles on it, probably made by Dave or whomever

had met with Rawlins when he requested the policy. She made a mental note of the date on the declaration sheet - October 20 of last year. This information would be added to her notes. Frankie closed the file, still dumbfounded, and carefully poked it back into place with the eraser-end of the pencil. Marjean returned, rosy cheeked, with a prancing Monarch, who looked lighter and sprightlier from his jaunt to the alley.

"Thanks, Francine. Any calls?" Frankie indicated no, said a sweet goodbye to Monarch and Marjean, and headed back into the Wisconsin chill.

Chapter 5

"Winter is not a season, it's an occupation."
- Sinclair Lewis

Back inside Bubble and Bake, Frankie shrugged out of her parka. She purposely placed her boots near the furnace vent for her next outing - putting on warm boots was a treat during the winter, since keeping hands and feet warm was an ongoing occupation. Frankie popped upstairs to her apartment to grab salad fixings, including a pouch of lemon pepper tuna for a boost of protein. Speaking of boost, she brought the salad downstairs to the shop kitchen a few minutes later, grabbed a coffee mug, and set her fancy-pants brewer into action for an afternoon pick-me-up. Checking the time, she shook her head and frowned at herself. It was getting late in the day and Frankie still needed to prep two batches of muffins for tomorrow, open three days' worth of mail, pay some accounts, and deliver the Butterhorns to the Library before 6:30. Any leftover time should be spent finalizing the menu for the Valentine's Romantic Getaway event and maybe calling her daughters. She wasn't one of those moms that needed to talk with her daughters daily, although she knew that her mother was apparently one of those moms, as she always made a point of chastising Frankie for not calling often enough. That was probably why Frankie vowed she would not be one of those moms.

She had to admit though that it always made her feel warm inside to hear from her girls, sharing their trials and celebrations made her feel important, still firmly connected to them. Sophie had graduated with a nursing degree two years ago, was happily rooted at UW Hospital in Madison as a floor nurse where she met Max, also a floor nurse. They lived together in an apartment near work and were busy carving out a life of their own making: friends to socialize with, concerts to attend, rock walls to climb, meals to cook together. All seemed to be going in a happy direction for them. Violet was only 20 and still unsettled. Moving away had been more difficult for her, unlike Sophie, who asserted her independence. Violet needed more support from her mother and luckily, as she chose to attend college at Stevens Point, her favorite uncle, Will, was a lifeline for Violet. Will worked as a forester for Stevens Point and surrounding Portage County and his wife, Libby, worked in one of the labs on campus, doing science research in Microbiology. Violet planned a career of some sort in environmental studies; she was passionate about saving the planet. Will and Libby looked in on Violet and invited her over for meals from time to time. Life in the college dorms had its ups and downs. Violet's freshman roommate, although a decent young woman, transferred out her sophomore year to a university closer to home. This year's roommate, Ashley, seemed nice but had established friendships in different circles than Violet. Ashley, a musical theater major, aspired to be a professional actress or singer; those aspirations kept her out late at rehearsals with most of her classes scheduled for afternoons so she didn't have to rise early, just the opposite of Violet's schedule. Violet frequently sounded melancholy when she called home, and Frankie knew she had Will and Libby to thank that Violet remained in college, instead of running home to mom where life was easy and safe.

Frankie took some leftover tuna to Brambles, who was sleeping contentedly in a sunbeam in the wine shop's cozy lounge area. Frankie loved the lounge - it made her happy inside every time she walked through it, knowing it had been a labor of love, made from the help of her family and friends. Going to rummage sales and auctions, she had ferreted out nearly all the furnishings for the shop, at the cheapest prices she could. The low coffee tables were in various degrees of dilapidation but had been antiqued and distressed to look like estate pieces. Everything was a mismatched assortment unified by their similar rich finishes, earthy colors, and hominess. One coffee table was an old army trunk with new, but distressed-looking, leather straps and pewter buckles. Pewter sconces adorned the walls with mason-jar lights that glowed a soft aqua blue, and complemented the pale blue and pale-yellow fairy lights adorning the beams from floor to ceiling. Finding couches and easy chairs in any usable condition proved impossible as the springs were almost always shot, and wouldn't safely or comfortably support her patrons. So, Frankie had hired Chelsey's father, Pete Mathis, to make simple Scandinavian framed couches and chairs. Pete was an expert furniture maker who opened his own custom workshop when Chelsey was a little girl. He had raised Chelsey alone as her mother left the family when Chelsey was only a toddler, so Frankie was like a true mother-figure for her. Many people, Sophie and Chelsey included, had tried to play matchmaker with Pete and Frankie, but the spark was never there. Eventually Pete found the right woman – Reena, who moved to Deep Lakes, opened a boarding kennel for dogs and other animals, and used Pete's skills to help construct the kennels. The two married a few years ago and were a happy couple that frequented Frankie's business. Frankie admired Pete's craftsmanship and knew he would charge a fair price for premium quality work. After Pete constructed the frames, Sophie and Chelsey, who sewed as a hobby, had made the overstuffed cushions for all the couches and chairs, in bright bird prints of aqua, yellow, tangerine, and lime. The soft lighting and dark woodwork muted the bright prints, giving the shop a natural, woodsy feel. LED-lit flickering candles of all kinds settled themselves in nooks, shelves, and on table-tops, completing the atmosphere of Danish hygge Frankie wanted to achieve. The wine, the bakery, the mellow music, and herbaceous scents provided the life force that magnetically drew in her customers and kept them coming back for more.

No time to waste admiring her shop right now though - Frankie needed to hightail it to the kitchen. Taking in the clean kitchen always brought a smile to Frankie's face; she knew how lucky she was to have a business partner like Carmen, who always left things tidy and organized, along with the other shop workers, trained by Carmen to leave the kitchen looking like a shiny new penny. Frankie grabbed muffin ingredients and occupied two mixing stations at once (thank goodness for stand mixers that made multi-baking easier - look, no hands!). One mixer was whipping up a batch of Double Butters - a butterscotch buttermilk muffin - while the other whisked away at a dark chocolate muffin batter to which Frankie would fold in dark chocolate chips. She readied the muffin tins, poured in batter, and shoved the pans into the ovens. As the muffins baked, Frankie opened mail and paid bills online on her laptop, perched on the kitchen counter. By the time the muffins had cooled enough to store for tomorrow morning, she had sorted her mail into piles for dealing with "soon" and "whenever", thrown away the "never in a million years" pile, and paid all the accounts she could. Frankie's business was paying for itself, though some months were better and greener than others. She was hoping, as her Business courses promised, that five years would be the magic number to bring about decent profits instead of break-evens. She could pay her employees but sometimes she and Carmen shrugged off the idea of taking a full wage - not good practice.

With a little time for herself, Frankie decided to peruse the *Watch* to see if any of the daily news was noteworthy. She looked for an article on Pastor Rawlins and seeing none, decided Abe must still be gathering information or maybe waiting on the autopsy report. Still, Frankie was surprised the death wasn't at least a blurb on the front page, but then he had a hot item already - the Whitman County police had made a big meth lab bust in the northern part of the county, between Cayuga Creek and Pike Junction. Because the police, including a couple undercover officers, had worked on setting up the bust for months, they were especially proud of the results, arresting 10 individuals involved in the cooking and the dealing of the nasty, addictive substance. This story would produce a lot of mileage for the paper as the defendants lawyered up, and multiple court proceedings filled the county docket. With 10 defendants now, and possibly more emerging as stories unfolded and plea bargaining was underway, numerous follow-up articles would litter the paper for months to come. On page two was a photo and interview of newcomers, Mark and Kim Hocherman, opening a meat market, From the Butcher's Block, north of town on Highway 404 in the old Gentleman's Club, Heads and Tails. Frankie was happy to see the club, closed down last year after some extra-curricular soliciting had come to light, opening as a new business, although some might laugh and comment the club had been a meat market before, and was going to be a meat market again. Frankie snickered at the thought but sincerely hoped the butchers would make a go of it. Local meats were back on most people's menus because they were higher quality, made to order, and originating nearby instead of somewhere unknown, containing possible mystery ingredients. Frankie made a mental note to pay a visit there soon.

In other news, community events were highlighted, beginning with the upcoming Valentine Jubilee at First Congregational. Other local churches hosted events, too, including Friday night Bingo at St. Anthony's and the Methodist Chili Supper on Saturday. Frontenac's annual Fisheree was set for the weekend, accompanied by all-you-can-eat chili and cornbread, and on the horizon was the Super Bowl Party at the Deep Lakes Community Center Sunday.

Anyone who thinks Wisconsin is a boring place when the snow and cold settle in, should think again. Many friends from warmer climates that visit during the summer, shudder at the thought of spending a winter here, but Wisconsinites take the cold in stride. Knowing how to "Winter" is the key. There might not be mountains here but there's many ski resorts offering skiing, snowboarding, and tubing on hilly terrain carved out by ancient glaciers. If that's too much physical work, snowmobile trails meander for miles across the state - all one has to do is suit up, glove up, boot up, and helmet up. Wearing all those layers means it's difficult to manage more than a clumsy caveman walk, but the reward of flying over wooded and open trails in the gleam of daylight or moonlight is worth the effort. Of course, there's also cold weather activities like ice fishing, sledding on a traditional sled, saucer or toboggan, ice skating, curling, cross-country skiing, and snow-shoeing to keep one's thick winter blood from freezing solid. Then there's the downright bizarre things normal Wisconsinites participate in to keep from going stir-crazy in the dark winter months. Sun Prairie hosts a festival dedicated to Jimmy the Groundhog on, you guessed right, Groundhog Day. Several civic organizations across the state sponsor a "Car on the Ice Contest" in which an old klunker, painted bright colors, minus its windows and engine, is parked mid-lake on the ice, and people buy tickets to predict the date the car will drown (sometime in March or April). But the icing on the cake just might be a polar plunge where the stout-hearted don swimwear and dive into an unfrozen lake, realize they are indeed still alive and desert that frigid lake as quickly as possible! There is nothing boring about a Wisconsin winter!

Personally, Frankie enjoyed watching hockey, a red and white Badger fan through and through. She could cross-country ski but not as aptly as ten years ago, and nobody was ever going to make her take a polar plunge, not while she had her right mind. Frankie loved being outdoors but not being cold, so most of her recreation took place at the Deep Lakes Wellness Center, where she had an annual membership (a gift from her mother) and participated in a few cardio, yoga, and strength classes. She usually worked out four times a week, but she suspected her investigative reporting into Pastor Rawlins' death was going to curb her exercise routine this week if she didn't take measures to plan her time more efficiently, something she wasn't doing right now.

Taking off her baking apron and tossing it into the laundry barrel in the stockroom off the kitchen, Frankie made her way upstairs to change into clean clothes before making the Butterhorn delivery. She threw on her favorite broken-in jeans and a northern gardener sweatshirt, heated up some leftover sweet corn chowder she'd made - when was that? - over the weekend maybe, and a piece of multi-grain bread with butter. That would have to do for tonight's supper, she guessed, vowing to eat healthier tomorrow - more veggies. She checked the temperature on her phone - already in the minus column, so the parka would need to be at her service again. Back in the kitchen, she grabbed the bakery box of Butterhorns and headed out the front door, across the street to the parking lot on Granite Street, one of five city lots for parking in town. The reliable SUV started up, blew icy air out of the heating vent that re-awakened Frankie's senses, and followed Granite Street three blocks to Jefferson where

Library of the Lakes sat on the corner. It was a three-story blonde brick structure, its front entrance enhanced by a garden and small statues of famed storybook figures - Peter Rabbit, Wilbur the Pig and Charlotte the Spider, Tortoise and Hare, all four Little Women, and Tom Sawyer. Frankie saw numerous cars in the parking lot, probably because the library was finishing up with patrons before closing for the evening. Frankie saw Patsy Long getting out of a truck in the carport; Frankie wondered if Patsy was on the Board or a Friends Member. She hurried out of the SUV, so she could try to catch up to Patsy, but didn't quite make it as the automatic door closed before she reached it. The truck was still idling in the carport, so she looked inside and noticed Patsy's husband, Duane, tapping on his cell phone.

Frankie was about to knock on the truck's window but to her surprise, the window opened a couple of inches to Duane's voice: "Hey, are you going in the library? My wife forgot her bookbag. Could you take it in with you?" Frankie, who was balancing her own bookbag, her purse and the bakery box, gave Duane a small smirk. Who did he think she was anyway, Wonder Woman?

But, Frankie saw an opportunity to get a little information, so she shifted her bookbag over her shoulder beside her purse, saying, "I think if you can just hold this box for me, I can get Patsy's bookbag, too."

Duane appeared to notice Frankie's load for the first time and he looked a little embarrassed. "Oh, yeah, sure," he said, opening the truck door and coming around to the passenger side to take the bakery box. Frankie knew Duane as one of the locals who worked at the Triple Crown Marine plant where her brother Nick was a foreman, making boat motors. Tall and lanky, Frankie figured he must be in his 30's, same as Patsy.

Duane seemed skeptical that Frankie could handle all those objects and started walking to the door with her, but she stopped, looked up at Duane and asked, "How is Patsy doing anyway? I mean, with Pastor Rawlins' death and all?"

Duane stopped cold and scoffed at Frankie's question. "Patsy'll be much better off now that she's not working with him," Duane spoke without weighing his words, an indication that Frankie might prod a little further.

"Oh, so you didn't care much for the pastor?" The lighted carport showed the darkening look on Duane's face.

"Nope. Not much of a pastor if you ask me, not my kinda pastor anyway," Duane said. He seemed more guarded at Frankie's second question, so she decided this public place, with more people walking toward the entrance, was not going to work for further interrogation. But Duane's comment left Frankie's mind wondering. Marjean had basically said the same thing about Pastor Rawlins. Why didn't people care for the man? The automatic door opened, Duane set the bakery box on the table just inside the entrance, turned and headed back to the truck. At least having Patsy's bookbag would give

Frankie a reason for a brief conversation with her.

She poked her head into the meeting room on the left, across from the library's electronic walk-throughs. Her gaze met Patsy's and she held her bookbag aloft as a signal. Patsy left her chair to meet Frankie by the doorway. "Hey, Patsy. You left this in the truck, so Duane caught me coming in and asked me to bring it to you," Frankie smiled.

Patsy thanked her, "Guess I'm a little forgetful these days," she admitted.

This was the perfect in-road to Frankie's question, "How are you doing anyway?"

Patsy looked down sadly at the floor, "Oh, I don't know. There's so much to do right now at the office. There's been so much activity and phone calls, then there's the Valentine event coming up and it's just been terrible. So much to organize and the volunteers haven't been able to arrange their schedules to get stuff done…" Patsy trailed off, helplessly.

Frankie thoughtlessly offered her help. "I can come in and help you organize and label the raffle baskets," she said, giving Patsy a hopeful look. Immediately both fireflies lit up on Frankie's shoulder, vying for attention, even though they said the same thing. "You'll do no such thing," the golden one chirped. "You've got your own Valentine event to organize, Sister." The pirate nodded, "You don't have the time, Girlfriend."

Frankie shushed them both as Patsy's reply came out

joyfully, "Oh that would just be great. You know how to organize and…" Frankie cut her off.

"But, I can't come by until Monday, and only for two or three hours, Patsy."

Monday was just fine with Patsy, "I can't even think about it until Monday anyway with the visitation and funeral to plan," Patsy said, looking sadly at the floor a second time. The funeral? Yes, there was that, but was there already a date for the funeral? Patsy explained the council wanted closure as soon as possible on the accident and urgently requested the county to step up their autopsy so the body could be released. Her voice wobbled on the words "the body" but she told Frankie the funeral was set for Friday at 11 a.m. It would be in the newspaper tomorrow.

Frankie gave Patsy a reassuring pat on the shoulder. "Don't worry about the raffle right now. Just do what you need to do for the funeral. I'll see you Monday around 9?" Frankie asked.

"That'll be good. Thank you so much," Patsy said.

Frankie delivered the Butterhorns to Sue Pringle, the Library Director, who took a deep sniff, smiled brightly at Frankie and handed her a check for the bakery. Frankie headed back into the cold night air, the little fireflies resuming their commentary. "You're not even a member of that church, Francine."

"Oh, be quiet for once, Golden One," Frankie said, hugging her arms around her jacket hood and pulling her scarf up around her mouth to keep the wind at bay.

Chapter 6

"Life is a long lesson in humility."
– James M. Barrie

Wednesday dawned with a rosy sky when Frankie lifted the wooden blinds on the back window overlooking Sterling Creek. She had awakened early again, unable to keep all the bits of information about Pastor Rawlins' death from floating around her restless mind. Who had met him that fateful day on the lake - Dave Kilpatrick or some other "Patrick"? What kind of argument or struggle had ended in the pastor being smote by an ice auger? What was the sweet air freshener smell all about? Why the business card for Briggs and Baker Law Firm in Milwaukee specializing in Criminal and Personal Injury law? Why didn't Duane Long like the pastor? And, maybe most important, why did Pastor Rawlins have a million-dollar personal liability policy? "And why do you care anyway?" the golden firefly squawked, interrupting her jumbled thoughts. Somebody hasn't had their morning coffee, Frankie mused to herself, then grabbed a quick shower and dressed in her typical bakery garb: jeans, a Bubble and Bake tee, and Sketchers. Frankie sprayed some bouncy volumizer into her straight, flyaway mop, then zapped it with the blow dryer set to cool, coaxing it with a round brush into a turned-under bob. She looked in the mirror and sighed, "it'll have to do." Her own number one critic, Frankie actually liked her red-brown tresses that would transform in the summer sun with some golden highlights, but she always managed to find fault with her body. Those who wanted to score points with Frankie referred to her as petite, and while she could barely claim a fifth foot in the height column (she thought about switching to the metric system to sound taller), she wasn't tiny by any means. To Frankie petite meant a size 2, which she most definitely was not, in fact, she wasn't a size 6 either, so she'd settle for average or medium and continue to exercise and watch her consumption of sweets - well, most days.

Dressed for the day, she flew down the steps to the kitchen and welcoming coffee maker, which she could hear whirring away from the hall. Swinging the door open, she was surprised and happy to see Carmen, who already had one batch of dough rising near the heating vent, while working on a second at the counter. Carmen grinned and handed Frankie a latte.

"What brings you here so early?" Frankie asked, double-checking the time to be sure she'd registered correctly upstairs. Yep, it wasn't quite 6:15 yet.

Yawning, Carmen's answer came out garbled, "Ioy got up to helllp Ry wid tha sheep," then more clearly, "Ryan has to go to Wausau this morning, so I got up with the boys to help him get out the door on time. Figured I might as well get here and get going." Carmen explained Ryan had a Lamb Council meeting - he had been appointed to the Lamb Board two years ago - and getting up with Ryan meant a 4 a.m. alarm. The shop partners usually made some kind of yeast dough for Thursdays, so getting an early start was helpful. Since the wine bar would also be open Thursday evening, the kitchen would be buzzing most of Thursday and Friday to prepare weekend bakery for mornings, and quiches for evenings. Carmen was working on yeast donuts, which would get three kinds of glazes just before tomorrow morning's trip to the bakery case: vanilla, maple, and chocolate - something for everyone. Frankie gratefully drank her latte and began preparing a large sheet pan for apple coffee cake, an easy addition to the yeast donuts that might yield a few leftovers for the wine bar customers craving something for dessert. Carmen already had pie crust dough thawing from the freezer for the quiches - those would be prepared later that afternoon. The wine bar had a limited menu of pizza, quiche, and a cheese and cracker board. Any leftover bakery from the morning was also for sale at half price. The quiches were made in advance for the whole weekend, while the personal pizzas were made to order.

Frankie hired two interns each semester from Madison Area Technical College's Culinary Arts and Hospitality programs. This created a mutually beneficial relationship for all involved; the interns were granted real world experience, while Frankie and Carmen were rewarded with employees who didn't have to be paid high wages. Not all interns are created equal, however, and some of their choices needed more guidance, reminders, and sometimes a scolding, but overall it was a win-win situation. The interns did food prep on Thursday, Friday, and Saturday nights, taking turns working the front of house as servers, and in the kitchen making pizzas and plating quiche or cheese and crackers. Both interns cleaned up after closing. Frankie, Carmen, and Frankie's mom, Peggy, ran the wine bar, offering tastings to customers, ringing up wine sales, serving up full bottles or single glasses of wine, and providing wine advice to patrons who wanted to know which wines go best with certain foods. Since Peggy always worked Thursday nights and Sunday afternoons (the wine shop only opened from 1-5 p.m. on Sundays), Frankie and Carmen filled in the Friday or Saturday evening slot, so each technically had time off every weekend. Technically, because Frankie found it hard to stay away from the business when she lived upstairs and often found herself popping in unannounced - a bad habit she knew she needed to quit. She trusted her co-workers, after all, and nothing produces low confidence levels like checking up on your staff, even if that's not what you mean to be doing. Peggy, like any mother, was forceful toward her daughter, insisting that Frankie "find something else to do because everything's fine here." Peggy's commands were easier to follow during the spring, summer and autumn months when Frankie had vineyards to care for, along with a garden and small orchard. The winter months, not so much.

Her New Year's resolution was to leave her apartment Thursday nights and Sunday afternoons and do something, so she'd been practicing yoga at the Wellness Center with Stormy, a yogi of perhaps 30 who had the free spirit of a flower-child from the 1960's. Frankie appreciated that Stormy referred to yoga as a practice because Frankie was certain that was all she'd ever be able to do was practice - not perform. Some Thursdays, Frankie would walk the track at the Wellness Center - she didn't enjoy using the equipment and couldn't remember how some of the machines worked from one day to the next. Frankie was not gifted when it came to machinery or operating anything that required more than two steps to remember, so she mostly tried to go to the variety of classes offered. The other problem with walking the same track for an hour was that it produced boredom; Frankie found her mind wandering to the baking that needed to happen, so she'd head back to the shop and start preparing baked goods for weekend orders. But first, she'd call the shop to let them know she was coming in. Well, Frankie was trying to keep her resolution anyway.

Now she and Carmen talked happily about the sheep farm, which was a booming business thanks to the natural fiber yarn-crafting craze that had returned to America, and the desire for local meats. Lamb was becoming a coveted culinary item on many posh menus around Madison and other cities. The O'Connors ran a true family business as the twins were literally raised in the sheep pens and began caring for them under the guiding hand of Ryan since they could walk and talk. Frankie recalled a favorite photo of Kyle and Carlos holding twin lambs one spring, each of the twins about the same size as the lamb he was holding, with laughing faces, Carlos pulling on the black wool of his lamb, while Kyle was gently nuzzling the neck of his white wooly friend. Nobody who was a stranger to Deep Lakes would imagine Kyle and Carlos were even brothers, not to mention twin brothers. Kyle looked so much like Carmen, brown skin, black silky hair, with intense dark brown eyes. While Carlos was the spitting image of his dad - they have the same laughing blue eyes, fair skin, and dark wavy hair. Carmen said they decided on the names after they were born, assigning the name the opposite way most people expected, just to throw them off. "We don't want people making assumptions about our kids," Carmen had said. Frankie knew Carmen had sometimes been stereotyped so she thought it was clever to turn the tables on people, keep them on their toes!

By 6:45 a.m. there was a small line waiting to get in the bakery and Carmen grinned wide, showing one dimple. "Somebody from the Library meeting spread the word about your Butterhorns is my guess," she gestured toward the front door. Since the bakery case was loaded anyway, the two opened the door early to let those customers in from the frigid cold. The grateful customers all grabbed coffee while waiting their turn, and the Butterhorns were the first to leave the case, boxed or bagged.

Frankie and Carmen experienced tremendous satisfaction in making goodies people raved about. With the bakery part of the shop only open a few hours, the two enjoyed serving customers, greeting regulars, and meeting newbies. Except for the occasional problem patron, most customers were easy to deal with. Bakery seemed to make people smile - wine had the same effect. Today, however, Frankie was less than thrilled to see the arrogant face of Bram Callahan, real estate tycoon of Whitman County. There were very few property deals in the area lacking Bram's golden touch, and it was widely known he didn't mind getting his hands a little dirty either. Raised in the business with both parents investing in expensive property ventures in Lake Geneva, Bram could smell capital a mile away, and he had no qualms about taking advantage of his clients. Domineering, superior, and clueless about good manners perfectly described Bram's public persona, which was all most people knew about him. Today, he walked right in front of poor Esther Brockton, throwing the elderly woman off balance as she leaned on her walking cane.

"I'm in a hurry, Francine. I need a dozen of those things. Morning meeting you know." He jabbed one fine leather gloved finger at the Butterhorns.

"Good morning, Mr. Callahan." Frankie was being extra polite for the moment. "I'm sorry - if you'd just wait your turn. I believe Mrs. Brockton is next. Good morning, Esther," Frankie said, turning her full attention in Esther's direction and completely away from Bram Callahan's. No doubt Esther could hold her own against someone with poor manners though. Deep Lakes' retired meter maid once towered over most people, but a dowager's hump took her down a few inches, leaving her with a stooped gait. Frankie recalled Esther's younger days, wearing a smart black skirt and short jacket, oversized police cap with the badge in the middle, guarding parking meters as time trickled to zero, then issuing tickets to vehicle after vehicle in downtown Deep Lakes. When offenders tried to wriggle their way out of a parking ticket, she wouldn't back down, and her almost 6-foot height (along with fashion boots adding three more inches most days) loomed over any adversary.

Taking her time on purpose, Esther couldn't decide exactly how many Butterhorns she needed this morning, her bent fingers calculating the number one-by-one several times. She settled on a dozen, leaving only six remaining for Bram. Esther turned a repentant face toward the realtor, her steely blue eyes looking directly into his, even though he was occupied with his cell phone. "Sorry, Mr. Callahan. You'll have to get here earlier next time," Esther's voice boomed to capture his attention. The comment didn't register with Bram at first until

Esther turned her gray permed head back around toward the bakery case, pointing to the all-but-empty tray of Butterhorns while Frankie boxed up her order, looking down so she wouldn't burst into a broad smile. Esther took the proffered box, then decided to order coffee and sit awhile to enjoy one of her purchases. Esther was a regular customer, coming in for what she called "good coffee" as opposed to Dixie's "burnt bottom" brand, but today she pretended to linger over her coffee decision, happy to pay back Bram for trying to cut in front of her. Coffee in hand, Esther made one more passing remark to Bram. "I hear the muffins are good."

There were only a few muffins left by closing time. "You know, Frankie, you should make Butterhorns every week or maybe we should market them," Carmen schemed.

"No way," Frankie said. "Too labor intensive. Besides, they wouldn't be special if I made them all the time, now would they?"

Carmen was on clean up today, so Frankie untied her apron and headed for her apartment stairs when Carmen called out, "Hey you! Where you off to in such a hurry?"

"Sheriff's Department," came Frankie's reply and she didn't wait to see the frown Carmen presented when she heard.

As Frankie headed up Meriwether and turned right onto Kilbourn Avenue, the locale for the sheriff's

department's new digs, she marveled at how this week
was going along at a crawl and a blur simultaneously. She
faced a full docket of preparation for the Valentine's event
while finishing up batches of wine at the vineyard, which
would have to be bottled and labeled before February
17th. Yet here she was chasing down a suspicious death,
a possible murder here in her small hometown, and the
victim a pastor no less! The full parking lot indicated the
sheriff's office was having a busy day, or maybe there were
lots of visitors at the jail - Frankie didn't know, but had
to park in one of the last stalls far away from the doors.
She figured she needed the extra walking steps anyway,
reminding herself she must go to the Wellness Center
today sometime. She took a quick look in her overhead
mirror, plumped her hair a bit and sighed. Frankie only
wore make-up on the rare occasion that demanded it,
believing it to be a waste of her precious time. Just now
she wondered why she was even noting that to herself -
was it because she was going to see Garrett Iverson and she
was actually concerned how he might view her appearance?

"Never hurts to look your best at all times," Golden
firefly buzzed in Frankie's ear.

"Oh, God help me from my mother," Frankie snipped,
getting out of the SUV and briskly walking to the
entrance. Once inside, Frankie set her purse in the plastic
tub before heading through the metal detector. She didn't
know the young female officer posted at security but gave
her a friendly smile and said hello.

"What's the reason for your visit today, Ma'am," the officer asked.

"I have an appointment with Officer Lazaar and the coroner," Frankie explained, handing over her driver's license, silently steaming about being pegged as a "ma'am"- a title she believed suited her mother, not her. The officer handed her a visitor's badge as Frankie picked up her purse and headed up the stairs to the second floor. She dreaded the idea of running into Officer Pflug and even Alonzo, who had seemed somewhat cool toward her at the accident scene. With any luck she could avoid both. Shirley Lazaar was manning the reception desk, probably because she filled in for officers on vacation or sick leave and didn't have an office of her own. She looked up as Frankie approached and gestured toward an empty room just behind her desk on the right. Frankie was grateful they could meet in a more private setting, making it less likely she would have to encounter Pflug and Alonzo. Frankie took out her phone, opened her notes and handed a small white sack to Shirley at the same time.

"What's this?" Shirley asked, opening the bag and making a non-committal half-grin at the Dark Side Chocolate and Cherry Almond muffins inside. "No Butterhorns left, eh?" she asked. Frankie shook her head, trying to decide if this woman liked her or thought she was just a pest, like an insect she'd like to swat but she wasn't sure what kind of insect it was yet. Shirley opened the manila file folder she had brought with her from the desk, getting right down to business. "Okay, here's what I can release on this case and this is all I can tell you so don't ask me for more. Already saw Abe Arnold from the *Watch* and I told him the same as you," Shirley looked Frankie straight in the eyeballs.

Time of death was about 8 a.m., plus or minus 15 minutes. Because of the blood smear outside the shanty and other evidence gathered, the police were treating this as a possible homicide and interviewing anyone who might be connected to Pastor Rawlins. Frankie rolled her eyes, imagining the long list of people connected to the pastor the police would have to contact - he was the pastor of a fairly large church after all. Of course, the department hoped the press would seriously implore anyone with information to come forward. Frankie said she was sure Abe would mention that in his article. "What about you, Francine? Your article?" Shirley asked. Frankie admitted she wasn't sure when her article would go to press but yes, she would include that information in it.

Frankie decided to ask questions anyway even if they bore no fruit.

"Can you tell me what other evidence you used to determine possible homicide?" she asked in her business voice. Shirley looked at the file, deciding what she was able to reveal.

"Well, you know the auger was a hand drill, so it's pretty irregular for somebody to get the kind of injury the pastor got." Shirley paused. "Possible, but far-fetched."

She went on, "Then there's the blood smear. Somebody tried to wipe that up, making sure there was no footprint. We found fabric fibers stuck in the ice." Frankie looked surprised. She'd missed seeing those fibers when she surveyed the scene, not once, but twice.

"Did you find any fingerprints at the scene?" Frankie asked.

Shirley hesitated; would she be giving away too much information that might help a murderer escape justice? She gave the safe response, "Nothing we can discuss at this point." Frankie didn't find that helpful.

"Any other evidence?" she asked.

"Fishing gear was all normal. The thermos and breakfast sandwich could be tested but since we know the auger caused the death, we think that would be a waste of taxpayer money," Shirley offered. To Frankie, that last comment seemed obvious and she wondered if she was being dismissed or sidetracked by the wise Shirley Lazaar. Frankie decided to test the waters once more.

"Anything on the business card from the Milwaukee lawyers?"

Shirley gave her a blank look. "Hmm. Fact is we don't know without looking deeper. There was a print on the card but only a partial," Shirley trailed off. Frankie saw a small advantage.

"So, I take it the print didn't match the pastor's," she stated rather than questioned.

Shirley lifted her chin a little, looked toward the office

doorway then said in a low tone, "That's right, but not for publication." Shirley stood up, signaling she was done being questioned. Frankie stood too, thanked Shirley for the information, and asked her if they could speak again as new facts came to light. Shirley said that was fine, but again, Frankie couldn't tell if she was being sincere or something else.

"You're such a rookie," the pirate firefly chastised Frankie. As she left the side room, Frankie bumped into Alonzo, who was heading to his back office with a case file box. He looked surprised to see her and not a bit pleased.

"Hi Lon," Frankie said quietly, testing his mood.

"Good morning, Frankie. Sorry I can't talk. I've got a lot of work to do," Alonzo's short reply sounded tired and irritated. What could Frankie do at this point? Nothing.

"Have a good day then," she said, headed out the door and down the hallway to the door marked "Coroner."

"It's open," came Garrett's voice on the other side of the door as Frankie rapped. Garrett looked up from his computer screen as she entered, smiled warmly and offered her a seat across from his desk.

"I hope you like chocolate muffins," Frankie said, handing him a small sack. Garrett proffered a genuine nod and another smile. Frankie sat, deciding that she needed to get right down to business, she explained, "I've already spoken with Officer Lazaar, so I just need to fill in a few details."

Garrett looked disappointed and surprised by her

sudden formality. "Alright. Officially the cause of death is massive blood loss from severed left femoral artery caused by a puncture from a sharp object, namely an ice auger. It likely took less than 8 minutes from the time of the injury to the time of death. Blood on the tip of the auger matched the victim's, confirming it as the instrument that caused the wound."

Frankie interrupted him. "Well, what else could have caused the wound?" she wondered.

Garrett confirmed, "Well, there was broken glass recovered from the scene but that didn't cause the injury."

Frankie looked surprised, and suddenly Garrett looked as if he just stepped in something left on the sidewalk by a canine. "Didn't Lazaar mention the broken glass?" Frankie admitted that she hadn't. She didn't want to lie, and she also didn't want anyone to get into official trouble for revealing information to the press that wasn't allowed.

"Ok," Frankie continued, "I know this is off the record, but can you tell me anything about the broken glass? Was it from the shanty window or door?" Frankie thought she would have noticed a broken window or door pane when she surveyed the scene, but after missing fibers in the blood smear, she doubted her observational skills. Garrett apologized, but said he really didn't deal with evidence outside the body so he couldn't say. *Damn,* Frankie thought, *now I must speak to Shirley again.* She wished she'd been better at observing or sniffing out facts, like a seasoned reporter.

Getting her mind back on track, Frankie went on, "Was there any other trauma to the body?" She still wondered what created the blood mark on one of the fishing benches.

Garrett smiled proudly at Frankie. "Good question, Ace," he said. "I looked for signs of a struggle, but because it was so cold, the pastor was covered virtually head to toe. He had on a Carhartt jacket, thick padded gloves, heavy boots, and a knit hat."

"Any blood on the hat," Frankie wanted to know.

Garrett shook his head no. "A little swollen spot on the back of his head when he fell to the ice but nothing major. No blood, only minor swelling. He probably slumped into his position on the ice, rather than falling hard."

Frankie wanted more details about a possible struggle. "Were there any marks on the pastor anywhere else? Any bruising from being hit or anything like that?"

Garrett was certain. "The sheriff wanted me to survey that body with a fine-tooth comb. There just isn't anything visible. Even if there was a struggle, it was masked by the padded outerwear." Frankie could tell that Garrett Iverson was invested in his profession, dedicated to uncovering any forensic evidence, no matter how small. Frankie nodded to herself, okay, so probably no other DNA evidence at the scene either. Frankie wondered if the blood mark on the bench had yielded any DNA. That was another question to ask Shirley.

Frankie backed off from reporter mode to look at the coroner. He had dark circles under his eyes and at least two days' worth of five o'clock shadow. "You must have been clocking in some long hours on this case, huh?" she said with empathy.

"Had to," Garrett remarked. "The church wants the funeral this week, so we need to release the body, plus the sheriff is boiling to move along this investigation. A homicide around here is about as popular as a skunk fight at a wedding," he finished, then added, "but it sure is nice to see a member of the press asking questions with bakery in hand." Garrett gave Frankie a wink that made her blush. She thanked him for the information, then turned to leave. Garrett's voice stopped her. "Are you interested in going to the Ice Races Sunday in Hustisford?" Ice races, just another wild winter pastime in Wisconsin. The Lake Sinissippi Ice Races were famous, held every Sunday at 11 in January and February - ice permitting - right by the Sinissippi Lake Pub. Of course, Wisconsinites mix pub grub with spectator sports!

Frankie wasn't sure how to answer, and she knew she'd begin to overthink the entire matter, so she went with her first instinct, "Gee Garrett, ice races are not really my cup of tea." Her words were barely out of her mouth when she caught the twinkle in his eyes - his melty caramel eyes - and he began to chuckle.

"How about a movie instead, a Sunday matinee at the local theater?" He offered instead.

Frankie, or someone who looked and sounded like Frankie, said "Sure. Yes, that sounds great."

"Alright then. I'll pick you up at the shop at 12:30 Sunday."

Heading back down the hallway to the sheriff's office, Frankie seemed to be floating outside herself. What just happened? Had she been asked on a date and agreed to go? The second thoughts were already coursing through her head while her feet seemed disconnected to the floor below. Both fireflies were alert and giggling. She was already at the sheriff's office, so this nonsense had to stop. She took a deep breath, reassembled her thoughts and opened the door, hoping Shirley would be at the front desk. She was and looked up at Frankie as if she was expecting to see her. "Can I ask you a few more questions, please?" Shirley stood and gestured to the room on the right again.

Frankie opened her phone notes. "First, were you able to get any DNA off the blood mark on the shanty bench?"

Shirley grinned. "Yep, and it's being tested so don't have any other info on that yet. Next?"

Frankie made a note and went on. "Where do you think the broken glass came from?" Shirley was clearly taken aback by this question and Frankie truly hoped she didn't know that Garrett had spilled the beans.

"So, you noticed that too, huh? You must have gotten a closer look at the scene than I thought." Frankie reminded Shirley she had taken pictures there and could zoom in for details. Although this was true, Frankie had not reviewed the photos closely, but she hoped this was a satisfactory explanation that kept Garrett out of trouble. "Can't tell you much about the broken glass. We're trying to print the two bigger chunks but not real hopeful. We're also looking at it in the lab, so maybe we'll figure out where it came from." Frankie made another note. She was beginning to greatly admire the minutiae involved with investigating a case - so much to keep track of, so many pieces to try to connect.

"I suppose the fibers in the blood smear are being examined in the lab, too."

Shirley confirmed Frankie's statement.

"But it all takes time, Francine." Shirley sat back and gave her a genuine smile. "You're pretty green at this investigating business, but you'll get there if you want to do it." Frankie became more at ease and thanked Shirley for her patience. She was beginning to believe she might have an ally in the department.

Chapter 7

*Geeks are people who love something so much
that all the details matter.*
- Marissa Mayer

Frankie was proud of herself. She woke Thursday refreshed from a decent night's sleep, which she attributed to a cardio dance workout with Jessie at the Wellness Center. The class, aptly named WERQ, combines fast-paced dance moves to pop, rock and hip-hop tunes, produces a good sweat, and thankfully most of the members don't take it seriously enough to judge others. Frankie was self-conscious the first couple of classes. Her middle name might be Grace, but she sure didn't have much, so she stayed in the back row until she no longer cared if she had the finesse demonstrated by the instructor. Frankie enjoyed the upbeat music and time flew by quickly. After class, Frankie ate a healthy supper, cooking a chicken breast and plating it atop a mile-high salad of field greens, herbs, carrot rounds, cucumber, yellow pepper, and pea pods. Then she headed to church choir rehearsal and sang her heart out, even though the Lenten numbers being practiced were often in minor keys with somber tones. Good for the soul, Frankie surmised. Everything does have its season indeed.

Today was going to be a busy one as Frankie planned a necessary visit to her vineyard on Blackbird Hill outside of town. She had four different varieties of wine percolating at the moment – these needed to be checked this week and moved into final stages for bottling before her Valentine's event. Frankie's interests in wine began as a teenager when her parents hosted several wine tasting parties at their home. Frankie was always allowed to taste – not to drink – and began to learn about the art of pairing wines with complementary foods. By the time she turned a legal drinking age, 18 at that time, she knew how to order wine successfully at a restaurant. When wineries began popping up around the Midwest, Frankie traveled on a few wine tours and wondered if she could learn to make wine. Her first attempts from kits were decent enough to impress her friends and family, who received bottles for Christmas, but she hoped to someday produce something with more flair and flavor.

Sometimes opportunity presents itself cloaked in bitter garb. Five years ago a fire broke out next door to Frankie's house in town. As the fire department waged war to contain the flames, the wooden fence between the burning home and Frankie's caught fire and an unfriendly wind blew the raging fire onto the small two-story home where Frankie had raised her two daughters. She and Violet (Sophie was at college) watched across the street in Frankie's brother's truck, wrapped in security blankets donated to the department for trauma victims, as the fire raced through their home, licking up the walls, blowing out the windows, leaping through the rooftop. They both stared, unable to look away - such is the hypnotic force of fire. They cried together, sobbing in each other's arms at the loss. They took the few belongings they had and moved in with Frankie's mother on the opposite side of town. Frankie's father, Charlie, had passed away less than a year earlier and being in her parents' home without her dad there made the loss that much harder. Peggy, of course, was in full-blown mother mode, happy to take care of someone, to feel useful, to be the rescuer. Violet loved how Grandma doted on her, and Frankie supposed that was a good thing - a safe place where her daughter could feel secure and have the balance of her world restored. But, Frankie felt like a little girl again and sometimes resented her mother's attention. Frankie found herself believing she was a rotten ungrateful daughter and there was tension at times between her and Peggy, tension that Frankie despised. She needed a fresh start and a new plan.

The house was a total loss. Fortunately, Frankie's homeowners insurance included replacement value coverage on the home and its contents. Investigators determined the fire began when the neighbor's teenage sons decided to barbecue indoors out of season, since it was December. The blaze from the charcoal grill caught the kitchen curtains on fire and the older home fueled the flames. Because of the neighbors' negligence, and with the expertise of Frankie's employer-lawyers, Ward Dickens and Jonah Probst, Frankie was able to collect insurance money from the neighbors' liability policy. She found herself with a nice little nest egg and wanted to make a smart decision before purchasing her next home.

Pursuing two of her passions, Frankie hatched the idea of buying the vacated landmark bank building downtown and renovating it into a combination bakery/wine bar. She enlisted the advice from her most trusted people: Carmen, Alonzo, and brothers Will and James. James agreed to sell a parcel of his property around Blackbird Hill for Frankie to start a small vineyard and winemaking enterprise.

Peggy was frightened for her daughter, frightened she might lose her shirt in an uncertain business and her whole world would come crashing down again. Frankie was Peggy's only daughter and she had seen her suffer enough, first from a devastating abandonment by her husband, then from the loss of her beloved father, then the fire. Peggy wasn't a fan of risk-taking and wanted to spare her daughter any further losses. But Frankie, like her father, was headstrong and once an idea formed, she would look down the road and see it to fruition, fully formed and thriving. She was like a runaway train. But in this case, older and wiser, Frankie knew to find business partners, to seek sound business advice, and to make a business plan. Carmen, well established in the family sheep business and with sons approaching their teens, had time and desire to add something new in her life. With her husband's blessing, she decided to invest with Frankie.

The corner building at #10 Granite and Meriwether had seen a number of failed enterprises over the decades, and the owner was anxious to sell it rather than continuing to lease it. He liked the idea of a sure thing, and Frankie negotiated a favorable deal. The building had the added advantage of the upstairs apartment with three bedrooms where Frankie could make her home, and an extra storefront on the Meriwether Street side, where the downstairs could be divided and rented out to another business. Two years ago, Rachel Engebretsen, an artist of many talents, opened "Bead Me, I'm Yours and Other Handcrafts" at #10 Meriwether and was doing well, not only selling crafting items but offering frequent workshops in jewelry making and monthly Paint Nights that featured Frankie's wines.

It was Frankie's brother Will, signing on to be her business partner for the vineyard, who convinced James to sell several acres of land to Frankie and construct the concrete block building for winemaking, and the pole building that would serve as storage and a tool shed for tending the vineyard and orchard. The acreage included some of the hillside and valley below, an excellent geographical configuration for growing fruits. After choosing a Southwest-facing flat area that offered the optimum sunshine for the short Wisconsin growing season, the soil was tested at UW-Stevens Point thanks to Will and Libby, additives were purchased, and sheep manure fertilizer was provided by Carmen and Ryan.

Two acres were prepared and planted in hardy white grape varieties. Edelweiss, which mimics a traditional grape used for Riesling, is perfect for sweet wines with its fruity and honey aroma. Along with La Crescent, known for its acidity and rich, crisp flavor. Like most Wisconsin vintners, Frankie would have to supplement her winemaking by buying juices from suppliers in California, Pennsylvania, and New York, where other grape varieties could thrive. Five years into the operation, Frankie now grew two other grape varieties - the red Frontenac and white Briana, both hardy through Wisconsin winters.

Her small fruit orchard included hardy all-purpose apples, pears, and peaches - some were used for baking, some for wine. She purchased pressed fruits and berries to supplement her own juices. The property also provided ample raspberry and blackberry bushes - enough to use for jams, pastries, and wine. Frankie hoped to add one or two more grape varieties in a year or two, but for now, she had enough on her plate. Mastering grape cultivation was no easy task, and she wanted to establish her delicate vines before adding more. She had wrapped up her fifth harvest this past fall and with Will's help, and the good graces of happy weather conditions, their vines were thriving. An acre of grapes can yield anywhere from 1,440 to 7,200 bottles of wine - a broad range for any farmer to bet on with precise certainty. A smart vintner cannot produce wines until vines are in their third year of harvest. Frankie and Will were ecstatic to yield about 3,000 bottles per acre their first production year and 4,000 the second. The elusive 7,200 bottles might come in a year or two when all the growing conditions were optimal - if that ever occurred. One thing that's certain about agriculture is that you can count on it to be uncertain. Farmers in her state lived by the adage, "if you don't like the weather in Wisconsin, just wait a day or two and it will change." Frankie recalled summer-like weather in both November and March, and snow-covered Tulips and apple blossoms in May.

As she drove south out of town on County K, she leisurely watched the winter landscape pass by while surveying the tall, bare trees and electrical poles for hawks and eagles on the lookout for a meal. Stark toasted brown fields of empty corn stalks lined the road - there hadn't been a fresh snowfall in a while, maybe a month, Frankie thought. She'd already heard talk among the locals about the winter drought, the need for more snow to supply the farm fields with moisture for crops, just one more thing to worry about when you make a living off the land. The naked oaks seemed to raise their ragged black arms to the sky, pleading for a reprieve from the bitter cold. Today was sunny and the ground sparkled where bits of snow remained in the field ruts and crooks of trees the wind had left alone. About three miles out, Frankie spied a majestic Red-tailed Hawk, its straight posture in perfect repose, as if it was settled in for the day. But she knew better. Frankie had seen a Red-tailed Hawk sail into a field, pounce on a smaller bird (maybe a Starling) with precision and grace, deftly ending its life with one sharp talon, announcing its prowess with a raspy screech. She marveled at the bird world with its many species and balanced hierarchy, and enjoyed watching and feeding them. Besides belonging to both the Wisconsin Natural Resources Federation and Audubon Society, Frankie was a member of her county bird club, the Whitman Seekers, attending club events and field trips when she could work it into her busy schedule.

Two miles further, she made a left turn onto Blackbird Marsh Road, noticing it was still partially snow-packed with sand spread on the icy spots, and some bare stretches where the sun hit the pavement during the afternoon hours. The road traveled straight along the marsh then curved around Blackbird Hill, straightening out again along the Blackbird River. Frankie's vineyard, Bountiful Fruits, was only a couple of miles down the road, a few miles west of the river. Her driveway was the first one on the property, the hand painted wooden sign announcing the vineyard's name at the entrance, and a wide gravel driveway between pine tree guardians on either side. Another 100 yards or so, the driveway widened to a gravel parking area large enough for five or six vehicles in front of a cement building that was the winery. The winery was partially nestled into the hillside, its dark red rooftop featured solar panels to help offset the cost of LP fuel. The driveway wound further down the hill where a large pole building stood, announcing the vineyards below.

Frankie saw a small gray vehicle in the lot, probably belonging to Nelson Raye, the interning vintner hired by Will. Frankie opened the heavy red steel door at the entrance, calling out as she walked in, so as not to startle Nelson. The building was well-insulated and warm, thanks to an energy efficient gas furnace, and Frankie welcomed the respite from the once-again bitter cold temperature. Nelson turned, gave her a small wave and immediately started rattling off statistics on the progress of the current wines being batched. Nelson looked all of 13 years of age, with his small stature and boyish face. Rounded black eyeglasses framed his gray eyes, and his hair was short, parted, and combed on the left side, baby fine hair that mimicked his baby face. Below his white lab coat, tan khakis peeked out above a pair of brown Hush Puppies. Frankie learned early in their relationship not to judge Nelson's competency by his youthful appearance. He was proving to be one of the best interns Will had found in the UW-Stevens Point microbiology program. Nelson had started at Bountiful Fruits in August and would be with them through December, thankfully, until he graduated midterm. He had already measured the specific gravity of the "Oh My, Apple Pie" and "Cupid's Cup" batches, explaining that additional cane sugar would be added to "Cupid's Cup" to achieve a higher alcohol percentage, a process called chaptalization. Using the hydrometer, he and Frankie measured specific gravity on the two other varieties, "Spring Fever Riesling" and "Crown Me Pineapple."

Jotting down numbers, Nelson smiled with satisfaction. "It appears all four tanks will be ready for bottling next week," he declared. Frankie was equally pleased. One big bottling party would mean all the wines would be available for the Valentine event, although, as Nelson pointed out, they would be improved with a month's rest in the bottle.

Frankie gave Nelson an appreciative grin. "You know that, and I know that, Nelson, but the people at the Valentine event won't know that. And, any bottles we sell that night, we'll mention that to our customers as a tip."

Frankie calculated approximately 800 bottles of wine would be corked at their next bottling party, and she would need to start rounding up family, friends and co-workers to make it happen. Her operation was too small to afford automated bottling, so she relied on manpower and 5 floor corkers to get her vintages from winery to customer. Usually that meant about four people or so per her four 200-liter stainless steel tanks. Two would fill bottles from the tank ports, one would cork the bottles, and one would heat attach the labels to the corked bottles. It was also nice to have at least one person loading bottles into cases and stamping each case with the appropriate name. With around 20 people inside the winery, there was just enough space to add a picnic table loaded with treats for the hungry helpers. The added perk of helping with bottling was being among the first to taste the new vintages and take a favorite bottle or two home. The winery included a large basement where the temperature was regulated to about 55 degrees, a perfect storing temperature for over a hundred cases of wine. Frankie's building in town had an even larger basement where more wine was stored - the batches traded out according to their date of completion for drinking, as well as supply and demand.

Nelson volunteered his bottling services right away, regardless of the date, adding he would be willing to bring along a couple of others from his department, if Frankie wanted them. Nelson was "psyched", as he put it, to be involved in commercial wine-making and wanted to publicize his bragging rights to fellow microbiologists. Frankie promised to let him know as soon as possible. Today was February 1st so she was thinking they would likely bottle on the 7th, a Wednesday night, since waiting until the weekend would create scheduling conflicts with the wine shop being open. She needed her shop workers to join the bottling brigade. That meant she had less than a week to get her helpers lined up. "Go ahead and lock down those department people you want to bring," she told Nelson, thinking she'd rather have too many volunteers than not enough.

Frankie paused in her thoughts, once again reminded

of the article she was trying to construct on the pastor's death. "Nelson, you're a smart guy," she began.

"Huh, I don't think anyone has ever referred to me as a "guy" before so I don't know if I should cheer or be insulted, Ms. Champagne." Frankie laughed a little, but not too much because Nelson had difficulty with social cues and she didn't want to make him uncomfortable.

"Well, I didn't mean it in a bad way. But, I'm working on a news story about a mysterious death that happened on Lake Loki Monday morning and I want to pick your brain, if I may." Nelson's poker face didn't convey any shock at hearing about a mysterious death; he simply nodded at Frankie, giving her his full attention. Frankie reconstructed the details as she remembered them, beginning with the pastor found dead inside his fishing shanty, stabbed by an ice auger. Evidence inside the shanty included broken glass, a bottle cap, and business card from a Milwaukee law firm. In addition, a bloody mark was visible on the fishing bench along with a lot of blood on the ice floor, and most suspiciously, a large bloody smear outside the shanty. Frankie also mentioned the noticeable vanilla-citrus scent inside the shanty, and finally, the scrap of calendar she found on the pastor's desk, indicating an 8 a.m. Monday meeting with "patrick".

As she recounted the details, she could see Nelson's brain at work, sorting the information into necessary file folders, almost like a computer. Frankie remained silent until Nelson spoke.

"Well, you can't assume it's a murder," he began. "After all, it appears there was a struggle so maybe the pastor attacked the other person first and that person used the auger in self-defense. Did the other person meet the pastor with the intention of murdering him? If so, why didn't that person bring or use his/her own weapon instead of the pastor's auger? An auger is not only messy, but it's not a very certain method for killing someone. The killer would have to have precise aim. Maybe the other person never meant to kill him, just fend him off. Furthermore, it appears the pastor chose the meeting place, so he would definitely have the upper hand in the situation." Frankie was grateful for Nelson's version of a logical scenario, ideas she hadn't entertained or thought through before.

Holding up one finger at Frankie, Nelson added, "Maybe the broken glass was from a bottle containing alcohol. Maybe the pastor wasn't a teetotaller, or intended to add liquor to his coffee to stay warm."

Frankie chewed on that for a moment, wondering if the silver cap could be from a liquor bottle, but no, more likely a flask, she thought. Hmm. "Well, Nelson, I don't know of any liquor that smells of vanilla and citrus, but possibly…" Frankie faltered, again racking her brain. Had there been any smell of alcohol in the shanty? She knew the olfactory sense was deeply connected to memories and she was keenly aware that she knew that vanilla-citrus smell from somewhere. She could only imagine the little yellow tree air freshener again, as she had ridden in a few vehicles with that particular scent. The smell nagged at her, as if she hadn't quite identified it correctly.

She asked Nelson how he would proceed if he were writing the article. He smiled. "Well, I would start talking to people in his church. Churches in small towns are full of gossips, and somebody knows something that could be a clue as to what happened. And, Ms. Champagne, don't bother talking to the men. It's the women who will likely know the right information."

Frankie giggled under her breath once more, "You are wise beyond your years, Nelson Raye." Frankie didn't tell Nelson she already had plans to do just as he suggested, starting with playing detective at the funeral tomorrow.

Chapter 8

Hades tempted Persephone first with the perfumed Narcissus flower. As she stooped to breathe in its intoxicating scent, the earth split open, the sky darkened, and the lord of the Underworld rose from the chasm in a dark chariot, trapping Persephone, capturing her for his very own ...
- Greek Mythology

Frankie breezed in through the back door of the shop and straight into the kitchen to see how things were proceeding for the day. It was just after 9 and the kitchen was hopping as both interns and Carmen were prepping baked goods for Friday, and quiches for the evening wine bar offerings. Tess was humming as she rolled out scone dough, her short round frame bopping to the beat of music. Tess, a 22-year-old African culinary student from Ethiopia, now living in Madison, was pure happiness in the kitchen. Frankie loved how Tess threw herself into any baking challenge; she loved to experiment with flavors, and Frankie found herself asking Tess to make some of her personal creations on a regular basis. Frankie was excited to learn from Tess, who brought new flavor combinations from her country to Frankie's shop. Today, her lovely brown hands were kneading the dough lightly as she added in coconut flakes and a sprinkle of curry powder. "That smells divine, Tess," Frankie complimented. "What else are we putting out tomorrow?" Tess, who looked down at the compliment, pointed to the oven where Chocolate Caramel scones were currently in progress, then waved her hand at the far counter where a batch of Lemon Basil scones were cooling on racks. Frankie gave her a thumbs up then, brushing past her side, she whispered, "You need to learn how to take a compliment, Tess. Don't you bow your head to anyone," she softly chided. Tess just smiled a small smile, nodded once and resumed humming.

The other intern, Adam, a tall long-armed 31-year-old from Baraboo, appeared to be rocking out to whatever his ear buds were playing, while whipping up one of Bubble and Bake's best selling quiches - Sad Tomato Pie, so named because the main ingredients were caramelized onions and roasted tomatoes, both making for big flavor. Frankie had prepped the pie dough into shells the night before, enough for 6 quiches. After Friday, her crew would reassess to see if more dough needed to be prepped for quiches on Saturday. Frankie motioned to Adam for his attention and he removed both ear buds and looked up, or rather down, at Frankie. "Your onions and tomatoes are just beautiful. Real good color on those, Adam." Adam beamed at the compliment. His specialty was working front of house, schmoozing with customers, keeping stock of needed supplies and refills, watching for any unhappiness among the clientele. But Frankie insisted that both interns have knowledge and experience in all aspects of running her shop, and that meant everyone would learn to bake, prep, clean, and provide customer service. Adam was a quick learner in the baking area and, despite a few disasters, he managed the recipes allotted to him. Tess was a little shy with customers so the experience every weekend would be a good confidence-builder. The two interns had only come on board right after Christmas, so they were still finding their feet.

Carmen arrived in the kitchen after finishing up with the bakery customers, rolling the big glass bakery cart with the leftovers to bag and box for sale that evening at half price. "Oh, hey there Frankie," Carmen said. "How goes it at the vineyard?" Frankie updated Carmen on the wines, suggesting they bottle on the 7th, if possible. Frankie usually employed the help of Carmen's husband, Ryan, and the twins so she hoped the date would be workable.

Carmen glowered in her direction and tsked. "Come on, Frankie, you know that Wednesday is catechism. The twins are working on Confirmation and you're in the choir," she said, as if Frankie had checked her brain at the back door. "Can we do it Tuesday night instead?" Carmen asked.

Frankie had to admit she wasn't thinking about church night: she had been too distracted by all she needed to accomplish before the Valentine's event and only the date registered with her, not the day. "I'm sure we can. I'll just fly a text to Nelson. He's going to bring a couple microbiology brainiacs with him," Frankie said. She waved at Adam and said to both him and Tess, "Can you bottle on Tuesday night? We could really use your help. We're going to put up about 800 bottles!" Tess affirmed immediately, and Adam checked his calendar, also nodding. She hoped Nelson and his crew could make it too.

Frankie dove into quiche-making, creating her signature pie, a mouth-watering bacon and asparagus dish loaded with French herbs and spices. It was her most popular quiche and she could make it in her sleep she'd done it so often. Carmen checked on Adam's pies and Tess's scones, gave her approval, and started on clean-up while Tess checked the rise of her dough for orange marmalade rolls. The dough needed a little longer to rise and Adam's quiches were baking, so Frankie and Carmen invited the interns to sit down for coffee and a meeting to finalize the Valentine Romantic Getaway event. There would be five wine pairings with small plates served in courses, each food item would be from a different culture. This could get tricky, making sure each item combined well with the next, so the palate didn't get too confused. The four huddled, searched their smartphones for recipe ideas and travel destinations, and agreed on a menu.

The night would begin with an appetizer from the United Kingdom, a Scotch egg with parsnip puree, and a pea shoot salad topped with lemon vinaigrette paired with Crown Me Pineapple, a semi-sweet white table wine, not exactly English, but oh well.

The second course would be a soup of pea pods and coriander, blended with Indian spices, accompanied by a traditional Samosa fritter for dipping in the soup. Spring Fever Riesling would pair well with this course, a refreshing crisp white wine with hints of lemon and lavender.

The third course would feature a Moroccan spiced risotto with tomato chutney, paired with the winery's new flavor bottled last fall, Persephone's Temptation, a Pomegranate Zinfandel. Persephone was the Greek Goddess of Spring who had been captured and taken to the Underworld to live as the wife of Hades. Her mother, Demeter, the Goddess of Agriculture, would allow nothing to grow on earth unless her daughter was returned to her, so Hades was forced to yield when Zeus intervened. Except, in his sly way, Hades tricked Persephone, deceiving her by offering her the irresistible pomegranate. To eat or drink anything in the Underworld meant one would have to live there forever. Persephone ate six pomegranate seeds, meaning she must return to him every year for the winter months, one month for each seed consumed. Frankie loved the story, but admittedly found pomegranates too large a labor for eating purposes. However, the taste of pom juice in wine was a discovered delight, which she capitalized upon, thanks to her juice supplier.

The fourth course, the entree, sparked a lively debate as

there were just too many choices and cultures to decide on just one. Adam was determined to execute fine Brazilian rodizio-style steak on large skewers. This would be served in a 4-ounce chunk, along with two Mediterranean grilled prawns with cilantro, lime, and chili sauce - two romantic destinations in one. Frankie's always faithful hearty red table wine, Dark Deeds, a black cherry Lambrusco was going to be a lovely pairing. The entree would be able to stand up to the Lambrusco, but she knew that some of her less-experienced drinkers might not be able to, this being their fourth glass of wine!

Finally, it was decided the dessert would be a trio of two-bite delights. From France, a Pear Galette (tart) with a crumble butter crust, then circle back to the United Kingdom for one of Frankie's favorite desserts, the velvety smooth Lemon Posset (a kind of pudding/curd) with Blueberries and a honey shortbread cookie, and finally, three hand-made truffles rolled in cocoa powder. The dessert course would end with one of Bountiful Fruits' sweet yet unpredictable wines, Cupid's Cup. This wine was concocted with multiple frozen fruit pulps that were leftovers from the previous summer harvest, so the taste changed from year to year, a quality Frankie absolutely loved about this wine.

Decorations for the event would be simple. Frankie purchased paper lanterns to hang from the rafters, and her team would load the bar top with LED candles in white and red. Each table would be adorned with the glittery bubble vases Frankie bought on clearance from a craft store going out of business. Whatever flowers she and Carmen could buy at an economic price would be going in those vases - definitely not roses since their prices spiked over the moon for Valentine's Day. While Carmen scribbled out a shopping list for foods, Frankie planned to stock the wine, call the piano player informing him of the countries featured in the menu so he could plan his play list accordingly, and order flowers. Plans were also in place for preparing all the dishes. The event was sold out at 62 tickets - the wine lounge area normally accommodated 50, but with the bar not in use for the night three more tables of four were added. Even at that capacity, Frankie had a waiting list of another 10 or so names. Sometime that evening, she would email all the reserved guests with the menu, requesting any allergies or special dietary needs. Anyone who changed their mind about the event could then be replaced by a waitlister, but that was unlikely as all reservations had been prepaid.

With the Valentine event firmed up, Frankie breathed a sigh of relief until Carmen reminded her, "We still have to tally the cupcake orders for Valentine's Day and decide who's going to make what and when." How could the cupcake extravaganza have slipped Frankie's mind?

The Golden firefly sparked to life immediately with the answer: "Maybe you're too preoccupied playing big-time reporter," she snarked, to Frankie's dismay.

Trying to drum up business their first year at the

shop, Carmen suggested taking orders for special filled cupcakes, jumbo-sized, for Valentine's Day. Although the two were already planning their first Valentine's Wine Pairing Night, they admittedly needed the money, and capitalizing on the holiday of love was a good opportunity to make some cash. The two made a little over 200 cupcakes the first year and that seemed like a breeze, so after advertising in the *Watch* and the local shopper, they capped their orders to 350 last year. This year, however, with the additional help of Tess and Adam and even Frankie's mom, they stopped taking orders at 600! Clearly, they needed a plan to accomplish this, likely including an all-nighter of icing and decorating on the 13th. Carmen pulled out the stack of unsorted order forms which she and Frankie sorted into three piles according to the three flavors they offered this year. Tess, a lover of all holidays, was ecstatic about every aspect of creating the lovely cupcakes, thinking of how much joy they would bring to both giver and receiver, but Adam was nervous and uncertain of his baking prowess.

Carmen reassured him, "Don't you worry, Adam. We can do the baking - you can help fill, make icing, box them. There's plenty to do." It was settled that each of the women would make one variety of cupcake to expedite the process. Carmen's brother, Esteban, managed a plant in Nekoosa that made boxes and napkins for every purpose and it was Esteban that offered the shop a deal on their everyday boxes and napkins. For the Valentine cupcakes, however, beautiful shimmery boxes the color of gold champagne were crafted at the plant, embossed with the Bubble and Bake logo, and a wine glass with a frosted donut hanging on the rim. Each box was the perfect size for one jumbo cupcake.

Frankie refilled her coffee mug, tired from planning, and checked the time. It was well past noon and she was hungry. With Tess back at work on the orange marmalade rolls and Adam out front stocking the wine bar ,which also offered regionally bottled beers from New Glarus, Madison, and Chippewa Falls, Frankie suggested she and Carmen go out to lunch. Just around the corner and down Meriwether was the MudPuppy, a bar and grill with giant juicy burgers and hand-cut fries. Frankie couldn't remember the last time she had splurged on bar food and Carmen was right along with her on that count. As they enjoyed their burgers and split an order of fries, Carmen asked Frankie about the pastor's death.

"You still working on that article?" she asked, more with accusation than curiosity, Frankie thought. Frankie filled Carmen in on her investigation and the details she gleaned from both Shirley Lazaar and Garrett Iverson. Carmen shook her head. "You know, I just worry about you. What are you trying to be anyway, Frankie? A hot-shot reporter or a business owner?" Frankie smiled and giggled at Carmen's show of bossy concern, but Carmen was relentless. "I mean it, Frankie. I'm in this business for the long haul and I want to make sure my business partner doesn't fly the coop, you know. Or something worse." Frankie stopped, mid-bite.

"What do you mean, something worse?" she demanded.

Carmen was candid as usual. "I mean you're sticking your nose in a homicide investigation. If there's a murderer out there, you might not be safe." Frankie said she didn't buy into that. "Okay, but you better keep your head down, is all I'm saying," Carmen warned, "and you know that cop don't like you either." Frankie couldn't argue with her on that one.

"Well, I'm going to the funeral tomorrow to scout out the scene, Carmen, if that's okay with you. It's not until 11 so you won't have to cover for me." Carmen just rolled her eyes and shoved a fat fry in her mouth as Frankie thanked her for being a wonderful friend and business partner. "You know you could come with me to the funeral. Two sets of eyes are better than one," she said, only half joking. Carmen said not her, no way.

Wanting to end lunch on a happy note, Frankie confided in Carmen that she accepted a date with Garrett Iverson to go to a movie Sunday. Carmen let out a low whistle. "Wow, big date. A movie, just a movie. No dinner?" She was mocking Frankie, knowing that she was gun-shy in the dating department. When she saw the hurt look on her friend's face, Carmen softened her tone. "That's really cool, Frankie. I'm glad you're taking a chance, even a small one. Just do me one favor please." Frankie cocked a brow at her friend. "Don't talk about the investigation or the

article, don't even bring it up. It's a date, remember that."
Frankie promised she would try to remember.

* * *

Back at her apartment, Frankie looked up the
Wellness Center's class schedule to see if she could fit in
a Yoga session before her evening plans. She was stuffed
from lunch and knew she couldn't make her usual class
work on a full stomach. Luckily, the center offered a class
at 5 p.m. that would work perfectly for her. Two hours
later, donned in yoga pants and a workout shirt, Frankie
bopped down the stairs, putting on her parka as she
walked through the wine bar.

"Well, if it isn't my long-lost daughter," Peggy's voice
came from behind the bar where she was busying herself
setting out wine tasting glasses and checklists. Frankie's
mom always looked completely put together, her silvery
locks were expertly managed but made to look thrown
together, with her wispy bangs and feathery layers framing
her oval face. Her icy blue eyes dazzled under muted
mascara and highlighted eyelids while her complexion
still had a healthy glow, belying her 70 plus years. She
was taller than Frankie by a few inches and knew how
to dress to make the most of her figure. Today she was
dressed in black tweed-like slacks and a flowing fuchsia
tunic that hung asymmetrically across her waist and hips.
A long necklace of silvery flowers and matching dangling

earrings complemented her look. Peggy, whose formal name was Marit, declaring her Scandinavian heritage, remained a fixture in the lives of her five children, but was fiercely independent following the unexpected death of her husband, Charlie, five years earlier. Frankie didn't think she resembled her mother in any fashion, certainly not physically, but Carmen frequently reminded Frankie that like Peggy, Frankie was ferociously independent and knew her own mind. Frankie translated that comment to mean stubborn, or maybe opinionated, or both. Maybe she and her mother butted heads because they were more alike than either was willing to admit. Peggy's greeting reminded Frankie she hadn't talked to her mom all week and the guilt crept upon her, making her feel like a naughty child.

"Hey mom. How's your week been?" Frankie might as well acknowledge her failure to communicate this week. Peggy gave her daughter a meaningful look.

"Oh, just fine. What have you been up to?" Frankie felt like a fish on a hook. Obviously, her mother knew something, or everything, so she'd have to decide how much bait she was willing to swallow.

"Oh, I've been working on a news article on Pastor Rawlins' death and planning the Valentine's event along with running a winery and bakery. So, yeah, pretty busy week." She knew she came off as disrespectful, or shame-faced, or both, and immediately regretted it. Frankie adored her mother, admired her spirit and grace and greatly appreciated all of the help she had freely given her over the years, but who says love isn't complicated? Peggy returned her response with a small frown.

"I heard about your little investigation," she said, her voice tending toward shrill. Frankie didn't allow her to continue.

"I'm sorry. I've been caught up in this mysterious death and I just want the chance to write something meaningful, something that will show Abe Arnold he should take me seriously, Mom." Peggy patted her daughter's hand briefly.

"Okay then, go get 'em, Honey, but be careful." Then changing her tone again, "Where are you off to? You do have plans for tonight - I hope." Frankie said she was off to yoga class and hopefully later hanging out with Alonzo. Peggy raised one brow at the latter. "Alonzo, eh? It's about time." Frankie didn't have time to get into a discussion on the topic of Alonzo, a man her mother had chosen for her since her divorce from Rick many moons ago. Despite explaining repeatedly that she and Lon were dear friends, her mother wasn't one to give up on the idea of a romance. Frankie stopped back in the kitchen, grabbed two orange marmalade rolls with an apology to Tess, and headed out the front door again with a wave and smile to her mom.

At the Wellness Center, Frankie's yoga class was unexpected to say the least. She looked forward to her instructor's methods - Stormy was affirming, gentle, and encouraging. She always set the room up with flickering LED candles and New Age inspirational music. The room today had too much artificial light, even though the overhead fixtures had been dimmed, and the music playing was tinny with a lot of gongs. Instead of Stormy, Wendy Jarvis, the center's manager, entered the room in yoga clothes, unsmiling, clearly just going through the motions of announcing moves. During the hour-long regimen, Frankie could not find any flow or peace; she noticed her fellow compadres were falling out of positions, huffing and puffing rather than methodically breathing. There was a noticeable relief when Wendy abruptly ended class with an insincere "Namaste" delivered while the students were in the "downward dog" position, butts raised in salute to any gawkers at the tall glass windows. Wendy exited immediately, clearly not wanting to be engaged in any conversations. Everyone was too dumbfounded to speak, simply shrugging and exchanging alarmed looks as they left the classroom. Frankie wasn't one to be daunted however, and recognizing that something was amiss, she sought out Wendy's whereabouts.

Passing the front reception area, Frankie walked down the hallway where the trainer and instructor offices were located. The third door on the right had Wendy Jarvis's name on it and Frankie walked through the partially open door. Wendy, her dark hair pulled back in a ponytail, was staring at her computer monitor but didn't seem to be reading anything. "Hi, Wendy. Just wondering if Stormy is sick or something?" Frankie began. Wendy's head jerked, robot-like, in Frankie's direction at the question and she flushed red.

"No, Stormy is not sick. She's been dismissed."

Frankie's jaw went slack. "Dismissed. What? Why?" Frankie wasn't thinking, just reacting.

Wendy stood now and looked down at Frankie's incredulous expression.

With calm composure regained, Wendy responded, "Well, she was sleeping with my husband, so I fired her. That's why. Now, if you'll excuse me, I have to post an ad for her position." Frankie quickly left, wondering what changes would be coming since Wendy and her husband, Jeff, managed the center together.

Back in the SUV, Frankie dismissed the shock of the Stormy situation to focus on her next endeavor, meeting up with Alonzo at Hat Trick Sports Bar on Dodge Street, a couple streets over from the main drag of downtown. She pulled into the jam-packed lot, thinking everyone in Deep Lakes must be here tonight to watch the U.S. Olympic Hockey team take on Sweden. Hockey was almost as big as football around here, and had a more boisterous following than basketball for sure. For those unacquainted with hockey lingo, a hat trick means a single player scores three goals in the same game. Finding no place to park, she pulled back onto the street, but Dodge was lined with parked vehicles already, so she swung a right onto Doty, another street named for famous Wisconsinite, James

Doty, who proposed that Madison be the location for the state capital. Most Wisconsin communities had a Doty and a Dodge Street; Dodge named for Henry Dodge, the first territorial Governor of Wisconsin in 1836. Toward the end of the first block on Doty, Frankie spied one parking spot, but she would have to parallel park to get into it, and it had a jog, so that was out. She could barely parallel park in a long, straight, wide spot in the daylight, never mind anything more challenging. Proceeding into the second block, she pulled into the first open space that was two spaces in a row.

When she walked into the Black and White stucco building housing Hat Trick, she looked among the crowd, mostly males, and spotted Alonzo as he was waving her over to a small side table with two stools.

"Wow this place is hoppin'," Frankie said.

"Yeah, and you're late," Alonzo replied. Dressed in a Badger Hockey jersey and blue jeans, the sheriff looked like a regular guy, not intimidating in the least. Frankie decided this look almost brought him back to college age, except for a receding hairline that kept his light brown hair cropped shorter, and an extra twenty pounds in his mid-line region. He had an almost-empty glass of beer in front of him and was waving over a server to order another. Frankie knew she was only a few minutes late at most and informed Alonzo of the parking situation. He nodded, announcing, "I already ordered broccoli-cheese bites, onion rings, and cheese curds." Those were all Frankie's favorites and she nodded her approval. "Didn't know what you were drinking though for sure," he added. Frankie ordered a German Wheat Beer; Alonzo ordered a second pint of his local favorite. Frankie filled him in on the yoga class and news from the Wellness Center about Wendy and Jeff Jarvis. Alonzo let out a little whistle, "That's kind of surprising. I always thought Jeff only had eyes for Wendy. Never heard of him stepping out before." Frankie sighed.

"I guess you just never know. I mean it's easy to assume things about people, and then find out you were dead wrong." Frankie didn't want to bring up the Pastor Rawlins case, after all, she had called Alonzo this afternoon to get back into his good graces. But, that didn't stop Alonzo from raising the topic.

"I've known you a long time, Frankie, and I know what a go-getter you are, especially once you've made up your mind. However, I think involving yourself in a homicide investigation is a mistake." Frankie flashed a crooked-mouth look in his direction and narrowed her eyes, but before she chimed in, Alonzo held up one hand to make a point. "It's not because you're a woman so don't go there. You don't have enough experience with this kind of thing to make it your first big investigative story." Frankie paused to let this sink in. What Alonzo meant was maybe she would get in the way and cause the investigation to go sideways, was that it? She glowered in his direction again as the beers arrived with a basket of beer-battered cheese curds.

"So, you think I'm going to ruin your investigation?" she asked, accusingly. Alonzo looked into his beer glass. "You do think that!" Frankie couldn't believe it. "I'm not stupid, Lon. I think I know my limitations. I'm trying to do everything by the book," she said, defensively.

There went Lon's hand in the air again. "Whoa, okay. Please be careful and try to stay under the radar. You know Pflug doesn't like you anyway and I don't want him to give any crap to Shirley about you." Frankie still managed to feel offended, but the cheese curds and the beer were easing her defenses.

The rest of the appetizer baskets arrived and the two caught up on family life, amid cheering on the hockey team. Frankie mentioned the wine bottling party would take place next Tuesday and wondered if Lon would join in. "And ask Sue to come, too," Frankie added. Sue Clark had been dating Alonzo on and off for several months.

"Guess you didn't hear. Sue's seeing someone else, looks pretty serious, I guess." Frankie was embarrassed at being so out of touch with her dear friend.

"Oh, Lon, I'm so sorry. Everything okay?" His low under-the-breath chuckle made her a little wary.

"Oh, you know my luck with women. Anyway, we were never more than friends, just keeping each other company." By this time Alonzo was finishing his third beer and the alcohol made the otherwise cautious and inwardly emotional man a bit careless. "I'll still come to bottling though," he said. "Will Garrett be there?"

Alonzo asked the question so nonchalantly that Frankie was thrown for a loop. What had Alonzo heard and from whom had he heard it? She recovered enough to attempt an equally nonchalant reply.

"I'm not sure. I haven't asked him yet." What was going on here anyway - why was Alonzo testing their friendship so heavily these days?

Looking squarely at Frankie, he said, "Garrett told me himself that you two were going on a date this weekend. He seems pretty happy about it." Alonzo wanted to reassure Frankie that there wasn't idle gossip floating around the department. He hated the rumor mill as much as she did. As much as Frankie trusted Alonzo, she had no interest in discussing Garrett Iverson with him. Partly because she wasn't certain how she felt about him, and partly because this wasn't a topic she wanted to openly share with Alonzo right now. Something was amiss between them, and until Frankie could get to the bottom of what the problem was, she planned to keep him at arm's length. A true gentleman, Lon insisted on walking Frankie to her vehicle and told her to behave as a final passing comment. Well, she would have to see about that.

Adam and Peggy were tallying receipts for the evening when Frankie walked in the front door, just past closing time. "Hey, Mom. Hey, Adam, how'd it go tonight?" Peggy held up one hand as she concentrated on the pile of debit receipts she was calculating. Frankie looked around for any tidying up that needed to be done.

As her eyes adjusted to the soft interior lighting, she spotted Gordy "Red" Robbins, one of the town barbers, sitting at a corner table, a familiar parking place for Red. He was a member of the Jigsaw Buzzards, a club of old geezers that hung out Sunday afternoons at the wine bar, happily putting together puzzles or playing Scrabble. As Sunday afternoons could be dead, Frankie welcomed their business. Frankie hoped Red wasn't waiting around for her mother; she couldn't quite picture her choosy mother dating Red, who still lived in his childhood home with his 91-year-old mother, Thelma. Besides, with his waxed mustache, Red looked every bit like he belonged in an 1890's barbershop quartet. That thought made Frankie giggle as she realized the parallel between Red's appearance and his profession.

As if on cue, Peggy pointed a thumb in Red's direction, "Mr. Robbins wants to speak with you, Francine." Peggy was always formal around customers, a habit Frankie found at times annoying, knowing her mother was on familiar terms with 90 percent of the town. Frankie's father had been a customer at Red's Hometown Barber Shop for as long as Frankie could remember. She wondered what was so important that Red hung around past closing time to catch Frankie. Before heading over to Red's table, Frankie perused the opened bottles at the bar, choosing a nearly empty bottle of Dark Deeds, a black cherry Lambrusco, that seemed the perfect wine anytime, and poured herself a glass.

"What can I do for you, Red?" Frankie sat on a cushioned two-seater opposite Red. As a youngster, Frankie remembered going to the town barber occasionally with her brothers and father. In those days, Red had very red hair, the color of burnt pumpkin, hence the life-long nickname, despite the fact what little hair remained on his head was now a dazzling white.

"Well, see, here's the thing, Frankie," Red began, already working his hands while he talked. Frankie imagined the barber couldn't help himself, being so used to moving scissors and razors while relating stories and making small talk with his customers. But today had been a long one and Frankie wasn't much in the mood for a long-drawn-out tale.

"Go on," she encouraged him.

"Well, we - I mean the Buzzards - were wonderin' if we could meet here on Saturdays instead of Sundays?" Red looked sheepish and Frankie wondered why. She might be a generation or two younger than most of the Buzzards, but she was on comfortable terms with them and didn't feel the need to walk on pins and needles.

"Why would you want to do that? You know Saturday is busy in here - lots of bachelorette parties and tourists. Not exactly a good mix for you guys."

Red nodded at her, his hands ready to reanimate. "I told the guys you wouldn't like it. It's just Ol' Jim, well, he's going to have Euchre Club at the VFW on Sunday afternoons now and…" Frankie cut him off.

"What do you mean? Euchre Club is on Thursday afternoons." Frankie made it a practice to know the town activity schedule. Red was simultaneously shaking his head and nodding the affirmative, his cheeks looking like they might just shake loose from the rest of his face at any moment.

"Well, Ol' Jim wants ta have Euchre twice a week now." Frankie set down her wine glass and leaned in toward Red, looking him straight in the eye.

"I guess you guys will just have to choose then - Euchre or puzzles." Frankie didn't know if Jim Powell, the VFW Commander, was trying to make more money for his organization or what, but the VFW had never been open on any given Sunday, so she wasn't about to change her schedule. Anywhere from six to ten Buzzards showed up on Sunday afternoons, an otherwise slow day at the wine bar. Meanwhile, Saturdays were busy all day and sometimes a standing-room-only crowd waited for wine tastings or orders. Frankie didn't want to sacrifice table space for the Buzzards, bottom line. "I like having your gang in here on Sundays and I think you like being here, too, Red. So, I hope you can make it work." Frankie believed she and the club had a mutually advantageous arrangement - her cozy shop was the perfect setting for puzzles and games, plus she offered the Buzzards discounts on food and drinks, yet she had a guaranteed income every Sunday. Besides, the Knit Witches knitting club met at Rachel's store next door at the same time on Sunday - many of the Witches were wives of the Buzzards.

Red handed his empty beer bottle to Frankie, rose to put on his jacket and looked apologetically in her direction. "I'll talk to Ol' Jim. Maybe the VFW can have Karaoke more than once a month instead of tryin' to open up on Sundays." So, Frankie assumed, this must be about money. Seemed like every business, church, or civic organization needed extra money these days. She couldn't blame the VFW but then, the VFW commander couldn't blame her either for holding on tight to a sure thing, especially during the slim Winter months. Frankie managed a smile in Red's direction and bade him a good night.

Peggy had finished closing out the till and was donning her long cashmere coat with its faux fur collar. "Good for you for standing your ground. You really have a good head for business, Frankie. I'm sorry I doubted your business sense. This place is doing pretty well and I'm glad I get to be part of it. See you Tuesday at wine bottling." Peggy surprised Frankie, not only with her words of praise, but by grabbing her daughter and giving her a warm hug. Frankie hugged back, tightly. She'd never tire of having a real mom-brand hug. In fact, with the week she was having, the extra love was just what the doctor ordered.

Chapter 9

"Our feet are planted in the real world,
but we dance with angels and ghosts."
– John Cameron Mitchell

Groundhog Day brought brilliant sunshine to the morning with temperatures in the 20's for a welcome change of pace. Unfortunately, an hour from Deep Lakes, Jimmy the Groundhog saw his shadow in all that glaring sun, and before scooting back into his hole, pronounced there would be six more weeks of Winter - if only. Frankie always laughed at the idea of six more weeks of winter meaning a *late* spring. In Wisconsin, winter often lingered into the middle of April, sometimes later than that. Frankie recalled a Mother's Day not many years past where she took photos of several inches of snow piled onto the fragile tree Blossoms, weighing down delicate Lily of the Valley, reminding everyone that Winter wasn't quite finished with Deep Lakes, even though Deep Lakes was certainly finished with Winter.

Friday was one of the busiest mornings in the Bake part of the shop as customers congregated to buy pastries for weekend plans or visitors. The orange marmalade rolls flew out the door, along with the leftover yeast donuts from yesterday, and many scones as well. The leftover scones would likely be sold tonight at the wine bar, a nice accompaniment to a slice of quiche. Frankie went back upstairs to change into church clothes, leaving Tess and Adam baking away for Saturday and Sunday without her. Carmen had reluctantly given in to Frankie's pleas of going to the funeral with her, and she was changing in the downstairs bathroom.

Frankie satisfied herself with a black below-the-knee flared skirt and turquoise turtleneck tunic, black tights, and black boots. She wore her favorite locket for good luck - a Dutch Delft China oval with a spray of blue flowers - a present from her father Charlie when he returned from a business trip. Inside, Frankie had a picture of her 10-year-old self with Charlie, both grinning a wide happy smile, as if sharing a lovely secret. Whenever she wore the locket, she felt closer to her dad, still missing him sometimes as if he'd just passed away all over again. Frankie had much in common with Charlie: gardening, bird-watching, star-gazing, both in awe of the Natural World. This natural connection between the two seemed to carry on despite his passing. Frankie would spot a rare bird during migration or a flower blooming in the garden she hadn't planted and send a smile and thank-you upward to her father.

She met Carmen at the bottom of the stairs and the two set off in Frankie's SUV. "I think I like you in church garb, Carmie," Frankie said, admiringly. Carmen's shape hadn't changed since high school - she still had an ample chest, slim waist, and round bottom. Dressed in a dark blue shift with a cream-colored jacket and short cream heels, she looked like perfection. Her sleek black hair was pulled back into a low knot against her neck, complemented by a swirly blue and purple scarf.

"I still don't know why I'm going with you, unless it's to keep you from doing something you'll regret," Carmen complained, but only mildly. Frankie laughed at her friend.

"That's exactly why you're coming, of course. Besides, you know everyone in town so you're going to help me people watch." Frankie's eagerness about her mission at this funeral made Carmen a little worried, and she wondered what Frankie expected to find out by attending.

They arrived early - it was just about 10:15, but the service wouldn't begin until 11. Frankie wanted to look at the funeral flowers to see who was close enough to Pastor Rawlins to order a floral display, plus she wanted to hide herself upstairs in the choir loft before too many people arrived who might wonder why she would want to sit up there.

Pastor Rawlins' casket was placed in the sanctuary and was open, something Frankie didn't relish. Frankie believed the open casket custom was weird - why look upon a dead body, anyway? Especially if a person had faith in an afterlife - that body was now just an empty shell. And, if a person didn't have faith, death was the end

-the final departure, the big void. To look upon a dead body would just be depressing. Carmen urged her toward the altar, wanting to get this over with. Only a few people were in the sanctuary area, mostly members of the church council, Frankie surmised.

She and Carmen spoke in low whispers as they read the cards attached to the flower arrangements. There were only a few arrangements: one from the council, one from the women's prayer group, one from the women's Bible Study group, one from the choir, and one from the women's association. "Aren't there any men's groups in this church?" Carmen wondered in a loud whisper. Frankie also found it a little odd that all the flowers, except for the council and choir, were from the women. She also wondered why the pastor's previous church hadn't sent an arrangement or plant of any kind. She was going to jot that in her phone as soon as she got settled in upstairs. Carmen, according to custom, stopped at the casket to pay her respects and said a small prayer for the pastor. Frankie did the same but couldn't bring herself to give more than a passing look at the body, making a mental note that this morbid practice would not be part of her own funeral.

The choir loft, unlike at St. Anthony's, was near the front of the church and just to the right of the altar area. She and Carmen climbed the steps, noting the area was quite small, with several folding chairs, a small electronic organ/piano, two microphones, and a stand containing hymnals and other music. They pulled two chairs away from the grouping, setting them as far to the right and as near to the railing as possible for the best view below. Frankie wondered how many choir members would be there and if she and Carmen would be asked to leave the loft. She hadn't thought this through very well and was beginning to second guess her decision to come today.

At about 10:30, several choir members arrived in the loft, assembled pieces of music and made their way back down the steps, after throwing quizzical glances at Carmen and Frankie. Carmen looked at her hands, pretending to examine her nails while shooting a few accusing looks at Frankie. Frankie followed the choir's moves, noticing they were setting up just below the altar area on the far left, where another small organ was positioned on the floor. She breathed a sigh of relief. Maybe she and Carmen would have the loft to themselves, but that was too good to be true as more footfalls clopped up the stairs, followed by the uniformed figure of Donovan Pflug. He openly glared at Frankie and Carmen but took a seat on the opposite side of the loft. It appears investigators think alike, Frankie thought smugly. The Pirate Firefly was in attendance today, bowing at Frankie's thought with a little clap of his hands.

Frankie silenced her phone, but opened the Notes app and tapped in the information about the floral arrangements.

It was show time now. Officiating was a minister from

a Congregational Church in Neenah, according to the program, and he was followed by the procession of the choir and the church council, seated at the front section of the church. Frankie noticed the majority of the congregation was comprised of women. Carmen was counting members to herself and nudged Frankie as she came to the same conclusion. "Not many men in this church?" she whispered. Frankie shrugged. She noticed Patsy Long was sitting with the council, but she didn't see her husband, Duane, in attendance. Maybe there were a lot of men who couldn't take time off work to attend the funeral?

Most notably, Frankie's ongoing attention was pulled toward one of the back pews where a teary Wendy Jarvis was seated with two other women, a protective arm around one of them. Frankie didn't know either of them by name but knew she had seen them around. She and Carmen were texting now to avoid the evil eye of Officer Pflug, and Carmen gave Frankie positive ID's on both women. The thin woman on the end with more hair than face was Annette Sanders, 30ish, a Kindergarten teacher with two small children. Sanders, Sanders...Frankie's brain was churning. She texted Carmen: *Related to Kevin Sanders?* She knew Kevin was a co-worker of her brother Nick at the Triple Crown Marine plant, and maybe a poker buddy.

Carmen's text: *Annette's husband but maybe not anymore. Separated for sure.* Annette seemed very sad as she wiped at her nose with a tissue, but Frankie couldn't make out any facial expressions because of her mass of long, softly curled tresses taking over her abnormally small face.

Carmen informed Frankie the woman being consoled by Wendy was Missy Geller, who was currently living with her parents since she and husband, Brandon, split last fall. Frankie couldn't remember seeing Missy around Deep Lakes, thinking she must be about Violet's age or just a little older, although she looked like a child. Missy's shoulder-length blonde hair was styled to the side, exposing her round doll-like face and pink cheeks; she even had a jeweled barrette in her hair, making her look like a middle schooler. Missy was openly sobbing, and not in the quietest fashion either. Sitting in the middle of the trio, Wendy's arm around her shoulder and Annette holding her hand, Missy seemed the most distraught of the three, yet they seemed to share a similar secret misery. To Frankie's question about Missy's age and origin, Carmen texted she was mid to late 20's and not from town. Carmen hadn't traveled in the same circles as Missy but knew the basic town gossip.

Frankie looked over at Pflug to see if he was making notes. As far as she could tell, he wasn't, but he was studying all the faces of the congregation to see what clues might be revealed. Frankie turned from the three women to the front pews. She noticed Patsy was composed, but looked as if a good night's sleep had evaded her the past few days. She must have a lot on her plate right now,

Frankie thought, at the same time puzzling over what her relationship to the pastor was like. Patsy must know more than anyone else about Pastor Rawlins and Frankie had a lot of burning questions for her.

The council members were difficult to read - they seemed to share the same somber faces, very likely worried about how this would affect their already cash-strapped church. She spent more time studying Dave Kilpatrick, a man who seemed more sullen than his companions, his face muscles taut, and a noticeable tick in his neck. The officiating pastor was delivering the eulogy, exalting Pastor Rawlins' rapport with his members, referring to the man as the Good Shepherd to his flock. This produced some sniffles among the women, and an audible throat-clearing from Dave who appeared to scoff then look down into his lap, red-faced. Dave Kilpatrick knows something about the pastor that he doesn't like, Frankie was sure, jotting her observations into her phone notes. Was Dave the person who met the pastor on Lake Loki that fateful day?

Her attention shifted to Milton Conway seated next to Dave, staring downward at his lap. Frankie continued watching Milton, trying to decide how she would record his expression in her notes. She frowned, studying him. He seemed resolute to remain looking directly down and, if Frankie had to name his expression, she'd say he looked like a cat that swallowed a canary. What was that smug look about?

The service went on with the typical funeral hymns of

eternal promise sung by the choir. As they sang, Carmen texted her observations. *Look at some of the younger women.* Frankie noticed again how the women in the choir were most affected by the pastor's death, not so much it seemed out of a spiritual loss, but a deeper emotional loss. A few choristers were visibly shaken, their voices breaking at certain points in their singing. The choir had only a few male members, whom, Frankie imagined, were singing the same as any other ordinary Sunday service.

Carmen texted again: *Nobody here from out of town. Don't you think that's weird? What about his past church?* Frankie did find this fact extraordinarily strange. Surely there should be other ministers and higher-ups from other Congregational churches here. And what about family and friends? Pastor Rawlins lived here just a couple of years - didn't he have friends from his hometown? Didn't he have any family? These questions were nagging Frankie and when she looked over at Pflug, she guessed he had already found the answers to a few them. She wondered if she could call Shirley Lazaar again or if she should simply pursue questioning others first hand.

When the service ended Frankie and Carmen stayed in the loft until the church emptied. She knew the congregants would file into the church's dining room for a luncheon, but she had no plans to make an appearance there. In the church narthex, Frankie bumped into Abe Arnold, who was gathering some information from the visiting minister. Frankie and Carmen breezed past - she didn't want to introduce herself to the minister and she already had a program where she could get his name and location. She had to admire Abe though - he would sniff out any and all information, sifting through the tidbits to put the whole picture together all in the name of good journalism. Abe followed Frankie out the door and brushed her arm before she got into the SUV.

"Hey, Francine. I saw you in the choir loft. What do you think about exchanging information on this one?" Frankie found the proposition interesting, but she shook her head slightly.

"No. I don't think so, but thanks." She was playing her cards close to her vest this round. She imagined Abe had plenty of information that would be news to her but for this particular investigation, she wanted the pride of earning those facts for herself. She told Carmen just that as they drove back to Bubble and Bake.

The afternoon passed with running errands, making phone calls, and rounding up willing helpers for wine bottling. Frankie stopped at Shamrock Floral, a few doors down on Granite Street, to discuss and order flowers for the Valentine event. Meredith Healy, the owner of Shamrock, looked up from a pile of yellow and white carnations she was trimming at a long work-table adjacent to the front counter. Her smile was a bright welcome to Frankie after the funeral and all the questions the funeral drummed into Frankie's mind.

"Hey, Frankie. I thought you'd be around soon to talk

flowers." She motioned for her to have a seat at a small empty wicker table by the front window. "I've got tea on. I'll just go grab some cups and my February flower list." Frankie relaxed in the lovely little shop that had once housed a doctor's office back in the early 1900's. Meredith and husband, Glen, ran the business together the past ten plus years, and made it profitable by adding greenhouses onto their rural property where they sowed annual flowers, vegetables and herbs, selling them at the shop and local farmers' market April through September.

The shop's interior was crafted into a garden setting with a gazebo, picket fence, and a small waterfall surrounded by silk greenery and twisted grapevines. Besides flowers, the shop offered gardening tools, planters, decorative items and a nice selection of herbal oils, balms, and teas. "Glen's out at the greenhouse today. Can you believe it's time to plant pansies already?"

Frankie sighed and smiled deeply. "That's the best news I've heard this week with this freezing weather. Thinking about flowers growing just makes me feel better somehow," she mused.

Meredith poured tea, offering honey and milk to Frankie, who added some of each to her cup. "I know what you mean. This winter seems to be relentless."

The two women discussed the approaching holiday and how busy each of them would be in their respective ventures. Meredith and Glen would have their hands full for a few days before Valentine's Day, preparing and nurturing their supply of roses, the biggest money-maker for the holiday. Orders were piling up for bouquets and arrangements with little teddy bears or other cute stuffies attached. So Meredith's sister, Marlena, would be on hand to help her out, along with Jovie Luedtke, a local who worked for both Meredith and Frankie as the opportunity arose. Jovie was a talented, artistic individual who knew her way around both a kitchen and a bunch of flowers, so she was wonderful to have on call. Checking her February floral inventory list, Meredith indicated she could get bulb varieties at economic prices. Frankie was thrilled.

"A touch of spring this time of year will be nice. Let me see - I'll need 16 bunches. How many do you think per table, Meredith?" An eye for aesthetics, Meredith said that three Tulips tied with a ribbon would be lovely in the vase that Frankie brought along as a sample. To demonstrate, she grabbed three silk Tulips from a display, tied them with a piece of floral tape and stood them up in the glass bubble vase. Frankie agreed with the suggestion, ordering half of the Tulips in a cherry red with white stripe, and half in a bright pink color. She bought a spool of white floral ribbon to tie off the bunches.

Their business complete, Meredith asked Frankie why she had looked so glum when she first walked in the door. When Frankie explained attending Pastor Rawlins' funeral and her role there as a snooping reporter, Meredith looked thoughtful. "You know, I probably shouldn't be saying this, but the pastor used to come by here often to pick up flowers. I got the feeling he was giving flowers to more than one person. None of my business, I suppose, but he came in here pretty regularly." Frankie raised her brows at the information. She was already beginning to speculate that the pastor was a ladies' man and while buying flowers didn't verify her suspicion, it was another fact that supported it.

She thought of something and asked, "Meredith, did he always buy the same kinds of flowers every time?" Frankie knew that most women had their own personal favorites. Meredith thought, and her mouth opened in a little "oh". She got up from the table, pulled out the order ledger she kept under the counter and brought the black binder back to her seat, opening it to the pastor's customer page.

"Come to think of it, he did. There was a kind of pattern where one week he would buy pink carnations, one week mixed bright-colored daisies, one week a single red rose with Baby's Breath. There were other times on and off when he purchased a bouquet from the cooler, but those first three I mentioned were part of a routine." Meredith rose again, returned the binder to its place and shook one finger at Frankie, her brunette curls bouncing for emphasis. "Please keep this between you and me. I don't want my customers to think I blab about them. Flower giving is fraught with secrecy and I have to be the secret-keeper." Frankie assured Meredith her secret was safe.

"It's probably not important anyway." But now the pirate firefly was poking Frankie's shoulder with his peg-leg, willing her to store away the information for later.

"It means something," Pirate hissed in her ear. Frankie couldn't ignore his insistence, even as she left Shamrock Floral huddled inside her jacket to keep the cold air at bay.

That evening, Frankie busied herself with customers at Bubble and Bake, selling the remaining scones and nearly every piece of quiche from the kitchen by closing time. Garrett Iverson had come into the shop at 9, allowing himself to be schooled by Frankie's wine knowledge, as he tasted several varieties of whites and reds, then ordered a glass of Two Pear Chardonnay, a slice of Frankie's signature quiche, and a lemon-basil scone. Frankie heartily approved of his choices, deciding that the two had similar taste in foods, a checkmark on the list of pros she was mentally crafting in her head about this man. She ignored the two thumbs up she received from each firefly, wondering why they were corroborating on this enterprise - were they making a secret wager about Frankie's prospect? Frankie's internal voice spoke up now - *people will call you crazy if you continue thinking this way. It's bad enough you have squabbling fireflies for a conscience; don't give them any extra power,* the voice chided. Frankie enjoyed the rest of the evening, giving Garrett a resolute thank you for his visit and a pleasant "looking forward to Sunday" goodnight. Frankie took the upper hand here - she didn't want to possibly give Garrett the opportunity to suggest she show him her apartment, let alone have a nightcap together. Besides, she had one more place to be tonight. She left the clean-up and final closing tasks to Adam and Tess, then grabbed her parka to head out into the night.

An interesting aspect of a Midwest winter, also known by its moniker "the quiet season" in the business world, Friday nights wind down hours earlier than in the warmer months. Although a couple of bars still had customers, Frankie noticed the streets were still and nearly empty. A languid snow flurry was drifting around the night air with no particular place to go, the stars watching from above along with the pale half-moon. Deep Lakes was sleepy and restful most winters, as if it needed to hibernate and re-energize for another tourist season on the spring horizon. Frankie liked this about her community, even though she relied on tourism, as did all the other area businesses, she felt herself overcome with resentment that Pastor Rawlins' death had ushered in a shaky disturbance to this peaceful place.

Frankie was on her way to her brother Nick's duplex, a newly built income property among others of its kind in a subdivision on the outskirts of town. James, who owned her father's construction company "Nothing But The Finest", had purchased the parcels for a cheap price following the burst real estate bubble in 2008. His endeavor turned out to be a wise one as most of the parcels were sold, and his company was bustling to keep up with construction of new homes and duplexes there. Good for James, thought Frankie, as she turned into the subdivision, where all the streets were names of birds. This had been Frankie's idea and she beamed about James' decision to adopt it.

Turning onto Bobolink Lane, she stopped at the white duplex with brick accents, saw a soft light was still on, and a car on the street in front of the house might mean Nick had company. "Oh well, at least I won't be waking him up," Frankie thought.

Frankie parked in Nick's driveway since there was space, bounded up the front steps to the porch and punched the bell. Cherry Parker emerged from the bathroom perhaps? Wearing a long-tailed button-down shirt that Frankie suspected was Nick's, she looked a little tipsy, or was it sleepy? Frankie wasn't sure, but one thing was certain, she didn't look embarrassed and neither did Frankie, who was used to her brother's escapades. Nick was the pretty-boy of the Champagne family. He stood at six feet, kept his body in impeccable shape, and didn't look his mid-40's age one bit. His sandy blonde hair was kept neatly in a slicked-back style off his forehead, accentuating chiseled facial features, and icy blue eyes that could have leapt off the cover of a trashy romance novel. Nick had numerous romantic affairs but never a permanent relationship. Frankie had lots of theories about why this was so, but now wasn't the time for entertaining those - she was here to glean information.

"It's a little late for a social call, isn't it Sis?" Nick

was grinning to let her know it didn't much matter to him and whatever activity was happening here, Frankie hadn't interrupted it. Nick was in black boxers but disappeared for a minute to grab a pullover and sweatpants. Meanwhile, Frankie said hi to Cherry, a local girl who graduated sometime after her youngest brother, Will. Cherry sometimes helped at Bubble and Bake - she was flirty and flighty simultaneously. Rumor had it that she recently suffered a bad break-up with her live-in, so maybe she sought solace from Nick - a willing participant in the solace department. For Frankie, however, Cherry was someone who could be counted on to serve customers at the wine bar, especially in the busy summer months, and her persuasive tactics meant bigger wine sales. Not that Frankie promoted exploitation of any kind, but Cherry emanated sensuality the way a dog wags its tail - instinctively.

Frankie sat down at Nick's breakfast bar, moved aside two empty cocktail glasses, took out her phone and opened her notes app. Nick surveyed the situation as serious and took a seat across from her, leaving Cherry completely isolated and forgotten.

Frankie began: "What can you tell me about Kevin Sanders?" Nick couldn't hide his surprise but recovered when he saw Frankie's game face.

"Okay, well, I work with him. He's on my shift but not in my department. What else you want to know?" Frankie asked if Kevin was reliable at work, assuming Nick would know if he wasn't since Nick would be the personnel manager dealing with complaints about employees. "He's never been reprimanded as far as I remember. No attendance issues, no safety issues, no co-worker disputes." Frankie prodded Nick - he must know more.

"What about his personal life? What about Annette?" The light dawned then.

"Oh, yeah. Kevin was devastated when they split a few months ago. He stopped coming to Poker Night. Told us his gambling was the reason they split. Said he'd do anything to get his family back together. They have two kids, you know." Frankie was a little confused to hear this; she suspected that Kevin was at fault and didn't imagine he had attempted to reconcile.

"So, what happened? Why didn't they get back together?" Nick thought for a bit, got up and poured some filtered water from the fridge, then sat back down.

"I'm trying to remember, Frankie. I think he said Annette wouldn't go to counseling with him. She was seeing her own counselor." Nick shrugged, "I think that's what Kev said. It never came up again." Frankie wanted to know if Kevin was back in the Poker Night club. Nick shook his head. "He has his kids most weekends and can't afford to play poker with child support, I suppose."

Frankie's opinion of Kevin rose a notch. She even felt sorry for him to a point. Frankie wished Rick had fought for their marriage and their family. She wondered what made Annette give up. What makes anyone give up?

There are so many individual circumstances; this she knew.

Frankie needed to ask about Duane Long next, another co-worker of Nick's. Triple Crown Marine was a gigantic operation, employing hundreds of workers so Nick couldn't know everyone, but he did have an active social life, so Frankie hoped for some insightful information. Nick only knew Duane by appearance - their paths did not cross at or outside the plant.

"I know Duane. I went to school with him." Both Frankie and Nick turned to the voice that seemed to have arrived out of thin air. Cherry was sitting on the living room sofa, just around the corner from the breakfast bar - out of sight but not out of earshot. Frankie hoped Nick was ashamed at his virtual dismissal of Cherry, but that was unlikely - Nick was charming but could be quite superficial. Frankie hopped off the stool, gave Nick a sisterly look of disapproval and strolled into the living room to sit across from Cherry.

"So, can you tell me anything about Duane?" she prompted. Cherry conveyed that Duane was a nice guy, a "straight arrow", she called him.

"He and I were at the same church camp one summer when we were sophomores," Cherry explained. "I thought he was kinda cute, so I tried to kiss him one night on the way back to our bunkhouses after prayer service, but he brushed me off, said he had someone he liked and wanted to be true to her. I thought that was so sweet, I never forgot it." Frankie had the impression Duane wasn't

much for church - he seemed to have a genuine dislike
for Pastor Rawlins and didn't attend the funeral. Perhaps
she was wrong - again.

Did Cherry know Patsy? Yes, she was in the same
class in high school, too. "Patsy was kind of smart, but
sort of frumpy. She was kind of a wallflower, if you know
what I mean. Patsy and I didn't travel in the same circles."

Frankie suppressed a smile but inwardly commented,
"I bet you didn't." Frankie thanked them both for their
help. On her way out the door, she turned. "Oh yes. I'm
bottling wine at Bountiful on Tuesday night. Can you
come, please?"

Nick nodded, "You know I'm always up for that."

With a mischievous smirk, Frankie added, "Oh,
you're invited too, Cherry. The more the merrier." Cherry
smiled playfully, but Nick just scowled as Frankie's figure
hurried away.

As Frankie started up the SUV, she noticed the
swirling snow flurries had intensified. Her view through
the sunroof showed only faded stars peeking out here
and there in the dark sky, looking lost and cold, Frankie
thought. Just then a large shade crossed over the ghostly
half-moon, obscuring it completely for mere seconds,
stealing the tiny light left in the darkness. Frankie shivered.
Groundhog Day had begun and ended in shadow.

Chapter 10

"Let us remember that Lucifer, too, was once an angel, appointed with the task of guarding the most holy throne in Heaven. Yet, within him, a sinful nature was uncovered."

The light snowfall from Friday night coated the sidewalks, roads, and trees with just an inch of pure whiteness, somehow dressing up February shiny and new again. The light snow did not deter the bakery customers Saturday morning, who swept through the doors for pastries, coffee cake, and the tasty apricot and raspberry tarts Tess concocted Friday night after the wine bar closed. People were not rushing today, lingering in the lounge area with coffee and an extra goodie or two before heading off to another activity, which could be snowshoeing on the fresh white coating, or a visit to nearby Gibson, hosting its Ice Sculpting Festival this weekend. Ice sculpting attracted experts from all over the Midwest, who transformed giant blocks of ice into wizards, dragons, princesses, or popular cartoon characters or, for something more fun and unusual, a Harley-Davidson, jumbo cheese wedge, or tropical palm trees. Frankie used to bring Sophie and Violet there annually as a much-needed break from Winter's monotony. They enjoyed watching the images emerge from the large cubes and being able to vote on the best each year.

Today, Frankie was enjoying a little down time of her own - she had the whole day practically to herself with Carmen at the helm on the night shift working with Tess and Adam. She spent the morning holed up in the shop's kitchen, preparing more quiches for the weekend wine drinkers, allowing herself to test out Tess's tarts, or so she announced to no one in particular. Brambles the cat had settled into the shop most comfortably, loving the sunbeam that radiated extra warmth in one corner of the kitchen. Carmen scolded Frankie for breaking her own strict rule that no animals would be allowed in the kitchen area, but Frankie was wishy-washy. When the kitchen was bustling with people and activity, the cat of the month was relocated to another room. When not much was happening in the kitchen, well then, the rules were bent, to say the least. Currently, Brambles was snuggled under the raised chef's ovens while the quiches were baking away - a self-made kitty spa, what a smart kitty indeed.

Frankie noticed that even after yesterday's funeral, which usually placed matters to rest, customers continued to chatter about the death of Pastor Rawlins. She supposed this was a phenomenon in Deep Lakes, a death surrounded by speculation about a man who was virtually unknown. Despite being part of the community for two years, few people seemed to profess a friendship with the pastor and, while Deep Lakes wasn't always the most welcoming town, after two years' time much more should have been known about Rawlins. The snippets of conversations Frankie picked up on mostly involved rumors about the shoddy financial condition of the church and Rawlins' unconventional ways.

Frankie spent time in the afternoon at her computer, fitting together the facts as she knew them for her article, typing out a second column loaded with questions and speculations. Beginning tomorrow, she was determined to embark on a fact-finding mission to fill in as many blanks as possible.

As luck willed out, St. Anthony's Sunday morning mass was led by the youth – a once a month affair in which the high school students performed the readings, announced the prayers of the faithful, and ushered at offertory. The youth service was always followed by fellowship of coffee, milk, juice, and donuts, also set up and manned by the high schoolers. Frankie rarely stayed after church service, deciding she socialized enough with the community during the week, and she certainly didn't need an extra donut either. Because she sang in the choir, she usually filed away her music after service, then quietly descended the stairs and exited out the side door. Peggy would often chastise her daughter's antisocial behavior, commenting that parishioners ought to be greeting Father

Donnelly and complimenting his sermon. "Goodness, Francine, I raised you better than that" or something similar was Peggy's usual remark.

Today, Frankie planned to surprise her mother by joining fellowship. She caught up to Peggy as she was exiting the sanctuary in a line of fellow parishioners waiting to shake Father Donnelly's hand. Peggy looked surprised, then delighted, to see her daughter and she pushed her in front of her place in line to speak to Father first. Frankie suspected she either wanted to hear what her daughter would say to the priest, or she wanted to chime in an added remark or fun fact, or more than likely, both.

Father Donnelly extended his hand to Frankie and smiled broadly at her. "Well, Frankie, isn't it nice to see you after church for a change." Father winked as he spoke; having been the priest at St. Anthony's for more than two decades, he knew Frankie's entire family fully.

Before Frankie could utter a word, Peggy piped up with, "Oh Father Donnelly. I told Frankie she should have better manners. What's a mother to do!" There stood Frankie, once again, demoted to child status.

"Great sermon, Father Donnelly. It's nice to see you face to face." Frankie decided being candid with the priest was a safe bet.

He stifled a chuckle, "And the choir sang beautifully as always." Frankie took the church bulletin proffered by a high school student she didn't recognize and began walking down the hallway to the fellowship room, hoping to spot Carmen and Ryan so she wouldn't be waylaid by her mother.

As luck would again have it, Kyle and Carlos were putting out coffee cups and juice glasses on the long table inside the room, where Carmen and Ryan were already seated on folding chairs against the back wall. Peggy had been sidetracked talking to one of the youth about the proper way to knot a necktie, then proceeded to fix the youngster's tie as he looked down, mortified. Frankie said hi to the twins and allowed Carlos to pour her a cup of coffee while Kyle handed her the creamer. Frankie offered them a smile of pride - these boys were becoming young men and turning out to be good ones.

Carmen motioned Frankie over by her and Ryan, knowing full well why she decided to come to fellowship. Gesturing discreetly across and speaking quietly, Carmen said, "Over there, Frankie. The Kilpatricks." Frankie smiled her thanks.

"Show time," she said. Ryan didn't even pretend to understand what the exchange meant, as Frankie carried her cup across the room, picking up a donut along the way. Nan Kilpatrick was talking to June Thompson, the church secretary, something about ordering enough palms for the Palm Sunday service this year, so Frankie attempted a conversation with Roger, Nan's husband. The weather was always a safe conversation starter.

"Hi, Mr. Kilpatrick. How is this Winter treating you?" She tried to sound chummy. Roger tried, too.

"I guess it is what it is. We live in Wisconsin, we must like it, or we wouldn't stay." A long pause ensued, followed by another attempt on Frankie's part.

"Do you sing?" Roger stared at Frankie as if she had sprouted a second head, clearly bewildered at the query. "I mean, we always need more men in the choir, especially tenors." The comment came out in bumps and wobbles.

June Thompson's attention left Nan and now she turned toward Roger and Frankie. Roger looked relieved and perused the area, looking for someone worthy of conversation. Frankie made a valiant effort to speak to Nan.

"Hello Mrs. Kilpatrick. How are you?" Nan was fine. Frankie, prodded along by the Pirate Firefly, took a small leap into the abyss. "I think I saw you at the First Congregational Church a few days ago," she began. When Nan began shaking her head in dissent, Frankie went on. "I was pulling into the parking lot and you were pulling out. I went to drop off a donation there for the Valentine Jubilee. You, too?" Nan was caught off guard.

"No, I certainly was not." Frankie heard something in Nan's voice that urged her forward in her mission.

"I was there when the secretary found out about Pastor Rawlins' death. It was a terrible shock. But I imagine you heard all about it from Dave." Nan's face went ashen. Roger, hearing the mention of Pastor Rawlins by name, turned harshly toward Frankie.

"Some Pastor he was," Roger said in disgust.

Nan chimed in, "More like a homewrecker." Nan's

voice broke in emotion on the last word, prompting Roger to steady her arm. Frankie knew the conversation was about to come to an abrupt halt, so she ventured one last question.

"What do you mean by homewrecker?" Roger's head snapped sharply in Frankie's direction.

"This is not the time nor place, and it's none of your business," Roger was getting hot under the collar. He took Nan's arm and led her away.

Peggy was standing near Carmen, watching the scene unfold. She reached Frankie in a few long strides and there was nowhere for Frankie to escape. Peggy looked perturbed. "What was that all about, Francine?"

Frankie presented her most demure expression. "No idea, Mother. Here, would you like my donut? I think it's time for me to leave."

Seated in her SUV, Frankie rewound the conversation again. Somehow, the Kilpatricks were involved in Pastor Rawlins death, but how and why? Or was Frankie just jumping to false conclusions - her lack of experience playing out. Frankie had no evidence as a basis for her conclusion. Nan and Roger were respected members of Deep Lakes and lifelong residents. Dave Kilpatrick was a respected insurance salesman. None of the three had a single black mark on their record as far as she knew - they were not even the subject of town gossip - except for Dave's marriage to Glenda. Frankie reviewed what she knew on that story. The Kilpatricks were lifelong members of St. Anthony's, serving several roles in the church. Nan and Roger had two sons, but Mark, the older of the two, had been killed in a car accident his senior year of high school. Frankie recalled there had been drinking involved. Just before graduation, Mark had attended a senior class party out in the boondocks somewhere, and flipped his car going around a curve too fast. The only blessing was that he was alone in the vehicle. The family was devastated. Nan became over-protective of her now only son, Dave. She wasn't happy when Dave agreed to join Glenda's church, converting to Glenda's religious faith. Frankie could only imagine how unhappy Nan and Roger were when Glenda left town a few months ago, their marriage seemingly broken beyond repair. Where had Glenda gone and why did their marriage fail? And, the question swimming around in Frankie's brain, what does Pastor Rawlins have to do with their failed marriage?

Frankie laid out the information she knew, wrapping her mind only around that which involved the Kilpatricks. There was Nan angrily driving out of the Congregational church parking lot on the day the pastor died. There was the paper from the pastor's calendar with a scheduled 8 a.m. meeting the day he died with someone named "Patrick." There was Glenda and Dave's separation. There was the look of suppressed anger on Dave's face at the funeral. There was the personal liability insurance policy for a cool million sold by Dave to Rawlins. What did it all mean - how is it connected?

"Maybe it is not connected," Golden Firefly was filing her nails, looking smugly at Frankie. "Life is full of coincidences. You don't have anything concrete, my dear." Frankie had to admit the Golden One was right.

"So, I need to keep digging," came Frankie's rebuttal.

* * *

Five o'clock came and went with Frankie still marching back and forth from her closet to her bedroom mirror, trying on different outfits to wear on her "date" with Garrett. Frankie was becoming agitated with her indecisive behavior. This isn't like you, her inner voice weighed in. Frankie usually didn't spend a lot of time trying to look like a fashion model. She had her go-to outfits that she felt comfortable in and that suited her best. She couldn't understand why she was making such a fuss about this. After all, Garrett had already seen her a few times - he couldn't have been disgusted by her appearance or he wouldn't have asked her out. She needed to get a grip in a hurry. Looking at her previous selections piled on her bed, she pulled out the nicer blue jeans and the black leggings, either of which would be just fine for going to a movie. Would she be underdressed in the jeans? Would she look wonky in the leggings?

The Pirate Firefly, tired of playing along with this parade of outfits was mixing a cocktail. "If you ask me," he crooned, "what you need is a stiff drink to get rid of these jitters." This comment prompted The Golden One into action, the wingbeats blasting Frankie's eardrum.

"You be quiet over there," Golden One shouted. "You don't know anything about women, so just let me handle this." Pirate took a seat and sipped his drink, smirking.

Just like that, Frankie threw caution to the wind, donned her black leggings with a bold patterned long blouse in black, red and gold, added large black fashion boots that almost came to her knees, and dangling shimmery gold earrings that brushed her neckline. She looked in the mirror, smiled, gave her makeup a glance and decided not to add any, despite Golden One's prompting.

Garrett was sitting at the wine bar when she entered, talking to Adam about recent Olympic events. The bar had just closed, and Adam looked like the typical movie bartender, polishing glasses and wiping down the wooden bar as he chatted. Garrett stopped mid-sentence when Frankie entered, and he produced a low whistle that made her blush and Adam grin.

"Dang, boss lady," Adam said. "You clean up." Garrett laughed, putting her at ease.

"Yes. What he said," came Garrett's reply. "Ready?" Frankie nodded, Garrett helped her into her coat and they headed out the door to his waiting truck. "It's all warmed up, so I took a chance you wouldn't mind if I picked you up instead of us meeting there." Frankie said she didn't mind at all.

Garrett chatted with Frankie about the bakery

part of her business as they made the short trip out to Highway 5 where the Deep Six Movie Complex resided, accompanied by other newer businesses just outside of town, including a few chain stores and restaurants. The two discussed their preferences for hometown businesses over chains, the unique and personal touches the small businesses could offer over the blandness of big boxes, but admitted that the chains provided conveniences too.

Inside the cinema complex that housed six theaters, Garrett, insisting he was a traditionalist, purchased both tickets to an action-adventure flick the two had decided upon earlier. In the concession line, the cinema owner, Beau Collins, greeted Frankie from the other side of the counter.

"Hey, it's great to see my favorite baker and vintner!" Beau produced a giant smile for Frankie. They were both members of the Chamber of Commerce and had served together at a variety of local events. In addition, Beau was the Director of the Deep Lakes Players, the local performing arts group and wanted to discuss offering a small production at the Bubble and Bake sometime in spring. Beau was a striking man with dark hair that silvered around the temples; even more silver were his mustache and goatee. He laughed easily, and had a reputation for being charming, but hadn't been seen with any women since his wife passed away a year ago from a long battle with cancer.

"Hello, Beau. Good to see you. You haven't been

downtown lately. Thought you might have taken the winter off for somewhere warmer," Frankie teased.

"Nope. Winter is a busy season for movies and theater production. We've got two shows in the works right now." Frankie completely missed the fact that Garrett and Beau seemed to be sizing each other up. Frankie, like most other women in Deep Lakes, both single and married, would admit that Beau had a commanding presence. He was not a man to be ignored or easily forgotten. Available middle-aged men were about as common as a Blue Moon in the Deep Lakes area, so they tended to attract plenty of attention, both wanted and unwanted. Garrett tapped Frankie on the shoulder, drawing her focus back from the Beau haze and onto the important business of buttered popcorn, Twizzlers, and soda. Frankie realized she had been perfectly rude to her companion and intended to make it up to him. Beau didn't relish being dismissed, drawing Frankie's attention once more with,

"Hey. We still need to get together to discuss a show at the wine bar." Frankie barely looked over her shoulder.

"Yes, let's do that. Give me a call at the shop so we can arrange a meeting - you, me, and Carmen." Frankie hooked her arm into Garrett's, grabbed the popcorn bucket and headed toward Theater Number 5. Garrett looked contentedly at Frankie's hand on his arm and she appreciated those gooey caramel eyes lingering in her direction.

Later that night, under her covers in her flannel

pajamas, Frankie assessed the evening, giving it a solid B plus. Mentally calculating the pluses, she felt comfortable with Garrett at the movie, with the compatibility of their concession choices and film selection, with their conversation and with the brief kiss that capped off the date. Now for the minuses. Well, Frankie supposed a real date should include dinner or some activity that offered more opportunity to become better acquainted. Also, most of their dialogue was surface-level, nothing intimate. Frankie questioned her motivation at that thought. Did she want something more intimate? She just wasn't sure. Finally, they said goodnight without making further plans. Was this a one and done? Frankie didn't know the answer to that question either and she hadn't taken matters into her own hands by inviting Garrett to wine bottling on Tuesday so… Suddenly, Frankie decided to change the grade for the night to a B minus. Definitely time for some sleep.

Monday morning brought revival to Frankie's spirits as she headed to the kitchen, donned an apron and set about baking for tomorrow. First, she went into the wine bar and turned on the aromatherapy atomizers with some vibrant mint and eucalyptus. Back in the kitchen, the smell of rising dough permeated the place as Irish music echoed lively around the room from Frankie's MP3 player. She filled Brambles' dishes, finding a small piece of leftover ham for the grateful kitty, who rubbed enthusiastically around her ankles. Covering the dough with tea towels,

Frankie planned for an evening of baking sticky buns and hand pies. Pie dough was improved by allowing it to rest several hours, relaxing the gluten to make a tender flaky crust. Her Kringle dough would have to rest overnight so she and Carmen would be busy Tuesday morning putting up Kringles. When Frankie made the official pastry of Wisconsin, she did so in batches, to make the most out of the baking process, as the time-consuming Danish layered coffee cakes could be frozen for up to four months. Frankie used her grandmother Sophie Petersen's Kringle dough recipe, which she said traveled across the ocean to America with her Danish mother in 1902. Frankie so wished she had more family recipes in her collection, but many dishes were prepared from memory, never recorded, and if they were not passed down, eventually lost.

Her Grandmère Champagne, Felicity, had left a pittance of her collected memorized recipes behind when she died, leaving Frankie to marvel at her mémé's talent in cooking complex French dishes. Frankie searched for other people with her similar heritage - French, Danish, Irish - hoping they would share their recipes. She imagined her ancestors gathered together, eating special family dishes. Frankie believed in the bond of food - a common denominator transcending all differences among people, a unifying force more powerful than enmity.

Carmen arrived just before Frankie was ready to depart for First Congregational Church, as promised, to help poor Patsy ready the raffle items for the Saturday event. Carmen was greeted with rising dough and an orderly kitchen, giving a satisfactory nod to Frankie.

"So, you seem well organized today. How was your date?" Frankie called it nice and Carmen gave her an uncertain look. "Nice? What exactly does that mean? You're not describing cheese or berries, Frankie." Frankie grabbed her coat from one wall hook.

"Jury's still out. I like him." Frankie's expression softened; she looked young, innocent, and uncertain. Carmen backed off for the time being. The two reviewed the shopping list for the week along with the bakery and quiche plans. Then Frankie left Carmen and headed back out into the wintry wind, a reminder to the idealist inside Frankie that not everything could be solved with food, as she was about to discover.

Patsy looked up gratefully when Frankie found her in the cafeteria where a large explosion of merchandise was spread over the tables waiting to be organized, boxed, inventoried, and labeled with a raffle item number. Right behind Frankie, Missy Geller entered the messy cafeteria, her mouth agape at the sight. Frankie was pleasantly surprised to see Missy there, thinking she might be able to garner more information about Pastor Rawlins from two women instead of one, especially since Missy had been overcome with grief at Friday's funeral. However, The Golden One reminded Frankie not to be her usual "foot-in-the-mouth" clumsy self with her direct questions, stressing sensitivity. For once, Frankie appreciated the counsel. But first, a plan of attack on the wares littering the tables was needed, for which Patsy and Missy seemed genuinely interested in diving into; nothing like a project to occupy a troubled mind.

By 11, all the items were sorted and packaged into boxes, crates, buckets, and baskets, ready to be numbered. Frankie suggested a break, and while Patsy made coffee, she approached Missy with a meaningful topic of conversation. "I saw you at the funeral, Missy. You seemed so distressed. You must have known him well?" It was a purposeful question but coated in a sincere expression from Frankie. Missy was wide-eyed and looking mournful again.

"Yes. Pastor Brad was amazing. I live in Cayuga Creek but came to church here because of him. He was - well - like no other minister I've ever known." Missy seemed eager to talk, maybe just the chance to share her grief left her unguarded. Frankie vocalized small affirmations to encourage her onward. Missy's voice lilted at every mention of Pastor Brad, saying she was part of his "angel" club, women who followed God's calling.

Outwardly, Frankie maintained her poker face but inwardly, she was finding Pastor Brad's ministry alarming. She broke into Missy's litany of Pastor Brad praise with a question. "Who was in the angel club besides you, Missy? Tell me more." Missy admitted she wasn't sure of all the club members but that she was close to Wendy and Annette, two of Pastor Brad's special angels. Missy explained that she and Wendy were on a mission to change the music in the church from the outdated hymnals to modern, upbeat music. Missy was searching for musical numbers online while Wendy was contacting area musicians who played guitar, drums, and electronic keyboard to perform at the church.

Meanwhile, Annette was creating an after-school program for children of working parents who needed a safe place to stay and get help with homework. Annette, a Kindergarten teacher at Deep Lakes Elementary, was a perfect choice to head the program. Missy said other angels were working on fundraisers to further grow the church. Frankie was skeptical - more like save the church as it seemed to be strapped for cash, she thought. Still, Frankie had to admit the after-school program sounded like a positive plan, but she wasn't too sure about the music changes. Most traditional religions followed regimented hymns; she didn't think drastic music changes would be done without approval from a higher level.

Turning the conversation to a new direction, Frankie asked Missy if she was married. Missy frowned, admitting she and her husband had split. "Brandon moved here a few months ago. He works at the Marine plant, so it was closer for him to live here." Frankie stayed in safe territory with her comments.

"I remember how hard it was when my husband left me. My daughters were little, and it was a painful time for me." Missy nodded, then shook her head, as if her situation was different from Frankie's.

"But he didn't leave me," Missy began. "I told him I didn't want to be married anymore." Frankie wondered at her decision. As if it was only natural, Missy told Frankie she was from a family where women are taken care of by the men. "We were having financial problems. You know, we made some silly mistakes right after we got married. We charged too much and just kept digging a deeper hole." Again, Frankie shared her own experience.

"I remember working two jobs when I was raising my girls, just to make ends meet. We made plenty of sacrifices." Missy looked incredulous.

"My daddy told me there is no reason for me to get a job. It's Brandon's responsibility to take care of us. Pastor Brad totally agreed with my daddy." Missy sounded like a ten-year-old school girl reciting the commandments. Frankie was dumbfounded. Was it still possible in this century to find people who believed the man was the sole provider for a family? She might understand this if Missy had children, but she and Brandon didn't, so she couldn't understand how Missy could just give up on her marriage, unwilling to work to repair their finances. Instead, she had followed the advice of her father and pastor, and moved back home with her parents.

The urge to nurture this naive woman was overwhelming, and Frankie being Frankie, couldn't help herself. "Look Missy. I know it's none of my business, but you're an adult woman. Maybe you should move out of your parents' home and find a place of your own, get a job. Isn't there something you want to do - something you dreamed of doing after high school?" Missy seemed uncertain and a little downtrodden, but admitted to Frankie that she always wanted to do hair.

"I was always good at doing all the girls' hair, nails, and makeup for Prom and stuff," she beamed.

Frankie suggested she investigate a program for Cosmetology, jotting down two area schools she knew of that offered the courses. "It isn't terribly expensive, and it won't take long to be certified," Frankie added hopefully.

Patsy arrived with coffee, cups, sugar, and creamer on a silver tray. She surveyed the cafeteria and thanked Frankie warmly for her organizing skills. They drank coffee and ate the leftover pastries Frankie had brought along, discussing the details of the upcoming Jubilee. Thinking about her own Valentine event, Frankie asked if they would be using flowers on the tables.

"Oh, I hope we can have carnations - they're my favorite," Missy contributed. Patsy said they would likely use the silk flowers in storage from past dinners unless Frankie knew of someone who would donate flowers to the church. Frankie doubted that any florist would have leftovers with Valentine's Day looming.

Missy's carnation comment hadn't escaped Frankie's notice. "I like carnations, too, Missy. They come is so many colors."

Missy nodded, "They do, but I have a weakness for pink. It's my favorite color. I love how carnations smell -

like, like," she faltered, "magical, I guess."

Frankie knew what she meant; "Yes they have a spell-binding fragrance," she said, certain she knew the recipient of Pastor Rawlins' pink carnation order.

Missy was ready to leave after coffee, but Frankie said she would stay long enough to help Patsy number the raffle items. Before Missy left, Frankie was urged on to make one last plea. "Missy, I hope you'll look into going to school and I hope you'll work things out with Brandon. It's not too late, you know." Frankie was sincere; she would have offered the same motherly advice to her own daughters. Marriage was precious, and Missy didn't seem to have a valid reason for giving up on hers so quickly. She wondered what kind of minister would encourage her to end her marriage based only on financial difficulties.

Now Frankie's thoughts turned to grilling Patsy and began with a determined set to her jaw; Frankie didn't feel like pussy-footing around her questions. "Patsy, can I ask you a few questions about Pastor Rawlins, please?" Patsy was caught off-guard and somewhat beholden to Frankie, since she had been so helpful to her.

"Sure," came Patsy's reply and the drilling began. Frankie wanted to know why Duane, Patsy's husband, didn't like Pastor Rawlins. Patsy turned a shade of deep pink. "What makes you think Duane didn't like him?" she asked.

"Because he told me as much the other night in front of the library. Duane said he wasn't much of a pastor and

that's not the only person who has said those words either."
Patsy faltered, searching for the right words to use.

"Pastor Brad was unconventional, I suppose…" she
trailed off. "Who else said they didn't like him?" she asked
defensively. Frankie didn't think it was wise or respectful
to mention her conversation with Nan and Roger
Kilpatrick. She tried another avenue.

"Why do you think he was unconventional? Where
did he serve before Deep Lakes?"

Patsy said Pastor Brad had come from Little Rock,
Arkansas where he was an Associate Pastor at First
Congregational Church. "This was his first church as
head pastor, so you know, he was learning as he went,"
Patsy offered.

Frankie progressed to her next question. "So, didn't
he have any family? Everyone at the funeral was local
except the officiating pastor." Patsy said she found that
strange, too.

"We tried to help the police locate next of kin and
came up empty. He never talked about family or anyone
from his past really." Frankie committed that fact to
memory, along with a few others she had learned that
morning.

Frankie asked what it was like to work for him
compared to Pastor Johnson, the previous minister who
served their church for twenty plus years. Patsy blushed.
"Oh, they were completely different. Pastor Brad was
so good to me, Francine. After my grandmother passed

away, he would bring little gifts to brighten my day . . . flowers for my desk sometimes, candy, you know." Frankie admitted that was very thoughtful, encouraging her to keep talking. "He was easy to talk to," Patsy went on, "I suppose that's why the women thought so much of him..." She trailed off again. Frankie decided specifics were in order.

"Did Missy counsel with Pastor Brad?" She tried to sound informal, like an insider, even though her words rang hollow in her ears. Patsy frowned.

"I don't think I can tell you that." Frankie shared bits of Missy's earlier conversation about her broken marriage, including Pastor Rawlins' agreement with Missy's father. She added what she assumed Patsy already knew about Wendy Jarvis' and Annette Sanders' broken marriages.

"Don't you think it's a bit strange how many marriages have broken apart since Pastor Rawlins came here?"

Frankie was blunt now and The Golden One shuddered on her shoulder, offering a gratuitous remark, "Whoa, Francine. This fish is going to swim past your hook if you're not careful."

Patsy looked away at some far-off corner of the room. Her voice was soft and low. "Yes. I guess so. And there are others." Frankie's ears pricked.

"Patsy, you kept his schedule. If there are women he counseled regularly..." Patsy produced another small nod.

"Glenda Kilpatrick. I think something was going on with her and Pastor. Their meetings were odd. I wasn't supposed to know anything about them." Frankie pressed her further, but Patsy said she didn't know anything, including the reason Glenda moved away. Frankie asked if Nan Kilpatrick had an appointment with Pastor the Monday of his death. She shook her head. "Not that I knew about, but she left in a big huff when I told her Pastor wasn't in on Mondays and I didn't know where he was."

Frankie had the feeling she'd just hit the jackpot of information and was only skimming the surface. Who knows more than someone's personal secretary? She was certain Patsy had her suspicions about the man, but felt disloyal in pursuing those doubts, much less openly discussing them. "Look, Patsy. Something doesn't seem right to me about Pastor Rawlins. I'm sorry if you feel caught in the middle but the man is dead, and it looks like there are a lot of ruined lives he left behind." Patsy looked down at her lap, ashamed.

"I don't know if I should tell you this, but there was a woman who called here asking for Pastor Brad. She would never say who she was, only that she was calling from his hometown and he would want to talk to her. He always shut the door when she called, and he never said anything about those calls." Frankie pressed her for more details, but Patsy could only say she called about once a month and she had a southern accent. Well, that narrowed things down to a large section of the country, didn't it, Frankie thought.

"Did the sheriff's department search his office?" Patsy

said they had but only removed a small box of items, she wasn't sure what items. Frankie remembered how clean the desk had been, making it easy for her to spot the scrap of calendar paper. No photos, no personal items that conveyed anything specific about the man. She guessed the police knew about the 8 a.m. meeting on the day he died too. But Patsy said she didn't.

"He didn't schedule any appointments on Mondays," she insisted. "Pastor's day of rest you know." How ironic, Frankie mused - his day of rest was more a day of rest in peace.

It was time for Frankie to go but she felt sad for Patsy, and for her own part in shaking her down for information. "I am truly sorry for what you must be going through, Patsy. I hope your next Pastor will bring healing to your congregation. I mean that." Then, on a brighter note, Frankie added, "I hope the Valentine Jubilee is a huge success." Patsy smiled and thanked Frankie again for her help.

"Will be you coming on Saturday? The food will be delicious. We have lots of wonderful cooks here." Patsy stood a little taller now, clearly proud of her congregation. Frankie said she just might show up, thinking maybe it was her turn to be less traditional and ask Garrett Iverson out on a date!

Chapter 11

"A guilty conscience needs to confess.
A work of art is a confession."
– Albert Camus

Frankie raced home to begin some fresh sleuthing, armed with the morning information gleaned from Missy and Patsy. Bubble and Bake was empty - she figured Carmen was still shopping the suppliers and would probably be arriving soon with goods to unpack. Frankie was hungry and scrounged the shop fridge first, knowing she hadn't done any proper grocery shopping for herself in a couple of weeks. All the quiche had been sold or confiscated by Adam and Tess who were encouraged to take the Sunday leftovers - one small perk of working at Bubble and Bake. Cheese was always in plentiful supply, thanks to Karlsens' store across the street, so Frankie nabbed a hunk of Colby, hacked off a chunk and grabbed a ripe banana from the counter. She was sure she had crackers upstairs. It would do for now.

As her computer revived itself from sleep mode, Frankie poured herself a large glass of water - she was in the habit of drinking a lot of water in between rounds of coffee - and located a box of nutty grain crackers. She dumped a pile on the counter, peeled and gulped the banana, then settled into constructing little cheese and cracker sandwiches. Her first internet search was for First Congregational Church in Little Rock. She was happy to see there was only one Congregational Church in Little Rock, now if only someone was there today to answer her call.

"Good afternoon. First Congregational Church. Debra speaking, may I help you?" The sweet voice with the Southern twang rang with the promise of genuine helpfulness.

"Hello. My name is Francine Champagne. I'm calling from Deep Lakes, Wisconsin. I'm writing an article about your former Pastor, Bradford Rawlins, and am hoping for some information." Debra didn't sound at all surprised to hear a caller from Wisconsin.

"Well, Sugar," she said, her voice suddenly changing from formal to folksy. "You must be the fourth person I've spoken with from your town this week. I sure am sorry to tell ya that I can't help ya out. We have never had a Pastor Rawlins here." Actually, Frankie wasn't too surprised to hear that either - she had all kinds of doubts about Pastor Brad since the funeral. She had a few follow up questions for Debra though. How certain was she that Pastor Rawlins never worked there? Debra was as certain as flies on a cow's tail. She'd been the church secretary for 11 years now and a member of the congregation her whole life, thank you.

"My momma and daddy had me baptized right here." The second question was trickier - did she know who the other callers were from Deep Lakes? Debra said two calls came last week, one from a man and one from a woman. "The man wanted ta inform us of the Pastor's death, so we could announce it here. He was purty shook up when I told him we ain't never had a Pastor Rawlins." And the woman? "Well, she called at least two, maybe three weeks afore that. She said she was tryin' to find the pastor and thought we'd know where he all might be." What was her reaction to the news that the church didn't know anything about him? Debra said she didn't seem surprised. She just thanked her for the information. Frankie pressed on.

"You said I must be the fourth person from Deep Lakes you spoke with this week. Can you remember anything about the other callers? Please - it's very important." Debra sighed.

"Lemme think now. Well your sheriff's department called this week too. I forgot about that. But, um, maybe a couple a months ago or so, a woman called here asking if Pastor Rawlins could be reached here. She didn't say where she was from, but I know she wasn't from around here. She was all-business, professional-like." That was all Debra could remember about the mystery woman. Frankie thanked her and told her she hoped nobody else would be bothering her church about Pastor Rawlins.

After she clicked off the call, Frankie stopped to tap notes into her phone. Well, she surmised the sheriff's department was doing its homework on Rawlins to piece together how he might have died and why. If she had to guess, she believed the man calling to inform the Little Rock church of the pastor's death was likely Dave Kilpatrick. But who were the two mystery women? Was one of them the woman that called the Deep Lakes church and spoke with Patsy on and off the past year? Frankie answered her own question - that didn't seem likely since that woman already knew where to reach Rawlins. Unless, she was fishing for information. But why? Was the other woman a member of the Deep Lakes congregation? Could it be one of the "angels", or maybe another woman who suspected Bradford Rawlins wasn't who he said he was? What about Nan Kilpatrick? Had she turned up some information on Rawlins and planned to confront him with it the day he died? New questions were popping up now. Who was Bradford Rawlins and why was he pretending to be a pastor? Who had a motive for wanting him dead? Frankie hoped the sheriff's department could find out those answers, but that felt like small compensation right now. Frankie was itching to know those answers herself, for the sake of the women "Pastor Brad" had bamboozled, the lives he had ruined, and the congregation he had left in tatters.

She did a Google search on Bradford Rawlins and came up empty. Not a single Bradford Rawlins in existence as far as Google knew. Just some hits on people named Bradford in Rawlins, Wyoming. Well, she didn't think it would be that easy. What to do next? She wondered if it would be possible to talk to Glenda Kilpatrick, find out what her relationship with Pastor Brad was all about. Except, Frankie had no idea where to find Glenda since she left Deep Lakes. And she couldn't imagine asking Dave, Nan, or Roger Kilpatrick, the three people who might know for certain. Frankie racked her brain, trying to remember if Glenda had any close friends in town. She really didn't know Glenda Kilpatrick; she might have come into Bubble and Bake on a few occasions, but Frankie wasn't on chummy terms with every customer who walked in the door. She did recall Glenda being a frequent visitor next door at "Bead Me, I'm Yours" crafting center on Paint Nights, where Frankie delivered wine and snacks from her own shop.

Frankie closed her computer for the time being and jogged down the stairs, out the front door and over one door to Rachel's. She knew Rachel was closed on Mondays as most Deep Lakes businesses were in the quiet season, but she suspected that Rachel was working on accounts and orders, two things Frankie was supposed to be doing as well. Frankie rapped on the door three times before Rachel emerged from a back room. At thirty, Rachel was a sprightly figure who managed to be a calming presence at the same time. She was a gifted artist in several mediums, and a patient teacher, making her workshops on painting and jewelry making very successful. Rachel was dressed in jeans and a blue plaid flannel shirt, her brown hair spiked at the crown, hanging in an asymmetrical cut off the side, longer on the right than the left. Rachel and Frankie had a comfortable relationship, making it easy for them to share a building and work together as the occasion called for it. "Hey, Frankie. Come on in." Rachel held the shop door open and gestured inside. "I'm working on bills. My favorite." Frankie laughed.

"Everyone's favorite, I think. Rachel, can I pick your brain?" Frankie asked if she remembered Glenda Kilpatrick. Rachel didn't hesitate.

"Of course, I do. She loved crafting. She came to several Paint Night workshops and also learned how to make jewelry. I was sad when she left town. She was a great customer." Frankie nodded.

"I don't suppose you know why she left or where she went?" Rachel shook her head.

"She just sort of stopped coming to the store. Of course, I heard rumors but nothing concrete." Frankie wondered if Glenda had any close friendships in town. Rachel frowned, thinking, then nodded. "Coral Anders took Glenda under her wing. Glenda was working on some special project. A gift maybe." Frankie knew Coral Anders fairly well. She was a retired art teacher who owned a lavender farm on the same road as Frankie's vineyard. Coral supplied the lavender Frankie used for baking and wine-making. The lavender farm housed Coral's art studio where she specialized in stained glass. A rush of adrenaline consumed Frankie from head to toe -

she needed to get in touch with Coral. She might just have the answer to Glenda's whereabouts.

"Rachel, you are a doll. Thanks for your help. When's your next workshop?" Plans were underway for a spring jewelry making and garden decoration workshop in March, and yes, Frankie's wines were an essential accompaniment to the workshops. "I should sign up myself," Frankie said. "My gardens could use some sprucing up." She spotted the workshop flyer and tucked one in her coat pocket, before heading back next door where she spotted Carmen's van parked out front with its hazards flashing and rear doors open. Carmen glanced up from the canvas bags she was holding.

"There you are, Frankie. I was wondering where you were when I saw your car parked here. I called upstairs but no answer." Frankie grabbed two crates from the back of the van, following Carmen into the shop.

"Let me help you unload then I've got a boatload to tell you." Carmen's look was somewhat disapproving, somewhat curious.

As the two unpacked and stowed produce and other shop supplies, Frankie revealed the details of the morning at First Congregational Church, ending with the phone call to sweet little Debra from Little Rock. Carmen was impressed. "So, what's your next move then?" she wondered. Frankie explained the information she just heard from Rachel next door.

"I think I need to talk to Glenda Kilpatrick. But then,

I don't know." Frankie admitted she didn't have a source who could provide her with access to locating the real identity of Bradford Rawlins.

"The police should have a database. You know, something where they can scan his photo," Carmen was certain. Frankie was skeptical.

"Yeah, right, but I can't just walk into a police department and announce that I want access because I'm a reporter. It doesn't work like that." Frankie sounded defeated. She wondered how Abe Arnold found out information that only the police knew. She wondered how far ahead of her Abe Arnold was in this investigation.

"What about Garrett Iverson? Or Alonzo? Can't they help you out?" Carmen interrupted Frankie's dejected assessment of her reporting skills. She informed Carmen in no uncertain terms would she take advantage of either her fledgling relationship with Garrett, or her long-time friendship with Alonzo. "Ok. Take it easy, Frankie. It was just a thought." Frankie doubted Garrett would be privy to the possible homicide investigation except as his expertise was called on. And as for Alonzo, well, she confided to Carmen that his attitude toward her of late had been pretty frosty. Carmen raised one eyebrow at her friend. "Hmm. I wonder…" she trailed off.

"Wonder what?" Frankie wanted to know.

"Well, your mom always says you'd make a good couple. Maybe Alonzo thinks so too. That could explain his attitude. Maybe he wants to be noticed as a *man,* or he's jealous of Garrett." Frankie said she doubted that was the reason.

"Alonzo and I know each other so well. We've always been friends, period, end of story."

Carmen shrugged. "Well, I'm going to start baking. You should get a hold of Coral Anders. Go on." She gave Frankie a little shove out of the kitchen. Frankie vacated, announcing she would continue the baking that night.

Upstairs, Frankie scrolled through her phone contacts, locating the lavender farm and Coral's number. Coral answered almost immediately. "Coral, this is Frankie. I need to talk to you. Can I come out to the farm?" Coral heard the definitive tone in Frankie's voice.

"What's this about, Frankie?"

"Glenda Kilpatrick," came the answer, short and direct.

Coral's melodic voice replied. "In that case, why don't you come over right now, if you can." Frankie didn't hesitate, donning her parka and starting up the cold SUV.

The afternoon was shaping up to be above normal, 35 degrees and sunshine that heated the frozen masses melting across the roadway. Frankie turned onto County K and passed her Blackbird Marsh fork, staying on K for another mile before the sign on the left indicated she'd arrived at Coral's Lovely Lavender Fields and Studio. The SUV swung down the gravel drive between now-sleeping lavender fields on both sides of the lane. Growing Lavender in Wisconsin can be tricky, like most agricultural enterprises. Lavender likes hot sun and desert-like conditions but, while it can tolerate a cold climate, it must be covered to protect the plants in their dormant stage. Coral grew varieties of both French and English Lavender, each one ideal for specific purposes, and marketed for different reasons. English Lavender is sought for its intensity of fragrance for oils, cooking, and medicines. While the lovely French Lavender is stunning for displays and decorations, sporting a long blooming season. Frankie loved the scent and taste of lavender, using it in teas, cookies and in her shop diffuser - lavender is known to have calming properties.

The long driveway ended at a rustic wooden house made from pine timbers. A wide front porch with log steps, and a side wooden ramp welcomed visitors to the farm and studio. Coral was already at the front door, waving Frankie inside, proclaiming, "I made some tea and I have some lavender shortbread cookies I took out of the freezer." Coral enjoyed baking almost as much as Frankie and the two exchanged herbal recipes from time to time. Frankie sat at the dining room table, an oval rustic plank with backless log benches for seats. "What's this about Glenda Kilpatrick?" Coral asked, pouring out tea and shoving a plateful of cookies in Frankie's direction.

On the drive out, Frankie pondered how to broach the topic of Glenda, her association with Rawlins, and her current whereabouts. Coral Anders was someone Frankie admired and respected; she was also a business partner of sorts and she didn't deserve to be deceived on any level. Frankie opted for the most honest discussion she could muster, stating her purpose in finding out information was not for gossip, but for a news article about the pastor's death. "He was a well-known figure in Deep Lakes and I just want to get to the bottom of what happened and why." Frankie decided to add in a tidbit, "I think he swindled his congregation." Coral's eyes widened at the last comment.

As she responded to Frankie's story, she seemed to choose her words carefully, pausing to think them over at times before proceeding. Yes, she had developed a fondness for Glenda as they attended some of Rachel's workshops together. Glenda wanted to learn stained glass, and Rachel suggested that Coral was the expert instructor in that endeavor, so Glenda had been coming out to the studio to learn the art.

Frankie decided to follow up, remaining in safe territory for the present. "What kind of piece was Glenda working on?" she wondered. Coral looked wistful, her eyes faraway and her mouth turned down.

"It was something special. She worked on it for weeks - a round vignette of two Bluebirds with a nest of babies amid lovely branches of apple blossoms." Frankie gasped, knowing she had just seen that very piece. Coral stopped musing.

"What is it?" she asked Frankie.

"It's just that I'm sure I saw that stained-glass piece today, at the Congregational church. I was helping sort items for the Valentine Jubilee raffle." Frankie couldn't imagine the painstaking work that had gone into designing such a beautiful piece of art and furthermore, couldn't imagine how anyone could part with it after making it. Coral looked down sadly once more.

"How sad that Glenda decided to part with it. She immersed herself in that piece, body and soul." Frankie couldn't stop there.

"Why would she leave it behind, Coral?"

Coral shook her head and confided, "Glenda was involved in something unhappy. I don't know what it was, but I know when she left Deep Lakes, she went to her sister's in Milwaukee. Maybe she can help you?" Coral added that Glenda often hinted at her personal situation but never fully entrusted Coral with the truth, only that it was something that made her feel shame and embarrassment and maybe anger, Coral thought. "I made her tell me where she was going when she left town, so I could stay in touch with her from time to time. Glenda gave me her sister's address, but I haven't spoken with her since she left," Coral admitted. She walked over to her small secretary's desk and pulled out a piece of paper, copying the address down for Frankie. "Please don't hurt Glenda, whatever you do. I feel like whatever is going on, she's already been through enough." Frankie promised she only wanted to talk to her, hoping to get some information about Rawlins.

Heading back into town, the shadows of the afternoon

crept back across the roadway from the evergreens on either side. The pines were entrenched in shadow, looking gray and black in places - the sun's business with the earth was finished for the day. The temperature dropped back into the 20's, growing colder by the hour. Two deer raised their heads in an empty cornfield Frankie passed, garnering what they could in the season of scarcity, waiting for new spring grass to emerge. The darkness enveloped the SUV, making Frankie feel small, invading her thoughts about the "pastor", his strange death, and Glenda Kilpatrick's stained-glass masterpiece. Frankie knew she was collecting pieces but had no idea if those pieces were part of the same puzzle.

Back at Bubble and Bake, Carmen was taking a large sheet pan of sticky buns, oozing with gooey cinnamon brown sugar syrup, from the commercial oven. "Wow, that smell warms my heart, Carmie." Frankie announced her arrival with the compliment and a small hug.

"What's that for?" Carmen wanted to know. Frankie shared her new knowledge from Coral Anders with Carmen.

"It just feels sad, somehow. You had to see the look on Coral's face. I think she suspects more than she's willing to say." Carmen patted her friend on the shoulder.

"Why don't you come to our house for dinner tonight? I've got the filling made already for the hand pies. You can bake them after dinner." Frankie was torn. She toyed with the idea of contacting Kris Duedenhoffer, Glenda's sister, as soon as possible and wasn't sure she wanted to wait until after dinner to do it. She knew going to Carmen's would be a distraction - the question was, would it be a much-needed distraction, or just procrastination? Frankie's stomach growled mid-thought, suggesting a home-cooked dinner wouldn't hurt at all, especially after the piddling food she'd eaten that day.

"Okay. Thank you, Carmen. What time should I be there, or can I come over right away and help you?" Carmen said she'd love her company and help throwing dinner together.

"It won't be fancy or anything, you know." Frankie tossed back her head and chuckled.

"Compared to what I've eaten lately, it'll be a feast. Trust me."

Frankie's SUV followed Carmen's van south out of town, past the hospital, Wellness Center, and surrounding fast-food joints that seemed to taunt those who work out to improve their health, then end up visiting a drive-thru on their way home. She made a mental note to get her own rear end back to the Wellness Center, tomorrow maybe. Traveling down County Road HH was black and quiet, accentuating the blandness of the winter season, where everything seemed to look the same. She mindlessly followed Carmen's van, turning right into the farm driveway just behind Carmen, parking on the concrete slab by the O'Connor's garage.

Vastly different from the dark, coldness outside,

Carmen's home was brightly lit and cozy. Ryan was in the large farm kitchen at the long trestle table, chopping up tomatoes, carrots, peppers, and cucumbers for a tossed salad. He pulled Carmen into a warm embrace and gave Frankie a friendly hello. "I already browned the taco meat," Ryan announced. "It's ready for you to add your magic ingredients," he teased. Carmen giggled, shrugging off the compliment. Checking the Dutch Oven, she headed to the spice cabinet, grabbed an armful of spices and started tossing and shaking ingredients into the meat. Another burner held Carmen's never-ending bean pot, so named because Frankie couldn't recall a time she'd been at Carmen's when a pot of beans wasn't in some stage of cooking. These were ready to be mashed into refried beans for dinner with the tacos, and of course, Carmen's homemade tortillas. Frankie said a person could live on nothing but the warm, thick savory tortillas with a fat pat of butter dripping off the edges. Comfort food was just what the doctor prescribed in Frankie's mind.

Working side by side, Frankie cut up winter fruit for a quick dessert salad, drizzled with honey and cinnamon while Carmen finished up the main dishes. Carmen noticed her friend was distracted by her thoughts. "What's going on in there?" Carmen asked, gesturing toward Frankie's head. Frankie sighed in reply.

"Just thinking about Valentine's Day coming and those ladies from First Congregational. Wondering if there's any chance their marriages will get a second chance. Especially hearing about Glenda. Nan Kilpatrick called Pastor Rawlins a homewrecker, you know." Carmen was about to chime in her own thoughts on the subject but was suddenly waylaid by a revelation.

"Oh my gosh, Frankie! Glenda Kilpatrick! She's one of the cupcake orders for Valentine's Day." Frankie couldn't hide her astonishment or her interest.

"Are you sure? Who ordered it? We need to find out right away." Carmen vacated the kitchen, returned with her laptop and placed it on the butcher block table. Carmen placed all the cupcake orders into one file folder under Bubble and Bake's accounting ledger, this one labeled "Valentine Cupcakes" with the current year.

"The orders are alphabetized so it should only take a minute…" Carmen paused, clicked, paused, clicked, then, her mouth dropped open. "It's from Dave. The message with the cupcake reads 'I still love you'. But there's no address for delivery. Huh." Frankie was undeterred.

"This is fantastic, Carmen! Don't you worry. I'll find Glenda and deliver that cupcake in person." First, Frankie knew she would be contacting Glenda's sister, and now she had a good reason to ask where she might find Glenda. Well, a reason anyway, even if it wasn't earth-shaking.

Frankie enjoyed the company of Carmen, Ryan, Carlos, and Kyle, thinking how wonderful family time truly could be. She missed that in her life, she realized; tonight, that little ache in her heart was relieved by unconditional friendship. Frankie helped clean up the leftovers, gratefully accepting a to-go container for her lunch tomorrow.

Back at Bubble and Bake, Frankie turned on her collection of Frank Sinatra duets, suitable company for swaying in the kitchen as she filled, baked, and glazed hand pies for Tuesday morning. Tuesday: how she was looking forward to wine bottling with her family, seeing Sophie and Violet, celebrating the fruits of their labor, toasting each other's lives. As her pies baked, Frankie searched her freezer shelves for the Kringles she knew were stowed away from the Christmas season. She was baking fresh tomorrow, but the frozen ones would be perfect accompaniments to the savory snacks at the bottling party, Frankie decided, choosing two almond, two apple cinnamon, and two peach Kringles from her supply.

Brambles was in crazed kitty mode, darting from the lounge area into the kitchen, chasing invisible spirits while Frankie baked. Frankie tried to bask in the moment of the entertaining kitty and enticing aroma of bakery, but found her mind wandering to tomorrow's agenda. She planned a visit to The Wellness Center, double duty, as she intended to exercise and see if she could find out anything else about Wendy and "Pastor Brad." First, she intended to call Kris Duedenhoffer - the need to accomplish that was compelling. If she had time, she would stop in at Garrett Iverson's office to ask him to attend the Valentine Jubilee on Saturday. And what else? There was always more to do as the day presented itself.

The kitchen cleaned, the bakery set aside to cool, Frankie shut off the lights downstairs and called it a day. She left Brambles happily pouncing on shadows as she went upstairs to her home.

Chapter 12

"Winter is the time for comfort, for good food and
warmth, for the touch of a friendly hand and
for a talk beside the fire: it is the time for home."
– Edith Sitwell

Tuesday morning dawned grayer than usual with a brooding sky full of clouds and a fierce wind whipping up dirty litter left from trash pick-up the day before. When Carmen arrived at 6:30, she found a smiling Frankie elbow-deep in Kringle baking - the oblong rings of dough lined up on the counters like thick oxen yokes, ready to turn a rich golden hue in the ovens as the fillings mingled within the layers of buttery dough. Kringle baking always conjured memories of Frankie's Grandma, Sophie Petersen, for whom her own daughter was named. Grandma Sophie had taken Frankie under her wing as a baking apprentice from the moment Frankie was old enough to lick the mixer beaters. First, she learned to make small cakes, then cookies, and finally worked her way into pastries and pies. Frankie was eternally thankful that Grandma Sophie had lived until Frankie was in college. Long enough for Frankie to take the reins in the kitchen, but never long enough for Frankie not to miss her presence - her sweet spicy smell, her steady hand, her cheery blue eyes, and dimpled smile. It was from Grandma Sophie that Frankie first heard the baking philosophy she transferred to her goodies daily: "remember to always add the secret ingredient in everything you make - love." Grandma had said, "just enough love to go around and you'll always have some left for the next batch." Maybe that's why Frankie's bakery was popular, at least she liked to think so.

Today Frankie was putting up Kringles to last into the Easter holiday, when they would be in high demand. She would need to set aside at least two more baking days before Easter to ensure there would be enough to sell. With Lent just around the corner, Frankie's baking agenda was lengthy. Ash Wednesday was on Valentine's Day this year - something Frankie didn't agree with and wondered why the Pope couldn't do something to change that. Not that Frankie didn't understand that the Lenten calendar complemented the lunar calendar, she just felt inconvenienced by a chocolate-indulging holiday on the same date as a solemn fasting day. To make matters more interesting, a Lent beginning on Valentine's Day meant an Easter Sunday landing on April 1 - All Fools Day! Seriously, Frankie thought the Pope would have vetoed that calendar.

Back to the baking agenda at hand. For a week before Ash Wednesday, Bubble and Bake would offer a Fat Tuesday classic pastry, the Polish Paczki (pronounced either poonch-key or paunch-key, depending on how the speaker likes to emphasize the "u" sound). Paczkis can be found in Illinois, Michigan, and Wisconsin, and maybe a smattering of other Midwest enclaves - and people clamor for them as a pre-Lent tradition of indulgence. Paczkis look similar to Bismarks, but are significantly fatter and puffier. Authentically they are stuffed with prune filling, but can be found in any variety of fruit fillings in modern times. Some Midwest communities have a named Paczki Day, which might be Thursday before Lent or Fat Tuesday. Bubble and Bake offers Paczkis from the Thursday before through Ash Wednesday morning, if there are any left by Wednesday. With the Paczki making, the Valentine cupcake extravaganza, and the February 17 Romantic Getaway event, Frankie decided she needed to sign up for cloning right away! She guessed now would be a good time to get Jovie Luedtke on board, working around her Shamrock Floral gig. Jovie already knew how to make Paczkis thankfully, because a novice baker simply doesn't start out on the Paczki challenge.

Carmen poked her head in the kitchen. "It's awfully quiet in here," then seeing Frankie standing deep in thought over a piece of paper, "Oh oh. I think I smell something burning." Frankie looked up, barely registering.

"Huh. Oh, yeah. I'm thinking about all the stuff we're supposed to accomplish in the next two weeks." Carmen nodded.

"Yeah, we really bit off a big bite this year. Whose

idea was it to take orders for 600 cupcakes?" Frankie and Carmen both pointed accusing fingers at each other, then laughed.

"I called Jovie. She can come in and help with the Paczkis starting on Friday."

Carmen groaned, "Dios mio. I forgot about those things." Carmen made it sound like they were deep frying cockroaches or something equally gross. Frankie added that Jovie would work around the Shamrock Floral schedule to help with cupcakes if needed, and they could definitely count on her to serve on the wine pairing night. Carmen sighed in relief. "And don't forget that the twins will be serving on wine pairing night, too." This would be the first official event the twins would be in service, and Frankie knew that Carmen was prepping them to be professional servers. Carmen also assured Frankie they could count on Tess and Adam, who were quick learners and shaping up to be two of the best interns since the shop opened. "I agree, wholeheartedly. Now back to work." Carmen pointed to the clock and Frankie gasped her surprise. It was already past 9:30 and the bakery was closed for the day. Carmen pulled the cart into the kitchen where she had parked it just outside the door. "Okay, you're done for the day. I'm making muffins for tomorrow. I know you have other things to do. Like a newspaper story," Carmen urged. Frankie nodded, finished wrapping up the cooled Kringles, and wheeled them into the shop's walk-in freezer.

"I have to go to *The Watch* with an article on the Wine Pairing event and new vintage. But first, I'm going to the Wellness Center to try a different yoga class. I hope Wendy Jarvis isn't leading this class." Carmen laughed and wished her good luck, before heading to the pantry for her needed ingredients. Upstairs, Frankie grabbed the printed copy of her promised article for the local paper. Funny, she wasn't good enough to be a real staff reporter for Abe Arnold, but he complained if she didn't submit articles often enough about Wisconsin grape growing and wine making business or other such features. Abe paid a pittance for Frankie's effort, but she figured it was good for her business and that would have to do. She changed into her comfy yoga pants and a loose tank top that read, "I don't sweat, I sparkle", then headed out the back door where her SUV was parked.

Entering the yoga classroom, Frankie immediately noticed the quiet atmosphere along with the calming essence of lavender and bergamot, broadcasting the good news that Wendy Jarvis was not in house for today's session. As her eyes adjusted to the low lighting, Frankie saw a diminutive woman with thick dark hair pulled back into a short braid. As she turned from setting up her music, Frankie could see she was perhaps Asian, maybe five feet tall at the most, and possibly in her early 20's. Frankie set up her mat as other women entered doing the same, also tossing curious glances toward the instructor, obviously a new employee. The tiny figure introduced herself as Fuji Vang, telling the women she was a Hmong-American with a degree in Health and Fitness. She would be teaching five yoga sessions weekly, while also teaching a full variety of yoga practices in Madison. After an hour of yoga led by Fuji, Frankie felt calm, stretched, and confident in Fuji's ability to successfully replace Stormy. Frankie couldn't help noticing Wendy had been certain to find an exact opposite of Stormy in her hiring choice.

Back at the welcome desk, Frankie chatted with her favorite receptionist, Taylor. Frankie could speak openly with Taylor, who had been friends with Violet in high school, yet another adopted daughter in her household. Taylor asked Frankie how the yoga class went, and Frankie gave a positive recommendation on Fuji's behalf.

"So, Taylor, is Wendy around today?" Frankie decided she might do a little fishing. Taylor shook her head.

"Not now anyway. She's in a meeting all morning." Frankie didn't travel down that road for information, instead asking straight out, "I haven't seen any flowers on the front desk in a while…" Taylor looked puzzled, then traced the comment back to memory.

"Oh, you mean the neon daisies?" Frankie nodded, yes, that's what she was thinking. "Wendy used to get them almost every week or so. She always put them out front to brighten up the place. But, I threw the last bunch away a few days ago," Taylor informed. Frankie pretended to be in the know.

"Oh, I suppose since she and Jeff are having problems,

she's not getting flowers right now?" Frankie realized she sounded girlish and catty, and she didn't like it.

"It's a dirty business, this investigative work, isn't it?" There was The Golden One in Frankie's ear, giving her a regular dressing down, enunciating the words "investigative work" as if they were swear words. The pirate jumped to Frankie's defense.

"A girl's gotta do what a girl's gotta do." Somehow, Frankie didn't feel any better to hear those words.

But then Taylor came back into the conversation. "I don't think those flowers came from Jeff," she said quietly, leaning toward Frankie conspiratorially. Frankie raised one eyebrow, questioning. "Jeff was never happy when the flowers were delivered. That's why Wendy put them out here, I think."

Frankie quickly asked, "So who sent them then?" Taylor shrugged.

"None of us out here know. We had our guesses, but nobody was brave enough to ask Wendy." Frankie decided the Wellness Center receptionists were a smart group not to mess with Wendy, both a formidable presence and their manager. Frankie wanted to pose one more question, even though she might be putting Taylor in a precarious position.

"Taylor, did you know about Stormy and Jeff?" Taylor looked uncomfortable and Frankie assured her it was okay not to answer. "It's really none of my business. It's just that when Wendy told me straight out why she fired

Stormy, I was shocked." What Frankie said was true - she had been shocked at Wendy's forthright proclamation about Stormy and her husband. Taylor shook her head; clearly she had not been shocked at the news.

"Jeff had a wandering eye and a bad reputation among the women. Most of us won't miss him." Huh, so much for Alonzo's faulty information that Jeff was a straight arrow, Frankie mused. Frankie decided she'd probed enough for one visit. Really, she wanted only to confirm that a regular delivery of bright colored daisies was being sent to Wendy. She was certain, thanks to Meredith Healy at Shamrock Floral, the flowers were part of Pastor Brad's pattern, a regular delivery to one of his "angels". Frankie made a putrid face as she left the building.

Back downtown, Frankie pulled the SUV into a parking space in front of *The Whitman County Watch*. It wasn't yet noon, but the day hadn't gained any brightness. The clouds deepened, lowering their threatening gray among the rooftops as the bare tree branches shivered and the street signs shook. Frankie wondered if a storm was looming, mentally reminding herself to check the weather forecast when she returned home.

She clutched the article to keep it from being torn out of her hand by the wind, opened the newspaper office door, and smiled at Chelsey Mathis. Chelsey stood from her desk, greeting Frankie at the front counter. "Hello, Frankie. Do you have a minute? Mr. Arnold asked me to let him know if you stopped in." Frankie pursed her lips but nodded at Chelsey, who disappeared to the back room. Frankie expected she couldn't avoid Abe forever; he'd been trying to pin her down for days following Pastor Rawlins' death and obviously wanted to coerce information out of Frankie. Which might mean he respected Frankie, or at least thought she had some worthwhile information on the mysterious death. Frankie straightened her posture and attired herself with a professional expression as Abe walked out. She wasn't prepared for Abe to hand her article back to her.

"Look, Francine," Abe said, peering over his wire framed glasses hanging on the end of his nose, "I don't think I have space for your article right now." Frankie was startled, then angry. So, this was going to be a game and now it was her turn to play.

"Well, you don't have to run it today. Really anytime this week or next is fine." Frankie pretended not to care. Abe folded his arms across his chest and gave Frankie an unimpressed look, as if she were a child who needed a reprimand.

"What I mean is that I don't think there will be room for it - period." Frankie decided it was game over now; she would play it straight.

"Stop the dance. What do you want, Abe?" Frankie was channeling those relatives who possessed a little chutzpah. Abe chuckled, perhaps appreciative of Frankie's candor.

"Tell me what you got on the Pastor Rawlins case. Come on - share what you know, and I'll add you as a contributor to the article I'm writing." Frankie was genuinely peeved now. She decided it was time to tell Abe Arnold exactly how she felt about being rejected as a serious reporter.

"A *contributor*? Wow, that's big of you," Frankie began, forcing herself to slow down her words so she didn't look like an emotional train wreck. "Look Abe," she used his own conversational tactic. "I'm working this story for Point Press. I'm not a staffer here so I don't owe you anything. I'm already a contributor. I contribute feature stories, just like you asked me to do three years ago." The last sentence came out in a series of staccato - one word at a time. Abe wrinkled his forehead in exasperation, but his voice didn't show any sign of anger, just reprimand for an unruly child.

"Ok, don't collaborate with me. Fine. But don't bring me any more feature stories. I can't use them." Frankie was fuming as she picked up her feature article.

"Fine," she managed in a huff. "I'll see if the shopper wants to publish them." She knew two things about publishing in the area shoppers: 1) Abe Arnold considered a shopper nothing but a waste of newsprint, and 2) The area shopper was a very poor substitute for displaying her articles, with low readership by people who mostly skimmed, looking for want ads.

Abe launched one more parting shot at Frankie's back as she went out the door: "You're too green for this story, Francine. You don't have enough experience. I could help you. We could help each other." Abe's words were drowned out by the slamming door and the whipping wind.

Frankie, a blustery bitter breeze, and several swirling snow clusters blew into the front door of Bubble and Bake a few minutes later. Frankie feeling about as bitter as the biting wind toward Abe Arnold. Who did he think he was anyway, putting the squeeze on her to divulge information he had no business asking her for? Why, it was a form of extortion. Frankie was tromping through the shop, muttering curses under her breath about the audacity of Abe. The fireflies had retreated to the netherworld, sensing now was not a good time for them to weigh in. Peeling off her parka and kicking her snow boots across the kitchen tiles, Frankie slumped onto a stool at the counter and opened the sub sandwich she'd picked up between the newspaper office and the shop. She felt like crying, and this feeling only heightened her indignation. She didn't cry; instead, she slid off the stool and ran a double shot of espresso through the coffee maker, grabbed full-fat half and half from the fridge, poured it into a stainless-steel cup and set the whirring steamer into action. Observing a potential change in Frankie's temperament, The Golden One attempted a comment.

"You know, Abe Arnold's refusal to print your article is really a small victory for you." Frankie's arm hairs stood on end.

"Oh, yeah. I'm listening. Explain." The Golden One heaved a sigh, as if this required a grand effort on her part.

"Abe Arnold obviously thinks you have some crucial information about the Rawlins case or he wouldn't bother holding your feature article over your head. Maybe he even regrets not hiring you." Frankie paused in her chewing to contemplate this possibility. Never before had The Golden One offered this kind of praise, or whatever this was. Still, it was quite a stretch to think Abe might regret not having Frankie on staff. No, more likely, Abe thought Frankie was easy to manipulate. The tamped down anger began to flare up inside again.

"Now look whach'juve done!" It was Pirate's turn. "It's so hot in here already, I could spontaneously combust!" He pointed his tiny pirate machete at The Golden One, who promptly stuck out her tongue in return.

"Listen to me, Frankie," she tried once more. "What do you care what a big blowhard like Abe Arnold thinks anyway? You just keep doing your own thing and forget about him." Frankie had to admit there was wisdom in that statement, at least about doing her own thing. She cooled down, finished her sandwich and turned her attention to the evening's bottling party.

Her thoughts were quickly interrupted by her ringing phone. Just her luck: this must be newspaper humiliation day, Frankie thought, seeing the caller was none other than her regional editor at *Point Press*, Magdalena Guzman.

"Hello, Magda," Frankie attempted to sound chipper. Magda was all business, as usual.

"I haven't heard from you in a few days. What's the deal

on your story? Is it ready?" In Frankie's defense, "Pastor Brad" had only been dead a week and the body had just been released four days earlier, so Frankie technically had spoken with Magda Thursday, right after she submitted a small factual article about the death and an investigation in progress. Frankie was fully aware, however, that a few days in the news cycle was a virtual eternity and she knew she should have kept Magda in the loop.

"Sorry, Magda. I have been juggling a few things here, but I've been doing a lot of investigating." She could hear Magda having a second side conversation, her hand over the mouthpiece of her phone. Magda was back, loud and clear.

"Oh, yeah. Well, is the story ready or what?" Frankie admitted it wasn't but said she was on the trail of a big lead and was about to launch into her discoveries when Magda shushed her. "Not now, and not on the phone. Look, you gotta get up here and meet with me so we can talk in person." Magda was paging through something on her desk, maybe a calendar. "Can you come up here tomorrow? Let's say - noon. Bring all your information with you and maybe a story, yes?"

Frankie wanted to make a good impression, but she knew she was still unprepared to finish the article. Finish it? Well, truth be told she hadn't even started it - all she had was a bunch of notes that needed to be pieced together. "Yes, Magda. I'll be there tomorrow, with everything I have. I have so much to tell you." But Magda cut her off with a click. Frankie felt humiliated. Carmen was right; her business was more important than some half-baked investigative reporter job. Nobody can really have it all, can they?

* * *

Frankie still had a couple of hours before she needed to gather up vittles for her bottling companions and head out to the vineyard, so she opened her laptop and pulled up her notes file on the Rawlins case. Her mind returned immediately to her conversation with Coral Anders from yesterday. She did a Google search for Kris Duedenhoffer in Milwaukee and hit unexpected pay dirt. Kristine Duedenhoffer was a newly hired attorney at the law firm of none other than Briggs and Baker, the same law firm named on the business card Frankie retrieved from Rawlins' ice shanty a week ago. A whole bunch of speculative claims unleashed themselves from the recesses of Frankie's mind. She could only rightfully imagine that three people would have the business card: Kristine, Glenda, or Dave Kilpatrick. Or maybe Nan or Roger Kilpatrick - but that was a longshot. Frankie's gut told her that either Dave or Glenda must have been at that ice shanty at the time of Rawlins' demise. But why? She couldn't wait for answers and tapped in the phone number of the law firm, asking to speak with Kristine Duedenhoffer as a matter of urgency. Frankie hoped she sounded as urgent as she felt, her heart knocking through her chest wall.

"This is Kristine Duedenhoffer, Ms. Champagne, is that right?" The professional smooth voice on the line sounded ready to be of assistance, or so Frankie's wishful thinking surmised. Driven by a need to prove herself to Magda tomorrow, Frankie decided she would explain honestly what her motive was for questioning Glenda's sister. She began with her intent to write a news article for *Point Press* about the mysterious death of Pastor Rawlins, along with a couple key pieces of information she already knew about Rawlins. She could hear Kristine scribbling notes on her end and tapping her pen methodically. Frankie laid her hand out in full.

"Ms. Duedenhoffer, I think Glenda may be in trouble here, and I want to get to the truth so I can write a fair article. I know there's something shady about Rawlins." Frankie had no idea if her approach was going to work, but she knew it was heartfelt. Kristine must have read Frankie's intentions correctly, at least to a point.

"I'll tell you what I can, Ms. Champagne, but not over the phone. We need to meet in person. Can you come to my office this week sometime?" Frankie agreed, was transferred to reception and scheduled an appointment for Thursday at 11:30, Frankie's day off. At least now Frankie would have more ammunition to offer Magda tomorrow.

It was time to gather up food goodies and hightail it to the vineyard. Frankie boxed up the Kringles she retrieved from the freezer, along with small plates and a serrated knife. Carmen would bring venison sausage sliced up thanks to her husband's and son's successful deer hunting season, along with her homemade garden salsa and tortilla chips. Frankie added a pile of fresh dipping veggies, spinach dip, baguettes, and cheese slices - all easily portable and ready throughout the evening. She loaded all items into her wheeled cooler, piled some disposable utensils, cups, and plates on top with a stack of napkins, then headed out to the SUV.

The temperature had risen to right around freezing, but the sky still looked threatening, and the wind was relentless as it pushed and pulled the SUV against the road shoulder. When Frankie turned into Bountiful Fruits, the sky had darkened a couple shades deeper and she feared an ice storm - worse than snow - might be on the horizon. Fighting the wind, she wheeled a bumpy track with the cooler through the snow cover to the wine-making building, heaved the door open and jostled the cooler through. Nelson Raye was already in the workshop along with his college cohort, a taller spindly young man with jet black hair that hung past his shoulders.

"Hi, Ms. Champagne. This is my lab partner, Zane Casey." Frankie smiled and held out her hand to shake his, which turned out to be an enthusiastic and firm pump.

"Nice to meet you, Zane. Glad you could make it. I'm a little worried about this weather though, so I think we should plan ahead in case of a storm." Frankie hung her coat on a wall hook and wheeled the cooler over to one of the three long folding tables lining the workshop room. Nelson and Zane both seemed oblivious to the threatening weather, so Frankie mentioned the dark sky and wind, precipitating the need to locate flashlights and check their function before the others arrived. Nelson emerged from the storeroom with five flashlights, which all worked well. Frankie instructed him to place one flashlight by each of the four wine tanks where the teams would be stationed. She took the fifth one and placed it on the long table where several empty wine cases were placed. Zane and Nelson continued bringing clean bottles in cases from the storeroom, calculating as they stacked them against one concrete block wall and stopping when the number of cases reached 84. With four 250-liter tanks to empty, Frankie expected to fill over 800 bottles of wine tonight - give or take a few that would be sampled and taken home by the helpers!

Nelson and Zane had already assembled the four floor corkers, positioned in the work station areas around the wine tanks. The deep stainless-steel sinks were filled with the cleaning agent in case the previously washed bottles needed one more going-over. In wine making and bottling, cleanliness is indeed next to godliness as the number one rule. It was almost four o'clock, and helpers were blowing through the heavy door every couple of minutes. Frankie grabbed her number one daughter Sophie, who came alone from Madison as her boyfriend

Max had taken extra shifts for vacationing nurses at the hospital this week. Frankie beamed at how healthy and happy Sophie looked, giving her a perusal before hugging her tightly. It was Sophie who spoke first.

"It's so good to see you, Mom. You look good but kind of tired." Frankie, realizing she hadn't spoken to either of her daughters since the Rawlins death, said she'd fill her and Violet in later.

"Let's just say there's been a lot going on in Deep Lakes lately." Will, Libby, and Violet came in a couple of minutes later and Frankie greeted them all with hugs. Her favorite brother teased her about her wind-blown hair, which Frankie hadn't bothered fixing since she walked in the workshop. She punched Will's shoulder, then wrapped her arms around Violet, doing a little dance. Violet looked happy, and Frankie, who worried about her more fragile daughter, felt relief - at least temporarily. Now was not the time to dig deep into any sensitive topics, so that would have to wait.

Carmen and her whole crew arrived next, the twins carrying in the food and setting it up on the long table beside Frankie's goodies. Adam and Tess came in together, announcing they had driven up from Madison in sleet. Sophie looked up, surprised. "I guess I missed that. It must have started shortly after I left." Alonzo followed right behind Adam and Tess, confirming what Frankie suspected, that a possible ice storm was predicted.

Frankie said she'd have announcements to make as

soon as the others arrived. "Everyone else should be here soon. They were working until 4 so…" Frankie was glad to see Alonzo, hoping his presence there meant their relationship was back on firm footing again. James arrived next, alone, noted Frankie. She supposed James' wife, Shauna, didn't want to help, as was mostly the norm. As if on cue, James explained that Shauna was working late to catch up on the business accounts. Shauna organized the projects and accounts at James' construction firm, "Nothing But the Finest Champagne Contractors" and, Frankie had to admit that Shauna was an astute business partner for her brother. Frankie forced a smile. "Well, tell Shauna we missed her." James nodded as the door opened to Nick and to everyone's surprise, Cherry Parker. At least Cherry missed the look of amusement on Frankie's face as she gave Frankie a little hug.

"Here I am, Frankie. Thanks for asking me to come. This is going to be such fun." Cherry chirped like a sweet little sparrow. Frankie looked beyond Cherry to Nick, who gave a noncommittal shrug.

"I'm really happy you decided to come, Cherry." Frankie gave introductions around the room like a school teacher. Just as she finished, the door opened one last time to reveal Frankie's mom, Peggy, on the arm of none other than Dan Fitzpatrick, Joe's brother and business partner at the bait shop and fishing guide service. Everyone of Peggy's family did their best to disguise their surprise since nobody knew their mother was dating Dan. The

Champagnes and Fitzpatricks had been long-time friends; Joe was a confirmed bachelor, but Dan and his late wife, Lois, had gone on weekend getaways with Peggy and Charlie for years. Dan lost Lois to a tough battle with breast cancer a little over a year ago - it should have been no shock that he and Peggy might keep each other company. Frankie retrieved Joe's conversation from a few days earlier, recalling how sheepish he looked when he said Dan might be seeing someone. Really, Frankie thought, how could she be so naive as to miss the hint he was offering?

Frankie broke the heavy silence first, remembering she was the hostess of this event, as she gathered the volunteers around her, placing them on crews of four to work one variety of wine for the night. She assigned the experienced helpers to fetch, hold, and fill bottles from the tanks - two people per tank - one to fill and one to fetch and carry filled bottles to the corkers. The other experienced workers would operate the floor corkers, a hand operation. This was the favorite post for the twins, who would manage two of the four corkers, with Nick and Adam posted at the other two. Frankie liked having her mother, Sophie, Violet, and Libby do the labeling as they tended to be fussier about perfectly positioning the labels on each bottle. Everyone else could place bottles in cases, labeling them with corresponding variety, and serve as floaters and relief workers when someone wanted a break.

Frankie also let everyone know where the flashlights

were in case of emergency. James quickly pointed out that, at his insistence, the workshop was equipped with emergency lighting and a corner wood burning stove in case the power went out. Frankie knew she was fortunate to have James as the contractor for the vineyard buildings - he was a consummate professional with a reputation for perfection. Before commencing the bottling brigade, Alonzo and Ryan followed James outside to the wood pile, each bringing in two bundles to stack by the corner woodstove. Their preparations turned out to be providential indeed as about 90 minutes into the process, icy sheets of rain began pelting roof and windows, followed by darkness as all power was lost. Helpers grabbed waiting flashlights and within a few minutes, the emergency lighting kicked on, albeit dimmer than the overhead LED lights installed in the building, but any light was better than nothing. Nick and Ryan sprang into action, getting the wood stove lit and stoked, while everyone else sat around the long tables, taking an advantageous food and beverage break. Frankie looked around the softly lit room, at all the contented faces enjoying food, wine, and company and smiled in satisfaction as the rain continued to fall.

This couldn't be more hygge, she thought, quickly interrupted by Carmen nudging her in the side. "I know what you're thinking, Frankie," she giggled. "You and your Danish hygge." Carmen loudly drew out the last word - "hooooo-ga."

Frankie had to laugh. "You are so right."

Discussion ensued about the favorite wines of the night amid details about each one's flavors, grape varieties used in each, subtle undertones, and food pairings. After about a half hour and still no sign of power, Frankie announced it was time to resume bottling, however carefully. Thank goodness for a manual operation in a small business! The only thing that could not be done was labeling because the labels and foil closures for the corks must be applied with a heat gun, and that ran on electricity. After the bottles were corked, they were immediately loaded into the labeled cases. Alonzo called into the sheriff's department dispatch and since the power in town was operational, it was decided the cases could be loaded up in vehicles and brought into the shop where the labeling and wine closures would be applied. A final count tallied 88 cases of wine, meaning at least five vehicles would be needed to do the hauling. Alonzo, Ryan, and Nick had large pickup trucks, which were loaded first, followed by Frankie's SUV, then Dan Fitzpatrick's Expedition. Knowing the roads were treacherous, a long caravan of vehicles headed into Deep Lakes at a snail's pace. The city roads were no better than the rural traverses, and the parade of vehicles had not seen a single county truck out sanding or salting until they crept into downtown.

With everyone arriving safely at Bubble and Bake, Frankie had to laugh at the arduous task ahead of them yet. To avoid parking on the entire street in front of the shop where they would be in the way of salt trucks, they parked in the lot across the street, then one by one, each vehicle pulled up to the shop front, flashers on, to unload. The pavement was coated in slick ice, meaning crossing the street and hauling cases of wine up the ramp was both amusing and frightening at the same time. Frankie and Carmen located the sidewalk salt and immediately scattered it up and down the ramp, the front walk and steps. At least the rain had ceased, and the wind died down, announcing the storm had passed.

With only three heat guns available, Frankie no longer needed 20 helpers hanging around, but with impossible driving conditions, plans must be made. Sophie, Violet, Adam, and Tess would spend the night with Frankie, who had three bedrooms and ample floor space. Peggy volunteered to put up anyone else who planned to stay, insisting that Nelson, Zane, Will, and Libby were in no uncertain terms driving the hour plus back to Stevens Point that night. Frankie dismissed Carmen and her family, emphatic their help was not needed, and they should get their behinds safely home.

Alonzo, Frankie, and her guests finished the labeling and capping just after midnight, toasting each other with one final glass of wine to top off the adventure. Frankie told Sophie and Violet to get settled in and help find places for Adam and Tess as well, while she finished cleaning up the shop kitchen.

With just Frankie and Alonzo left downstairs, she warmly offered her appreciation to him for all he had done that night but was dumbfounded by the serious look on Alonzo's face. Maybe it was the wine he consumed or the fact they were alone, and he wasn't in uniform that made Alonzo vulnerable and reflective. "It seems like life used to be so much easier. Frankie, do you ever wonder what it would have been like if we'd gotten together?" Frankie was not prepared to deal with that question, not because she had romantic notions about Alonzo - just the opposite was true - but because she didn't want to hurt his feelings. She decided to take a lighthearted approach to the topic.

"You and I would kill each other, Lon. We're both filled to the brim with determination." Alonzo just kept staring at the wall beyond Frankie's shoulder, inscrutable. "If you and I got together it would ruin our friendship," Frankie tried again, "and I am not willing to lose that," she proclaimed. Did Alonzo regret running for sheriff, she wondered? Did he have real feelings for Frankie, or was he just lonely? Or, like some men, was he having an adverse reaction to Frankie testing the dating waters with some other guy? The last idea couldn't be true; Frankie knew Alonzo for too long to believe he was a "guy" - he was loyal to Frankie through thick and thin, had come to her and the girls' rescue too many times to be anything but an upright man. Still, Frankie felt uncomfortable now, not wanting anything to change between the two of them. Alonzo's far-off look left his face and he stood up, smiling again.

"Yeah, you're right. We probably would fight like a cat and dog if we spent too much time together. Still, be careful. There's a lot of bad actors out there." What was he trying to tell her? Did he know something about Garrett Iverson that should make her worry? If so, why didn't he just come out with it? This was not the way Frankie wanted the evening to end, so she laughed it off instead.

"Don't worry so much, Lon. And thanks again - for everything." She gave him a long hug and he hugged back, squeezing her tightly.

"Well, I better get going," he said. "I should stop by the dispatcher and see how many accidents have been logged during the storm."

Before turning out the kitchen lights, Frankie basked in a long, gratified view of the fruits of her labors. More than 900 bottles of wine stood proudly in her kitchen - some of it from grapes she herself had nurtured and harvested. Each flavor was like one of her own children, and she needed to praise their attributes before retiring for the evening. There was her new achievement - Crown Me Pineapple - made from her own La Crescent white grapes with their citrus and pineapple undertones, the grapes combined perfectly with the pulpy sweet overripe pineapple must for a balanced medium sweet table wine.

There was Spring Fever Riesling - crafted from her own Edelweiss grapevines as well as some she purchased from New York, combined with vanilla, lemon, and local lavender for a unique flavor that couldn't quite be pinned down, but that customers said made them wish for Spring weather.

There was Cupid's Cup - an unpredictable wine because its flavors changed with every brewing. Made from leftover summer fruits of all kinds, and St. Pepin grapes, it was always sweet but not sickening or heavy.

Another of Frankie's pride and joy was the Oh My, Apple Pie! - blended from St. Pepin grapes, pressed orchard apples, and shot through with Cinnamon Liquor and Buttershots. It tasted like liquid apple pie that Grandma never made. The cases, piled against the kitchen walls, would make their way to the basement tomorrow, tilted on their sides for storage, but tonight, well, tonight was over, and Frankie was ready for a long winter's nap.

Chapter 13

*"What convinces is conviction. Believe in the argument
you're advancing. If you don't you're as good as dead."*
– Lyndon B. Johnson

Morning arrived in what seemed only minutes
after such a late night. After Frankie admired the fruits
of their labors, she tiptoed upstairs only to find Violet
and Sophie chatting away in school-girl fashion in the
spare bedroom. Frankie's eyes glistened as she stood
outside the bedroom, remembering earlier days when her
daughters would whisper and giggle some nights until
Frankie threatened some consequence or other. This time,
she paraded into the room, sat on the double bed and
joined in the conversation. Much was devoted to whether
or not Grandma Peggy was dating Dan Fitzpatrick, and
what exactly Frankie knew about it - which was nothing,
scout's honor. The girls both turned their attention to
Frankie's love prospects, including Alonzo. Frankie filled
them in on the mystery death, the investigation, her
somewhat shaky relationship with Alonzo and the article
she intended to pursue come Hell or high water.

Frankie couldn't remember when her daughters had

suddenly become her friends and confidants, but she thoroughly relished this new kind of parental bond and looked forward to more of the same. Still, Frankie was cautious about her newest prospect, Garrett Iverson. That relationship was too tenuous for her to discuss, along with the fact she couldn't even put a label on it yet. Frankie didn't know what time it was when sleep finally overcame her, but as the spare room quieted, she said her goodnights and crawled into her own bed, not even bothering to put on pajamas.

By six a.m., Frankie had showered and put on fresh clothes and took the stairs two at a time, unable to recall if the bakery was ready for the day. To her happy surprise, she opened the kitchen door to see Carmen, a latte in hand to pass to her, Adam and Tess already loading the bakery case with muffins. "I'm surprised you're up already," Carmen said, "I heard you and the girls were chittering away like little birds way after midnight." Carmen gestured toward Tess, the source of that information. Frankie smiled warmly.

"I guess Mother Nature had a different plan for last night than I did. It all worked out wonderfully." Carmen gave Frankie a little hug.

"So nice to have the girls home, huh." Frankie told Carmen that her plan for the day was to drive Violet back to Stevens Point for class, then meet with Magda Guzman, her *Point Press* editor. Gesturing at all the cases of wine piled against the kitchen walls, looking like a cardboard fort, Frankie said she'd be finding help in the afternoon to move it all downstairs.

Apologetically, she added, "I know it's Wednesday, Carmen, so leave when you need to, and I'll finish the baking when I get back." Carmen shrugged.

"Ryan can manage until I get home. I'll finish what you start. Let's get going while we have Adam and Tess out front."

It turned out to be a quiet morning at the shop with the whole town moving in slow gear following the ice storm. Everything had a shiny coating down to the tiniest twigs on the bare trees. The streets were salted but people were tentative about venturing out and the schools were closed, so more people had no reason to leave the safety of their homes. By closing time, only about half the muffins were sold, leaving Frankie with the decision to chill them, this would preserve their freshness and allow her to sell them Thursday for a reduced price. Most of the hand pies were gone, thanks in part to Georgia Harris, the education coordinator at St. Anthony's, who decided they would sell well at the Bingo night plate supper. St. Anthony's hosted Bingo once a month in the Fellowship Hall, and always kicked off the evening with a supper plate special. But for some reason, June Thompson, the church secretary, forgot to post a reminder in the bulletin for donated baked items so the church found itself without baked goods for the evening Bingo event. Well, everyone knows that no church supper is complete without dessert, so Georgia tooled down to the Bubble and Bake, hoping for the best. Frankie gave the church a deal on the hand pies and both parties were satisfied.

For the past three hours, Frankie and Carmen were preparing the Paczki dough and setting it in warm places to rise, then moving on to readying the fillings. Besides the traditional prune filling, Carmen made a lemon one, very popular in Deep Lakes, and Frankie started a custard filling, making the Paczki more like a Bismark. Three varieties would be offered for tomorrow morning and the work would begin anew and continue until Ash Wednesday, next week. Carmen promised to teach Tess the art of Paczki while Frankie was away that morning, and Adam chimed in that he would learn too. "Might as well. You never know when I might need that skill," he said jokingly.

Frankie passed along a final Paczki secret: "Don't forget the vodka. No Polish Busha would ever leave that out of her Paczki!"

Sophie had come downstairs during the dough-making process to say her goodbyes and head back to Madison with two bottles of Spring Fever in tow. Frankie shoved a bakery box of assorted muffins in her car, gave her a long warm hug, and wished her safe travels. Violet appeared in the kitchen, freshly showered, while Frankie was stirring the custard filling. Violet made a sweet version of a latte and grabbed a Lemon Poppyseed muffin, her favorite. "I miss your bakery so much, Mom. We can't get anything this good at school." Frankie beamed at her daughter.

"I'm just finishing up this filling and we'll head out. Pack up some muffins to go. We've got plenty," Frankie pointed at the bakery case.

A little while later, she and Violet were headed North on the highway to Stevens Point, Frankie looking professional in black slacks, a dark plum pullover top and lighter plum cardigan. She and Violet spent the next hour chatting about school and summer plans in general; Frankie tried to keep the conversation light, still concerned about Violet's uncertainty about college. As she pulled into the parking lot of Violet's campus dorm, she concluded her daughter's state of mind seemed positive and stronger than at Christmas. Violet reached over to hug Frankie and smiled firmly. "Good luck with your article. Go get 'em, Mom." Imagine that, Frankie thought, a pep talk from my daughter - a role reversal indeed. Frankie decided that was just what she needed.

Point Press was a few streets away from campus in the downtown area, which allowed Frankie time to gather her thoughts and rehearse her conversation with Magda. The gray concrete building on Minnesota Avenue housed the newspaper office along with other publications and a radio station. The entrance receptionist logged Frankie's information and pointed to an elevator on the right that would take her to Magda's second floor office. The newspaper receptionist brought coffee to Frankie as she waited for Magda, whose large corner office was down a short hallway, overlooking the busy avenue. Magda stood and offered Frankie a firm handshake as she motioned for her to sit. Frankie admired the fact that Magda began her newspaper career as a field reporter, then a department reporter, then an assistant editor before her promotion to regional editor two years ago. Frankie guessed her age to be under 30, quite a series of accomplishments for someone so young. Magda had a full face with large dark eyes and black hair pulled back, sculpted almost to her shoulders. She wore a black skirt and black jacket with a bright yellow blouse underneath, and black high heels to boost her height. Magda was a no-nonsense, assertive manager, who was very capable. Looking at Frankie, she picked up a pen, opening a yellow pad to a fresh page. "Ok, let's hear it. Tell me what you got on this story."

Frankie produced a print-out of her notes. So as not to waste her boss's time, she gave a short synopsis of being at the church the day Rawlins died to finding the scrap of calendar with "8 a.m." and "Patrick" on it that led her to interview Joe Fitzpatrick and Marjean at the Kilpatrick insurance agency, along with officer Lazaar and the coroner. She pointed out that her snooping at the insurance agency procured the existence of a million-dollar personal liability policy in Rawlins' name. Magda leaned forward and sharpened her gaze at Frankie before she resumed scrawling notes. She relayed what she knew from talking to the congregation ladies - Patsy and Missy - the counseling methods of Rawlins, the split marriages and Glenda Kilpatrick's sister, the attorney from the law firm on the card Frankie herself had found at the crime scene.

"And, I know Rawlins is an imposter. I called his 'claimed' former congregation and they never heard of him," Frankie ended out of breath. Magda's pen stopped abruptly as her eyes met Frankie's.

"Ok. Got it. What else?" What else? Frankie's mind raced. She thought she already had plenty to weave together, but she knew there were still loose ends, a detail she quickly conveyed to Magda. Magda reached across the desk, at the same time saying, "Can I see your notes, please?" Frankie didn't want anyone to see her notes, but she reluctantly relinquished them to Magda, who skimmed them like her hair was on fire. She handed the notes back to Frankie, one hand on her office phone. "I've got a lull here and a reporter with some time on his hands. I'm going to get him in here, so you can fill him in, then he can gather some missing information, so you can put this thing to bed." Frankie couldn't believe what she was hearing. The last thing she wanted was help, especially from a male reporter. This investigation, this story, was her baby and she wanted to see it through - alone.

"No, please Magda. I want to do this by myself." Frankie jutted her chin forward as she spoke, her tone determined enough that Magda dropped her hand from the phone. Her gaze invited Frankie to offer her more details - a reason she should allow Frankie to proceed on her own. From somewhere deep within Frankie, the reasons came forth resolutely.

"This story is about women, about how a man in a position of trust and power entangled *my community* and somehow - and I don't know how YET - came to his abrupt ending. I know I'm not polished when it comes to investigating, but I'm finding information that I'm sure nobody else has." She went on to explain her encounters with Abe Arnold and how badly he wanted to know what she knew. "I'm new at this but I'm invested in this story, Magda. I'm meeting with Kristine Duedenhoffer tomorrow morning and I just have a gut feeling that I'm going to be able to wrap this up, very soon." Magda let out a long sigh.

"The story's aging, Frankie. You've got to get me something before the weekend. Otherwise, I won't have a choice." Frankie stood up and shook Magda's hand enthusiastically.

"I promise I'll have something." Magda shook her finger at Frankie.

"If I see a story in *The Watch* before that, I'm going to boil." Frankie didn't doubt it for a minute.

Heading south now in the SUV, Frankie blew out a long breath she didn't know she'd been holding. In Magda's office, she felt confident, emboldened by her upcoming meeting, and by her collection of notes on the case. Now, however, Frankie realized her speech to Magda may have been nothing but bluster. Could she really find the truth about Rawlins before the weekend? Or at least something juicy enough to publish? Good grief, she still had many more questions than answers. Maybe her stop at the Sheriff's office would yield some unexpected information.

It was almost 2 o'clock when Frankie parked in the sheriff's department lot, trying to get as close to the entrance as possible to avoid her dress shoes connecting with the icy pavement, a recipe for disaster with Frankie's graceful track record. Looking around, she spotted Lon's official vehicle and Garrett's truck. Bad and good, Frankie thought, not certain she wanted to see Alonzo again so soon, but all aflutter about the prospect of asking Garrett Iverson to the Valentine Jubilee for Saturday. She took the stairs to the sheriff's department level, skirted past the offices as quickly as possible, hoping not to be spotted by Pflug or Alonzo, then walked quietly down the hallway toward the door marked Coroner. Just then, the sheriff department's main door opened, and Frankie heard approaching footsteps. She darted quickly into the women's restroom on the right and stayed still, listening for the footsteps to pass, which seemed to take an eternity. In fact, Frankie wasn't certain, but she thought the feet stopped right outside the restroom door. "Crap, crap, crap," Frankie's inner voice whispered. The Golden One had been alerted by Frankie's inner mutterings and was bored.

"What - are we going to just stand here in the bathroom all day?" she chided. Frankie decided The Golden One had an apt point. Frankie couldn't hide out indefinitely and didn't she have every right to be here anyway? This is a public building.

Frankie tentatively opened the door and stuck her head out upon an empty hallway. She smiled and lifted her head up as she walked fully out the door but jumped a mile when someone tapped her shoulder from behind. Closing her eyes meaningfully, Frankie dramatically turned her head and looked up at the figure of Garrett Iverson, who seemed to be thoroughly enjoying her discomfort.

"Are you on some sort of secret mission?" Garrett whispered, his melting brown eyes crinkling at the corners in amusement. Frankie's dander had risen by now.

"That's not very funny, Garrett. Why are you sneaking up on me, anyway?" Garrett didn't want to hurt Frankie's feelings.

"Hey, I'm sorry. What are you up to though?" Frankie was feeling a little ridiculous and nervous about her purpose for being there. After all, the real reason she stopped at the Sheriff's Department was to see Garrett and ask him out on a date. Best to equivocate, she thought.

"I want to get an update on the Rawlins investigation and I'm trying to avoid Officer Pflug. We aren't exactly on the best of terms." Garrett reassured her immediately.

"Don't worry about Pflug. He's been sent on a fact-finding matter in Missouri." Frankie's brain went straight to rapid fire. Missouri? Did this have anything to do with the Rawlins case? She filed away that fact for later.

Garrett interrupted her train of thought. "So, what

brings you down my hallway?" Frankie hesitated, and her tone shifted from business to pleasure.

"Well, Garrett, I was wondering… if you're not busy on Saturday night…would you like to go to the Valentine Jubilee dinner with me at the First Congregational church?" Garrett, who had been smiling and playful a minute ago, now looked down at the floor, almost in embarrassment, Frankie guessed.

"I can't, Francine. I'm sorry. I have plans already." Frankie was taken aback and uncertain what to say or how to end the conversation.

"Oh, okay. I understand," she giggled a little in her own uncertainty. "I should have asked you sooner. Sorry. And thanks for the heads up on Pflug." She whirled away from Garrett without giving him time to say anything more. Garrett called after her.

"I'll take a raincheck, Francine." Frankie felt deflated. A raincheck, sure thing. There's only one Valentine's Day, Garrett Iverson, and I guess you won't be part of mine this year. Frankie was mad at herself for this line of thinking. Jeepers, she'd only gone on one date with Garrett, what did she expect anyway? She wondered what his plans were for Saturday but decided it was definitely none of her business. Maybe she should find another date for the Jubilee because she knew she wanted to attend, but couldn't come up with anyone to ask off the top of her head. The Golden One was right there to make her feel worse.

"You're kind of pathetic, Francine. There's plenty of eligible men out there. Try a little harder, Dear." Just what I need, thought Frankie, another mother. Suddenly, Frankie found herself at the sheriff department door and her Jubilee musings were put on temporary hold as she reached for the handle.

Again, by some form of grace, Shirley Lazaar was manning the front reception desk in the department. When she looked up over her glasses at Frankie, she grinned. "I wondered how long it would be before you came back in," Shirley said, gesturing for Frankie to take a seat next to the desk. As if reading Frankie's mind, she went on, "Both the sheriff and Officer Pflug are out of the office for a while. I'm stuck out here until after lunch." Frankie nodded and sighed in relief. She wouldn't have to encounter Alonzo and face a possible confrontation. Instead, she opened her phone notes and got straight to the point.

"Can you give me an update on the Rawlins investigation?" Shirley's eyes met hers in a pointed manner.

"You know I can't comment on an ongoing investigation." Frankie retorted.

"I'm just asking if there's anything new, something official. It's been more than a week, Shirley." Shirley presented a half-smile.

"Let's just say that the investigation is heating up, so now is not the time to talk on the record. There's a lot of momentum and too much at stake. I don't have to tell you that the sheriff is under the gun to get this wrapped up asap." Frankie understood all too well the demands on a public official, especially one up for re-election in April. Still, she wanted to pursue a couple of points before her Milwaukee trip to see Kristine Duedenhoffer tomorrow.

"Can you confirm that Officer Pflug is in Missouri as part of the Rawlins matter?" Shirley's eyes narrowed but her smile was congratulatory.

"Off the record?" Frankie nodded her agreement. "Ok, he is. But I can't say more." Frankie continued.

"Did forensics turn up any blood match from the residue on the shanty bench?" Shirley shook her head.

"No match on file. I can tell you that the blood didn't match Rawlins'." Frankie raised one eyebrow, pleased that Shirley would even convey that much without her pressing for the information.

"How about relatives of Rawlins? Did anybody turn up?" This time, Shirley looked down at her paperwork and Frankie suspected someone did turn up, but Shirley wasn't going to comment. She was right.

"Can't say at the moment," Shirley said, disclosing in a roundabout way that some relative had turned up. Maybe in Missouri, Frankie wondered.

"Okay, thanks, Shirley. When do you expect Pflug back?" Shirley shrugged.

"He hasn't reported back anything yet. So, can't say for sure." Frankie rose to leave, parting ways as Shirley remarked: "Hey, usually you bring something baked and sweet when you want answers. What gives?" Although Frankie knew Shirley was just giving her a hard time, she promised she'd have something waiting for her at Bubble and Bake if she would stop by in the morning on her way to work.

"Hope you like Paczkis! 'Tis the season."

When Frankie returned to the shop, Jovie Luedtke was alone in the kitchen, humming an oldies tune from the radio, elbow deep in Paczki making. "Oh hey, Frankie! Good to see you. Carmen and Tess left me in charge. Hope that's okay with you." Frankie said it was definitely okay, glad that Carmen was able to help on the farm as was her Wednesday custom, and glad that Tess was returning to Madison after a long night Tuesday. Frankie frowned, looking around the kitchen at all the cases of wine that still needed to be transported to the basement.

She spoke absently aloud, "Maybe I better start wheeling these cases out the door." Jovie stopped humming.

"Oh, don't do that. Your brother Nick called and said he'd be here today after work to move the cases. Said he's bringing a couple of guys with him. He'll see you about 4 if you can meet him here." Frankie was happy to hear it. She tied on an apron and dove into Paczki assembly with Jovie, stopping to take pie crust out for quiche making in the morning. The two were almost finished filling and glazing some 12-dozen fat Polish donuts when Nick and three guys walked into the kitchen. Nick introduced his co-workers and exchanged hellos with Jovie. Frankie noticed Jovie's eyes lit up when Nick made small talk with her and her heart sank a little. Poor Jovie! Yet another female to lose her wits when Nick was around - he certainly had a commanding presence. Frankie's thought quickly led her to one much darker: had Bradford Rawlins used the same kind of charms to work his will upon women? She was certain he had, and that idea suddenly left her a little miffed at Nick.

"Hey, I don't mean to interrupt but can you guys get going on this before it gets dark?" Nick was taken aback at Frankie's sudden cool demand, but he acquiesced. Frankie realized her anger may be misplaced and called after the men, "There'll be fresh Paczkis waiting for you when you're done! Let me know if I can help with anything."

With four guys and three dollies, the cases were dispatched to the basement in no time, although Nick reported the basement was going to be a little challenging to navigate for a while. "I sure hope you sell lots of wine at the Valentine Pairing next week," he said sincerely, with a wide grin. Frankie, like all women in Nick's life, found that smile and sincerity irresistible. She grabbed him impulsively and gave him a squeeze.

"Thank you so much for coming down here and taking care of moving the wine. It would have taken me forever to get that done myself." She handed a platter of Paczkis to Nick and his helpers, who smiled delightfully.

The small talk resumed, Frankie asking Nick if he was bringing someone to the Family Pairing event, which Frankie hosted for her family immediately after the business event. Nick rolled his eyes, letting Frankie know that he'd prefer to come alone. "Well, it was very nice of you to bring Cherry out for bottling, Brother." Nick rolled his eyes again.

"You didn't give me much choice, did you? You asked her to come right in front of me." Nick's voice was mildly scolding, and he offered a wink in Jovie's direction, producing a little flush of color to Jovie's cheeks. Frankie had a brainstorm.

"Hey, maybe you could do me a favor?" Nick reminded her that he had just done her two favors, what else did she want? Frankie laughed. "Well, I want to go to the Valentine Jubilee at First Congregational Church Saturday, but I don't have a date. Do you want to go with me?" Nick actually brightened with enthusiasm.

"You bet. I'd love to go. What time should I pick you up, Sis?" Frankie was surprised at how easy Nick was making this. She wondered if her brother had too many Valentine invitations and was looking for a way out. She imagined herself his charity case sister who couldn't get a date so needed her brother's attention for the night. No matter, Frankie thought, she was now ready to do some more sleuthing work at the church Saturday.

Nick left, agreeing to pick Frankie up at 6 p.m. on Saturday. The expression on Jovie's face during Frankie's exchange with Nick was not lost on Frankie. "Jovie, why don't you come with me and Nick on Saturday night? It would be fun." Jovie looked down at the Paczkis she was glazing.

"I'm sure I can't go. There isn't anyone to take care of my mother. She needs her nighttime meds, and I need to get her into bed." Frankie couldn't help but feel terrible for Jovie, an only child whose father passed away when she was in high school. Since Jovie was between Frankie and Will in school, Frankie remembered how Jovie had missed many school activities, helping to care for her father, who had cancer. After high school graduation, Jovie attended college for two years, leaving abruptly when her mother became ill, insisting Jovie move back home to care for her, contending she was dying. Almost 20 years later, Jovie's mother was still "dying", never allowing Jovie to leave her alone for very long. All of Deep Lakes suspected Mrs. Luedtke was a hypochondriac, incapable of facing life without her husband and daughter, so Jovie was a virtual prisoner, unable to have any life of her own. Everyone who knew about the situation found it interesting that while it was fine for Jovie to work part-time, leaving her mother for a few hours at a time, Jovie could never attend a social gathering. People concluded that Mrs. Luedtke, happy to have Jovie's income on hand, was perfectly capable of caring for herself when called upon to do so.

Frankie wasn't going to give up that easily. "What time does your mother need her medication?" Jovie said she always took her nighttime pills with supper, then retired to bed about an hour later, maybe 7 p.m. Frankie suggested Jovie feed her mother early, say 5 o'clock, then put her to bed at 6. "Maybe Mrs. Thursten, next door, will look in on her or even sit with her until you get home." Jovie looked doubtful and Frankie quickly surmised she would make an excuse, denying herself any social pleasure. "I know Helen Thursten. She plays cards with my mother. I'll talk to her myself." Again, Jovie looked hesitant, but maybe a bit hopeful at the same time. "Let me take care of this. Just say you'll come with me?" Frankie didn't want to remind Jovie she would also be dining with Nick that night, not wanting her to be overwhelmed by the prospect. Jovie shrugged, nodding her head.

"Okay. That would be great. I actually cannot remember the last time I went out for an evening for fun." Satisfied, Frankie jotted herself a reminder to call Helen Thursten that night.

With 12 dozen Paczkis at the ready for Thursday morning, Frankie sat at her computer, reviewing the Rawlins investigation notes and preparing for tomorrow's visit with Kristine Duedenhoffer at 11:30. Checking directions on her maps app, Frankie figured she would need to leave about 9:30 to allow for time to park. The weather looked cooperative and the drive would entail nothing but interstate, no rush hour to contend with and 70 miles per hour as the speed limit, this meant most drivers would be cruising along at 75-80. She should make good time. Wanting Kristine to take her seriously, Frankie pulled a black skirt from her closet, remembering how commanding Magda had looked in her own black skirt earlier that day. She didn't have a black jacket except for a blazer from circa 1990, complete with shoulder pads. Yikes, that wouldn't do at all. She found a three-quarter sleeve, loose weave black cardigan with pearl buttons, which would work, worn with a knit turquoise turtleneck underneath. Jewelry was something Frankie never lacked - collecting it was one of her vices - so she selected a long looping silver chain from which dangled an open flower pendant. She had matching open floral earrings, and a pair of black semi-dressy flat shoes. Frankie couldn't be convinced to wear heels for any length of time, even though she often found some extra height could be useful to her.

Still thinking about her conversation with Shirley Lazaar, Frankie retired with the small satisfaction that, since the Rawlins investigation was ongoing, *The Watch* wouldn't be publishing an article Thursday, and hopefully not before the weekend either.

Chapter 14

*"There is no witness so terrible and no accuser so powerful
as conscience which dwells within us."*
– Sophocles

After two long days in a row, Frankie imagined sleep
would greet her tired bones and remain throughout the
night as a welcome guest, but that was not to be. Frankie
awoke three times, her mind awhirl with the answers she
would solicit from Glenda Kilpatrick's attorney sister,
Kristine. On the third trip of Frankie's mind merry-go-
round, she encountered a brand-new worry: how would she
convince Kristine to tell her where she could find Glenda,
especially if Glenda doesn't want to be found? Frankie
realized she needed a pretense of some kind, a valid reason
to see Glenda face-to-face. Her mind working overtime,
she remembered the Valentine cupcake Dave had ordered
for Glenda, professing his continued love for her. "That's
it!" Frankie spoke out loud, leaping out of bed, wide awake
and ready to spring into action. Scrambling into lounge
pants and whatever t-shirt she wore yesterday to bake
in, she jammed her feet into her moccasins and bounded
down the stairs to the shop kitchen. A sleepy Brambles,

stretched out as he padded into the kitchen from his warm spot by the shop furnace, took turns spreading one leg outward like a marching soldier, and peered up at Frankie with an exaggerated yawn and blinking eyes.

Frankie gave him a friendly scratch and chin cuddle, retrieved some ham from the cooler and broke it into tiny pieces for Brambles' cat dish. Then she proceeded to the pantry, gathering supplies for Red Velvet cake batter. She fired up the oven to Brambles' delight and mixed up batter that would fill her jumbo cupcake pans. One batch would make 10 giant cupcakes, which was the size used for the Valentine orders. Frankie figured she could freeze the other nine and serve them to her family. While the batter baked, she prepared the pastry cream filling, adding chopped Door County cherries to the finished mixture. The filling set aside, she decided to get a head start on the quiches, easing the workload for Adam, Tess, and Carmen later that morning. Rolling out nine crusts, pressing them into nine pie plates, Frankie recited the questions she would pose to Kristine.

Kitchen duties ended with Frankie filling the cooled cupcake, topping it with chocolate ganache, which hardened while she cleaned up her baking mess. Pulling pie shells out of the oven, Frankie grabbed a piping bag and thin white icing, scrawling "I Still Love You" on the cupcake's top, ending with a flourish of curlicues.

"Not bad for three a.m.," the compliment came with a muffled yawn from The Golden One. Frankie smiled a bit smugly. Maybe she was winning Goldie over to her side of thinking - then she reminded herself her firefly companions were not actually real! Three a.m.: Frankie was glad she hadn't given in to the temptation to brew a latte when she first arrived in the kitchen, for at least now she might be able to get some sleep before the 6 o'clock alarm. She shut off the light switch, glanced back at the oven to make sure she had turned it off, and prowled back up the stairs with Brambles in tow. That's what you get for waking a cat in the middle of the night, he's all yours now. Brambles reached Frankie's bed first, snuggling by the pillow on her side of the bed. Frankie didn't even care - she had crafted a plan to see Glenda Kilpatrick, and the best part of it all was that she didn't have to pretend. She had an honest reason to locate her.

Frankie slept through the six a.m. alarm, finally waking to the oldies station, one eye opening upon her clock, which read, thankfully, 6:20. Brambles had left her side, probably hearing the arrival of Bubble and Bake workers and hoping to garner additional ham for a second breakfast. Frankie showered and dressed in the clothes she selected the day before, grateful she had saved herself some valuable time in making those choices.

Carmen, Adam, and Tess all whistled and hooted as Frankie entered the kitchen, not used to seeing her "dolled" up for business. Frankie laughed then turned toward Carmen as her friend gestured widely around the kitchen.

"Looks like someone was busy last night. Did you stay

up all night baking or is your Guardian Angel working the night shift?" Frankie filled Carmen in on her restless sleep and brilliant idea of making Glenda's cupcake to deliver in person. "You better call me if you're going somewhere besides that lawyer's office, Frankie Champagne. I'm gonna worry about you getting in over your head." Frankie promised to keep Carmen apprised, then busied herself locating a fancy cupcake box from storage and a pastry box. Deciding she would stop by Helen Thursten's on her way out of town, Frankie placed one of each variety of the Paczki offerings of the day into the box to entice Helen to watch Jovie's mother on Saturday night. Frankie didn't want Carmen to think she was losing interest in their business, so she sat at the kitchen counter to chat with her partner about the day's menu.

Carmen smiled, clearly pleased to have Frankie's input. Quiches for the weekend would include: "This Little Piggy," a meaty delight of ham, bacon, two kinds of cheeses, and secret spices; "Toadstool Pie," a vegetarian quiche made with swiss cheese, three kinds of meaty mushrooms, and a crust of onions and saltine crackers; and "Mama Mia," a pizza quiche with sausage, Roma tomatoes, green peppers, basil, and parmesan. Apple, cherry, and prune fillings were underway for Paczki flavors for Friday, with Saturday fillings planned as blueberry, peach, and date. Frankie gave her hearty approval to all and bid Carmen farewell. "Please wish me luck?" Carmen patted her friend's hand.

"I know you're excited. Just don't get your hopes too high in case it doesn't turn out, Frankie. Ok?" Carmen raised both dark eyebrows sharply in Frankie's direction, but her small smile suggested she too was hopeful for things to turn out as Frankie wished.

"I promise to call you later," Frankie said warmly.

The SUV headed down Pine Tree Avenue in the opposite direction of the churches. Heading toward her old elementary school on Forest Lane, Frankie tried to remember the last time she had visited the all too familiar subdivision, where every street was named after some variety of tree. Helen Thursten lived on Maple Street, right next door to Jovie and Marian Luedtke. She had been Frankie's first grade teacher, in fact, she taught all the Champagne siblings, having been a fixture at Deep Lakes Elementary school for 50 years! Helen had attended a teacher training school just 20 miles or so down the road, during a time when only one year of school was required to earn a teaching certificate in Wisconsin. An older neighborhood, built in the 1960's when Deep Lakes constructed its new one-story sprawling elementary school, the streets featured the popular ranch design homes of the period and large trees now filled the yards of most of the houses.

Frankie turned onto Maple Street, driving slowly to pinpoint the Luedtke house, a small gray ranch home, with white trim and shutters. The Thursten house was before the gray ranch, set back a little deeper on its lot, two large fir trees on either side of the black-topped driveway, partially hiding the house front. Frankie pulled into the driveway, noticing pine swags hanging from the fieldstone front planter, and a Christmas wreath still perched on the front door. She rang the doorbell and in no time, Helen Thursten greeted her, looking chipper as ever, belying her 80 years of age.

"Why, hello, Francine Champagne. To what do I owe this visit?" Helen's eyes were sharp as a hawk's and went straight to the white box Frankie held in her hand, both sparse eyebrows raised in query. Helen was smaller than Frankie remembered the last time she saw her, recalling how she seemed to tower over others, also hawk-like. Helen could be very severe as a teacher, but she was dedicated and adept at her skill. Frankie remembered having her as a catechism instructor at church for Confirmation class; she had zero tolerance for chatty teenagers, and Frankie was often the subject of a tongue-lashing from Mrs. Thursten for her garrulous ways. On the other hand, Helen's husband, Lloyd, always seemed to be good-natured and laughed easily. He often produced Juicy Fruit gum or Chiclets from his suit jacket pocket at church, passing them out to kids to keep them occupied during mass. Lloyd and Helen never had children of their own and Helen was alone now since her husband passed away a couple of years ago. Still, Helen remained an active volunteer at St. Anthony's and the public library, where she tutored children with reading difficulties. She was also a member of a weekly Canasta card club, where she sometimes teamed up with Frankie's mother.

"I brought you a few Paczkis before Lent, and I wanted to ask you something. May I come in for a few minutes?" Helen opened the door wider and motioned Frankie inside.

"I do love Paczkis. Shouldn't be eating that junk though, you know. I'm trying to watch my girlish figure." Frankie wasn't sure how serious Helen was, but she stifled a laugh and complimented her on what great shape she was in.

"You're still so active, Mrs. Thursten. You haven't really changed that much since you were my teacher." Perspective is a remarkable device, Frankie concluded, remembering that she viewed Mrs. Thursten as "old" when she was in first grade, so she wasn't lying when she said Helen had not changed much. Still, Mrs. Thursten was never one for fluffy flattery.

"Never mind that, Francine. What is it you wanted to ask me?" Frankie conveyed that Saturday was the Valentine Jubilee and explained Jovie Luedtke's dilemma in being able to enjoy an evening out due to her sick mother. Helen instantly snorted at that. "Let me tell you something about Marian Luedtke. That woman was always 'delicate' in nature you know, even when her husband was still alive. She never worked much inside or outside that house." Helen looked over her shoulder, as if Mrs. Luedtke might be able to hear her insults through the walls and across the lot. She lowered her voice and continued. "If you ask me, there isn't a thing wrong with Marian except what she made up in her own head. That poor child has been taking care of her for some 18 years - and her mother just turning 70. Shameful, that's what it is."

Frankie was certain that, at 80, Helen Thursten, could work circles around Mrs. Luedtke and probably Frankie, too, so she could understand her perspective. She needed to get the conversation back on course, so she could be on her way to Milwaukee. "Yes, well I'm sure you can understand why Jovie would like a night out every now and then. She's been such a devoted daughter." Helen nodded emphatically.

"There's no denying that. So, yes, I'll come over Saturday night and sit with Marian, not for her sake but for her daughter's. You won't be out too late will you? I need to be up for church in the morning." Frankie assured Mrs. Thursten they would be home shortly after nine. Helen showed Frankie to the door. "When you pick up Miss Luedtke, you could bring me a couple more of those Paczkis, you know. Of course, I never imbibe during Lent, you know." Frankie said she could count on a Paczki delivery, patted Mrs. Thursten's hand gently, retreated to the SUV with a sigh of relief and a little cheer for Jovie.

Back in the SUV, Frankie pressed the car's phone button and asked it to dial Bubble and Bake. Carmen answered, surprised to hear from Frankie. "What's wrong? You can't be in Milwaukee yet?"

"Stop worrying, Carmen. I just stopped by Helen Thursten's house. Can you tell Jovie when she comes in that everything is set for Saturday and I'll pick her up about 6?" Carmen wouldn't let that go without further explanation, so Frankie filled her in on her date with her brother with Jovie as a third. Carmen couldn't resist weighing in.

"So, I wonder what Garrett is doing and who he's doing it with. And, I can't believe you're trying to play matchmaker with Nick and Jovie. They don't seem to have much in common, Frankie." Frankie was undaunted.

"I'm not trying to hook them up. I just want Jovie to have a chance at something besides taking care of her mother. It's only fair, Carmen. And, I'm not worried about what Garrett is doing. We only went out once." Frankie was a little offended, showing her sensitive side. Carmen backed off immediately and softened.

"It would be nice for Jovie to have a life. You're right about that." She didn't add anything further about Garrett Iverson.

Missing the morning commuters, Frankie was still happy she had padded her time allotment, encountering road construction that narrowed the interstate to one lane for several miles outside of Milwaukee. Heading toward downtown, the buildings loomed larger and traffic picked up. Frankie didn't frequent Milwaukee, but remembered taking a young Sophie and Violet to a children's ballet of *Bambi* at the Performing Arts Center, now the Milwaukee

Center. They had gone on a weekend getaway, splurging on a downtown hotel and going to the Milwaukee Public Museum, which was hosting a traveling exhibit of the treasures of Ancient Egypt – a stunning display of artifacts on loan from the British Museum. That was before GPS existed and Frankie wondered how she had navigated downtown without help. Now Frankie was instructed to exit onto Wisconsin Avenue, turn onto Old World Third Street, and park in the parking structure there. Because it was already past starting time for most people, Frankie traveled in circles for several levels, finally locating an open space on Level 5, just below the top level of the structure. Her heart racing, she glanced at the dashboard clock and noticed she still had 20 minutes to cross the street and walk one block down Wells Street to the gargantuan concrete modern structure named the Wisconsin Center, occupying about 4 city blocks.

Stepping out of her SUV, Frankie was frozen in place by a piercing cry that echoed throughout Level 5. Thinking the cry was more animal than human, or possibly bird more than animal, Frankie tentatively peered around the dimly lit surroundings, moving slowly toward the exit as she looked. Approaching the southwest corner near the elevator, Frankie distinctly heard a crunching sound and cringed, the hairs on the back of her neck standing at attention. Moving stealthily now, she kept a sharp lookout in the direction of the sound, as her eyes finally adjusted to the low light of the garage. Something shifted her focus to an upward direction and to her complete surprise, she spied a splendid Snowy Owl perched in the top corner on a horizontal beam, snacking on what appeared to be a chunky city rat, captured under its magnificent talons. Frankie's jaw dropped to the floor. She had always wanted to see a Snowy Owl and knew, through her bird club activities, the beautiful white birds were moving further south during the last few winters in search of abundant prey. She had read that Milwaukee parking garages were becoming a favorite perching and hunting spot for the owls, especially with the prevalence of city rats. Frankie swallowed hard, trying to decide if she was more horrified at the disheveled rat or the feasting owl with fresh blood on its front feathers. She couldn't stop staring at the scene, counting herself lucky, she guessed - it's not every day a person witnesses a Snowy Owl dining out after all.

Then Frankie remembered why she was here, hurried into the elevator corridor and punched the down button. She exited the elevator quickly and walked at a city pedestrian's pace to the Wisconsin Center. The majestic lobby featured a tiered 60-foot-high, five-story atrium garden environment, accentuated by lush greenery with rose-colored granite walls and floors. Frankie tried not to look like she just fell off the turnip truck and quickly checked her open mouth, firmly closing it and presenting a more business-like demeanor.

The front desk receptionist, whose name badge read "Oliver" and who was dressed like a GQ model, peered over his glasses at Frankie and asked, as if bored beyond belief, if he could direct Frankie somewhere. Frankie said she had an appointment with Attorney Duedenhoffer at the law firm of Briggs and Baker. In the same unimpressed tone, Oliver, not even looking at Frankie, gestured one hand toward his left, as if presenting prize cookware on a game show, "Take the first elevator to the 25th floor. Turn left down the hallway when you exit the elevator." Frankie supposed this was the crux of Oliver's job - repeating the same instructions all day long. Still under her breath, she couldn't resist muttering, "pretentious little snit" as she headed to the elevators.

Exiting the elevator, she gasped again at the view of the Milwaukee River through a long wall of glass windows, surrounded by more greenery. Turning left, she almost at once came to the bank of offices under the banner of Briggs and Baker. Hannah, the receptionist at a towering walnut desk, greeted Frankie in a friendly manner and offered her a beverage of choice. Frankie declined, hoping she wouldn't have to wait long to see Kristine, then realized she had no idea what condition her hair was in, having walked through a breezy section of downtown, a bracing wind blowing from the river.

As if reading her mind, Hannah discreetly asked if Frankie would like to freshen up after her drive and aptly walked her down the hall to a restroom. Frankie utilized the facilities, then glanced in the mirror, groaning. Why did her hair always misbehave? Winter was particularly cruel, turning her fine hair into a static magnet. First Frankie tried combing it but that only made her hair stand up straighter, so she resorted to wetting a paper towel and pressing it between her unruly locks and her face. She combed it lightly again and it stayed mostly in place, however, she had managed to get the front of her top wet, just in one spot, but it was visible and in an unfortunate location. Grimacing, Frankie turned on the hand dryer - one of those new powerful models and tried to position her chest within its confines. Thank goodness nobody walked into the restroom or Frankie would have been mortified. A few minutes later Frankie decided "what you see is what you get", exited the restroom and headed back to the waiting area, where Hannah looked up expectantly, raising an eyebrow in wonder.

A true professional, Hannah waited a couple minutes more, then announced that Ms. Duedenhoffer would see Frankie now. Kristine had an interior office without a view, indicating she was likely a newer hire, low on the firm's totem pole. Still, the office was handsomely decorated and decidedly masculine with dark walnut furniture, granite topped side tables, and burgundy leather chairs against a backdrop of striped wallpaper with gold gilt accents. If Frankie had to guess, she imagined Kristine was taller than her sister and probably the older of the two, though not by much. Kristine had lighter skin tone - Glenda always looked tanned, a longer face and darker hair that she wore cropped short in a modern layered style. She also seemed thinner than Glenda, but maybe that was what made her appear taller, or maybe it was the other way around. Frankie supposed it could be Kristine's outfit, a pencil skirt of gray pinstripe and dark gray boots, topped by an all-business pleated black shirt. Kristine's suit jacket hung on a nearby coat hook, reducing the masculine look, which was further helped by a lovely necklace of silver stationed pearls in white, gray, and black that draped her neckline down to the third button of her blouse. Kristine looked up at Frankie and warily offered her a seat, speaking first.

"So, you live in Stevens Point?" Frankie shook her head, confessing she was from Deep Lakes but worked as a regional reporter for the Press. Kristine looked a bit surprised and instantly guarded. "Oh! Deep Lakes. So, you're a local then." Frankie nodded, getting down to the business at hand.

"Can you please tell me what you turned up on Bradford Rawlins? I don't appreciate my home community being taken advantage of by a trickster." Frankie spoke forthrightly now.

With that point, she had an ally in Kristine Duedenhoffer. She relaxed a little and instructed Frankie to take notes, but insisting the information be off the record until the current situation sorted itself out. Frankie wasn't sure what to make of Kristine's remark, but decided it must have to do with protecting her sister, so she nodded her understanding.

Kristine began, scathingly referring to Rawlins as "that snake in the grass." "You're right about him, Ms. Champagne. Rawlins is not a pastor. In fact, he's not even Bradford Rawlins. His name is Scott Bradley, and he's wanted for fraud and embezzlement in Missouri." Kristine's face was tight as she spoke. Frankie allowed herself a moment to log the telltale word, "Missouri," surely the reason Donavan Pflug had been sent there.

"How did you find out this information?" Frankie asked. Kristine held a look of sisterly pride.

"It was actually Glenda who got the ball rolling. She found a file folder on her work computer with Rawlins' name on it. She was curious, so she opened it, discovered identity information, certificates with fake credentials and a variety of photographs of Rawlins, which were used to falsify his ministry papers. That's when she called me to see if I could find out who he really was." Frankie was shocked. Glenda was one of the office managers at Conway Quality Digital Printing Services in Deep Lakes, owned by Milton Conway, coincidentally a member of the First Congregational Church council.

"Did Glenda mention her boss, Milton Conway, is on the church council there?" Kristine nodded.

"Conway must know Scott Bradley, but I don't know how yet. I have a friend at the police department who has access to databases on criminals, so I asked him to look up Rawlins. Nothing turned up in Arkansas, so he looked him up on the National Database, using a photograph

Glenda provided. That's how we found Bradley in Missouri." Frankie frantically tapped the notes into her phone, her mind quick-firing questions as she tapped.

"Did your friend turn up anything else on Bradley?" Kristine nodded.

"You bet he did. He's also wanted for substantial back child support. Bradley has a son with a Gina Perkins, also living in Missouri." Missouri? Frankie wondered if Donavan Pflug was chasing down the same information she had just discovered from Glenda's sister. She also guessed Gina Perkins was the woman telephoning Patsy at First Congregational Church, having discovered the whereabouts of one Scott Bradley, aka, Bradford Rawlins. Looking at Kristine's patiently waiting face, Frankie guessed there was still more to tell. "The National Database also turned up two additional bench warrants on Rawlins under two different aliases, one in Nevada, and one in Montana. Five years ago, a Rowan Bradford was arrested at the casino where he worked as a Blackjack dealer for taking money under the table and cheating the casino out of $75,000. Somebody bailed him out, however, and he fled the state before trial. Seven years ago, Ronald Scott worked security at a bank in Montana, which was robbed under his watch. The thieves made off with around 100 grand and were never apprehended. Ronald Scott never showed up to work at the bank after the robbery and had vanished."

Frankie could hardly take it all in. To think a man like Rawlins, who was so slippery, landed a pastoral position in their small town was difficult to fathom, but then, he obviously had the help of Milton Conway for a reason yet to be determined. "So, what did you and Glenda plan to do with this information? Turn him into the police?" For the first time, Kristine looked away from Frankie, was silent for a time, then chose her words most carefully.

"Well, naturally we planned to turn all this over to the police." Frankie's radar was activated - she didn't quite believe Kristine.

"So, did you? Do the police know all of this?" Kristine looked trapped and her voice stammered.

"Well, not just yet. But we will." Frankie was mystified. What were they waiting for? Unless, unless - she couldn't put it together.

"I'm afraid I don't understand, Ms. Duedenhoffer. This information is crucial to the case. You must know that." Frankie spoke in her concerned citizen tone and meant every word. Kristine remained silent, thinking.

Frankie couldn't decide which direction to continue the conversation, fully aware she could be dismissed any moment from Kristine's office. "Where can I find Glenda? I need to speak with her. I have some welcome news for her, I believe." Kristine was too intelligent to be baited that easily.

"What is this welcome news? I'd love to share it with her." Since this was Frankie's only card in an empty hand, she couldn't reveal that the good news was nothing more than a cupcake love note from Glenda's husband.

Frankie couldn't be positive this would be seen as good news, after all.

She countered with, "I will share the news with Glenda myself when we connect." Frankie sounded much more confident than she felt. Kristine rose from her chair, signaling their meeting had come to its conclusion.

"Well, I hope I helped you with your article. Good luck putting the rest of the pieces together. I'm sorry I can't be more helpful." She extended her hand to Frankie, who ignored the gesture.

Instead, Frankie retorted, "Oh, I think you could be more helpful but for some reason, you're hiding something. I hope whatever it is, Ms. Duedenhoffer, it doesn't cost you your law license." Frankie felt a renewed strength at the comment that had come from some inner place Frankie wasn't sure she could locate. Kristine bristled, making Frankie aware the remark had hit home.

"I'm sure you're not threatening me, Ms. Champagne. Certainly, you must have heard of attorney-client privilege?" Frankie imagined Kristine was more than a sister to Glenda, likely her acting attorney. But for what? Divorce proceedings?

Unable to leave Kristine on sour terms, Frankie rose, held out her hand to the attorney, saying, "I do appreciate the information you gave me, and I truly hope that Glenda isn't in any kind of trouble. I mean that." Reading her sincerity, Kristine shook Frankie's hand without further comment and walked her to the reception area. "I'm just going to stop at the restroom before I leave. Long drive, you know." But, Frankie had one more plan to put into play first. She saw Kristine, briefcase in hand, put on her jacket and get on the elevator, probably going to lunch or court, Frankie imagined. Heading back to the reception area, she asked Hannah if she could make a phone call, explaining her cell phone battery was dead. Well-trained in customer service, Hannah smiled warmly, told Frankie which button to push for an outside line and discreetly disappeared somewhere. In two rings, Patsy Long answered at First Congregational Church.

"Patsy, this is Frankie Champagne. I need a huge favor from you and I need it in a hurry." Patsy was willing. "Could you give me the address and phone number of Glenda Kilpatrick's parents, please? It's important. I figured you would have it on file from Glenda's wedding and church records transfer." Frankie wanted to be helpful and knew Patsy would be unprepared for the request. Patsy asked Frankie to hold on while she went to the file cabinet to search. Thank goodness for Patsy's organizational skills as she returned quickly to the phone with the desired information, which Frankie jotted on a sticky note, thanks to Hannah's stocked desk. Looking down the hallway for Hannah's return, Frankie rapidly punched in the number of Patsy's parents, hoping her hunch would pay off.

"Hello, Duedenhoffer's," an older woman's voice was on the line.

"Yes, may I please speak to Glenda?" The voice paused momentarily, then, "May I say who's calling?" Frankie clicked the receiver. Bingo. Glenda was staying at her parents' home in Dubuque, Iowa. Frankie strode to the elevator, out the front door, and onto the street, never looking back. Checking her phone, it was 12:30 and she knew she probably had a three-hour drive ahead of her to Iowa, but nothing was going to stop her from making that trip.

It's now or never, she said to herself in the parking garage, just before walking past the corner where she had seen the Snowy Owl. She looked up - the owl was gone, but the remains of a carcass were lying on the pavement. Frankie shivered from the inside, recalling the Native American legend of the white owl symbolizing wisdom, patience, secrets, and observance. Specifically, the white owl represented a desire for pure unfettered knowledge. As Frankie climbed into the SUV, she wondered if she was meant to see the Snowy Owl - maybe as some kind of spirit guide in her quest to find answers about Rawlins and Glenda Kilpatrick. Even if the owl wasn't there to guide her, Frankie knew without a doubt that Glenda was involved in Rawlins' death in some way. She could arrive at no other logical explanation as to why Kristine and Glenda hadn't gone to the police with the information they uncovered. Kristine was obviously protecting her sister. But what about Glenda? Was she protecting someone or herself? Did Glenda go to the ice shanty to

meet Rawlins? Or was Glenda protecting Dave or Nan or
Roger Kilpatrick?

Frankie's mind was a swimming pool of swirling
thoughts and facts as she made the drive down the
interstate in Southern Wisconsin. Her GPS indicated she
would arrive at her destination in 2 hours and 23 minutes,
calculating out to about 3 p.m.. Frankie checked her gas
gauge, deciding she'd need a pit stop to gas up and fill her
own tank with something. About an hour later, she pulled
into a Kwik Trip, gassed up, grabbed a latte, a couple
bananas and a two packages of peanut butter crackers.
Well, it's better than nothing, she figured. Back on the
road, Frankie tried to look at the rolling scenery on either
side of her to calm her troubled mind. The southeastern
and south-central area of the state was sometimes hilly
and sprawling with large farms, making for wide open
spaces of pasture land. In the summer, it was particularly
lovely with varying shades of emerald green, with black
and white, and brown cows grazing serenely in the
sunshine. The area is one part of the National Ice Age
trail, which extends some 1,200 miles of walking area
throughout Wisconsin. The trail, one of only 11 national
scenic trails, traverses forests, bluffs, and river valleys
carved out by glacial ice more than 12,000 years ago
providing a haven for nature seekers, hikers, backpackers,
bicyclists, and this time of year, snow shoers. Although no
green grass was to be found, today was sunny and near 30
degrees, downright balmy weather for February.

As Frankie neared the mighty Mississippi River area, bluff formations jutted upward along the drive, adding interest and beauty that kept her going for the final leg of her trip. Occasionally, she looked up from her window, searching the bluff clefts for a perched Bald Eagle, expecting to see one at any time since the majestic birds thrived along the Mississippi, and mating season was in full swing. Her focus shifted as, entering Dubuque, she turned off the interstate and onto Highway 52, slowing to watch road signs for Peru Road, her next turn that would lead to the Duedenhoffer farm. Heading west on Peru, the narrow road was coated with sand in spots from winter plowing, but was in overall good driving condition save for the unexpected potholes marring the surface. A mile more, the faithful GPS flashed the upcoming destination, counting down in hundreds of feet. Frankie saw a large painted sign, proudly proclaiming, "SunnyVale Farms, Duedenhoffer Family since 1872," with a painted figure of a Holstein Cow on it. Swinging the SUV into the farm lane, Frankie saw fields on both sides with barbed wire fences, cows munching from feed troughs on her right, a brown stubbled field where feed corn grew on her left. At the end of the lane, she could see the farmhouse growing larger as she approached, a typical large boxy white house with black shutters. A large addition appeared on the right side, probably added to the house sometime in the last 40 years. The farm was equipped with a three-car garage, a large dark red barn with field stone foundation, three pole buildings, and four silos, telling Frankie the Duedenhoffers had a large operation and were probably quite successful.

She parked, carefully took the bakery box from the floor in front, and walked up a pathway that led to a side door, the one that looked the most used. She rang a bell and a short woman with salt and pepper hair opened the door. Frankie put on her brightest smile. "Hello. You must be Loretta Duedenhoffer. I'm here to see Glenda." Frankie sounded sure of herself and was pleased to see the door opening wider for her entrance into the family kitchen.

Loretta called to another room, "Glenda. The lady from church is here to see you." Frankie felt the first flutter of doubt now. She didn't want to be allowed in under false pretenses and wondered who the expected visitor was supposed to be. She shook her head.

"No, Mrs. Duedenhoffer, I'm not…" but her words were lost when the family dog, an energetic Sheltie, bounded into the kitchen, barking and trying to leap on Frankie. Luckily, Loretta came to Frankie's rescue before the treasured cupcake took a nasty spill or Frankie's outfit was dirtied.

"Down, Bella, down!" Loretta grabbed Bella's collar, opened the door and gave her a friendly shove outside. "So sorry about that. Bella's a hyper girl but she isn't mean. Just let me go find Glenda. Please have a seat." She indicated the round kitchen table and chairs. Frankie tried to get her attention once more.

"Thank you, but you see…" Mrs. Duedenhoffer had already paraded out the kitchen and into another part of the house where Frankie could hear bits of conversation. Glenda sounded as if she didn't want to talk to anyone from the church, but her mother was insistent, leaving Frankie guessing that Loretta was concerned for Glenda's well-being - hoping she would either seek counseling from their church or participate in some good old-fashioned soul-healing activity of some kind. Glenda relinquished and entered the kitchen on the heels of her mother, who suggested Frankie come into the living room where they would be more comfortable. As Frankie rose, her eyes met Glenda's and recognition crossed her face. A small cry of surprise emerged from Glenda, stopping Loretta in her tracks, who looked from Frankie to her daughter, in confusion.

Frankie knew she needed to get her words out first and quickly. "I'm sorry. I tried to tell you I'm not from church. I'm from Deep Lakes. I have a delivery for Glenda and some news." At the mention of Deep Lakes, Loretta Duedenhoffer darkened, glowering at Frankie.

"And who are you? You tricked me. You should leave at once." Her words came out like punctuated nails from a nail gun.

"I'm Francine Champagne. I own a bakery in Deep Lakes. I'm delivering an order to your daughter. Please, I don't mean any harm," Frankie hoped her cajoling tone would work. Not budging an inch, Loretta stood in front of Glenda, blocking Frankie's view of her, as if Loretta expected Frankie to tackle her daughter. Finally, Glenda broke the stand-off with a voice that resembled a defeated, cornered mouse.

"Never mind, Momma. I know Francine. Just let her tell me why she's here." Loretta turned and looked sharply at Glenda, shaking her head, clearly worried about Frankie's presence. Before she could speak, Glenda added, "It's okay. We know each other. Francine and I worked together at a charity event last year. She's not a bad person."

Charity event? Oh yes, Frankie recalled, she and Glenda had worked together at the Deep Lakes Cancer Golf Event the past May, manning the charity auction area with other volunteers. She didn't remember talking extensively with Glenda, but there was something specific, wasn't there? Glenda brushed past her mother, turning toward the kitchen counter to grab two coffee mugs from the cupboard.

"Would you like tea or coffee, Francine?" Glenda asked, still facing the counter. When Glenda swept past her, Frankie caught the faint scent of her perfume. Suddenly, as if a dam broke, a vivid memory gushed full throttle into Frankie's mind. Back at the charity auction, Frankie was taking a bathroom break. As she exited the restroom stall, Glenda was standing at the sink, touching up her hair and make-up. Frankie, meaning to make small talk, had jokingly complained about the excessive use of air freshener in the bathroom. Glenda smiled wide and gushed, "Oh, I think that's my perfume you're smelling. It's my signature fragrance, layers of vanilla, citrus and musk. It's called . . ."

But now Frankie was speaking out loud in the Duedenhoffer's kitchen, "Dark Secrets." A confused Glenda turned toward Frankie. "I'm sorry, what did you say?" But, Glenda's confusion was cut short as she realized Frankie was staring at Glenda's stomach, clearly revealing a baby bump under her flared shirt. Flushing red, Glenda turned away again, silently facing the counter. So, Glenda was pregnant? If that was true, who was the father? Frankie knew she needed to regain control of the situation at hand or face being booted out the door. Remembering how she had made tea for Patsy at the church when the pastor's death was announced, Frankie decided to take the reins again.

"Why don't you sit down and tell me where I can find tea and things? I'll make it and then we have to talk, Glenda." Frankie spoke calmly but firmly, looking decidedly at Loretta Duedenhoffer. "Would you please allow us to speak alone, Mrs. Duedenhoffer?" Frankie knew she was taking a big risk in asking. Mrs. Duedenhoffer looked doubtfully at her daughter. Something in Glenda's expression showed resignation, surrender perhaps, Frankie couldn't be certain, but Glenda's mother began walking toward the living room.

"I'll be right in here if you need anything at all," she said tightly.

Tea in hand, Frankie sat opposite Glenda at the kitchen table, having spent the last few minutes scripting her questions so as not to spook Glenda into silence. How to break the ice was at the forefront of Frankie's mind, but Frankie being Frankie, she took the straightforward route. "You were there, at the ice shanty that day." Although Frankie spoke softly, Glenda looked up into Frankie's face as if she'd just been struck.

"How do you - what do you . . ." Glenda couldn't formulate her response.

Frankie cut in. "Dark Secrets. Your perfume, Glenda. The ice shanty smelled strongly of it. The police found broken glass on the ice and a bottle cap. Your perfume bottle." Frankie spoke certainly, but still softly.

Glenda began crying, trying to muffle her sorrow so her mother wouldn't come into the room. When she spoke, she sounded regretful and a little angry. "I should never have agreed to meet him there." Finishing one thought, she began crying harder and laid her head on the table, burying her face into her arms to mute her sobs somewhat. Frankie didn't know if she should approach Glenda, to offer her a comforting pat on the shoulder or a hug. Instead, she decided to wait a few moments to see if she would regain composure. Momentarily, Glenda lifted her head, took the napkin Frankie offered and wiped at her eyes. Glenda's breathing regulated so Frankie decided to tell Glenda something that would hopefully make her feel that Frankie was an ally.

"I know Pastor Rawlins was a fraud. I know about his other identities." As Glenda looked shocked, then relieved, Frankie proceeded with her next question - the big question. "Can you tell me what happened?

Glenda looked as if she might erupt into a second crying jag, but instead, she took a large gulp of tea followed by a deep breath. "I called Rawlins and asked to meet him. I planned to confront him about what I knew about him. About who he really was. I wanted to meet him at the church, but he said he would only meet me in secret. At his ice shanty." It was clear to Frankie that Glenda was perturbed about the meeting place, that she viewed his attitude toward her as an insult. Frankie wondered if they'd had a long-term love affair, if Glenda was a woman scorned by the discovery of his real identity. She asked Glenda if Rawlins knew why they were meeting. "Only that I had something important to discuss with him. I wouldn't tell him anything more." Glenda stalled, thinking.

Frankie began to prod. "Did you intend to blackmail him? Threaten him? What were you hoping for?" Frankie realized she sounded like a police detective doing an interrogation and thought she should back off a little. Glenda seemed to deflate again, but looked appalled.

"No! No!" Well, those were not the right questions to ask, Frankie thought, again patiently waiting for Glenda to say more. "I didn't want anything from that man. I just wanted him to tell the congregation the truth and leave town!" Frankie imagined Glenda would operate nobly, but she wasn't dealing with a righteous man in Rawlins, so Glenda's tactic would never work.

"And Rawlins refused, right?" Glenda nodded, some indignation returning to her voice.

"He accused me of threatening him. Then he said I needed to get rid of the baby." Glenda's voice broke on the word "baby", opening a new round of tears, but she continued talking, anxious to convey feelings she must have bottled up for some time.

"I counseled with Rawlins because I was so depressed. Dave and I had been trying to have a baby for years and were constantly disappointed every month. It was so hard on both of us, on our marriage." Now Glenda was gulping in air, readying herself to say more. "Rawlins said all the right things. Made me feel so good about myself, so - special. I fell for him. I'm so ashamed of myself." Frankie felt sorry for Glenda and all the other women who were taken in by the charms of that dirty scoundrel. She patted Glenda's hand.

"So that's why you left Deep Lakes? Because you were pregnant?" Glenda nodded, looking miserable. Frankie wanted to ask if Dave knew, if the Kilpatricks knew, but she felt like that would be prying too deeply. Anyway, was that relevant to her article or the investigation? She thought she better file that question away for later. "Then what happened at the shanty, Glenda?"

Another sharp intake of breath from Glenda as she

continued. "I was so mad that he wanted to dismiss me as if I were nothing, the baby was nothing. I told him if he didn't come clean, I would tell everyone in town." Her memory triggered a little look of triumph on her face, quickly erased and replaced by a dark frown. "He came toward me, threatening me not to tell anyone. He shoved me quite hard and I lost my balance. There's not much room in there, you know. I fell against the bench." Glenda rubbed the back of her head at the memory. Frankie guessed the blood on the bench came from Glenda's fall and that DNA tests would confirm it. "I guess a smart person would have run away at that point, but I was too mad to. How dare he threaten me when he was the big liar, the fake?" Poor Glenda - it must have been horrible for her to confront a man she believed in wholeheartedly, a man who would be the father of a child she wanted so badly for so long. Frankie couldn't blame her for staying in the shanty, for not backing down. Glenda must have been in shock, full of conflicting emotions. Frankie wondered what she would have done in Glenda's position. Frankie's musings were interrupted by Glenda's sad whimper. "But I was a big liar, too. I lied to the people I loved, to my husband. I was just as much to blame as Rawlins."

While that might be a somewhat truthful statement, Frankie decided Rawlins, acting as a pastor, was held to higher moral standard than Glenda, especially in his role of counselor. Her dander was rising. "Glenda, you were duped by this man and you are not the only woman he tricked." Glenda nodded - she was likely aware there were more victims than her.

"I know that," she said, "that's why I wanted him to tell the truth." Frankie was trying to turn the conversation back to the sequence of events at the shanty, however.

"What happened after you hit your head on the bench?" Glenda retreated to her memory center again.

"I remember getting up and going toward him. I was going to give him a piece of my mind before I left, but he picked up the ice auger and came at me. I couldn't believe it. I dove at him and tried to grab the auger. It was like a tug of war." Glenda began laughing a little and Frankie concluded she was heading toward shock or mania at the horror of the event. "I imagine we looked so silly, in that tiny shanty, slipping on the ice, trying to hold onto the auger. I don't know how it happened, but I gave him a huge push away from me. He fell backwards and the auger and I both fell on top of him. When I got up, the auger point was in his leg. There was blood everywhere. At first, I didn't know which one of us was bleeding." Glenda's climactic re-telling traveled the gamut from hysterical, to frightened, to overwhelmed - leaving her exhausted. Urged on by Glenda's pale face, Frankie came around the table and hugged her tightly, as she would her own daughter.

"It's going to be okay, Glenda. You didn't do anything wrong - it was an accident." Actually, Frankie believed she could make a case for self-defense given the circumstances. Reassuringly, she added, "Please let me help you. Let me take you to Deep Lakes, to talk to Sheriff Goodman." Glenda began shaking her head, but Frankie persisted. "You know it's the right thing to do, Glenda. You have to. You're a good person and you won't be able to live with yourself if you don't tell the truth." Loretta Duedenhoffer, who had likely been listening in to their whole conversation, entered the kitchen.

"Thank God, Glenda. This has to be over." She embraced her daughter and the two cried together. Frankie knew her own mother would have sheltered Frankie the same way Loretta had sheltered Glenda, just as Frankie would have sheltered Sophie and Violet. Frankie smiled, feeling a flood of emotions, but mostly gratitude. Grateful she had pursued her leads, grateful that Rawlins had not been murdered in cold blood, grateful that Glenda would be able to heal now. Then she remembered the cupcake. If there ever was a time when Glenda needed hope, now was it. Taking the white box from the counter, she set it in front of Glenda.

"I brought this for you. It's from Dave," she said simply. Glenda's furrowed brow indicated she couldn't even imagine what could be in the box, but as she peered in at the message on the cupcake, she looked like an excited teenager and another tear rolled down her cheek.

"Do you suppose Dave and I have a chance, even now?" Glenda looked down at the growing baby bump. Frankie grinned, and her words were genuine.

"I believe in second chances, Glenda. Looks like Dave does, too."Frankie hoped that Dave was the kind of man who would be willing to be a father to someone else's child and that the love he and Glenda had for each other would be enough to warrant a second opportunity for a successful marriage.

Chapter 15

The two-hour return drive to Deep Lakes passed like a lightning streak for Frankie, as Glenda needed the stress release of fully confessing all she knew about the Rawlins case, and Frankie had earned the status of trustee to that information. Before leaving the Duedenhoffer farm, Frankie placed a call to Alonzo at the sheriff's department, but had to call his personal cell phone as it was nearing six o'clock already and the office was closed except for dispatch. He picked up almost immediately and Frankie requested he return to his office until they arrived, offering the briefest of information: "I have Glenda Kilpatrick with me and you're going to want to talk to her about Rawlins' death. We have a two-hour drive to get there."

Alonzo merely breathed an exasperated, but surprised exhalation into the receiver, followed by, "Okay. I'll be there." Meanwhile, Glenda packed an overnight bag with clothes and necessities, imagining the worst - she might be arrested for Rawlins' death. Even if she wasn't held in police custody, she would not be allowed to leave town and she couldn't envision Dave or the Kilpatricks offering her a place to stay. Frankie could hear the ongoing regret in Glenda's voice each time she discussed her relationship with Rawlins and her marriage difficulties.

Loretta Duedenhoffer interrupted her daughter's fears. "As soon as your dad gets home, we're driving down to Deep Lakes. We'll take care of finding a hotel. Don't worry, Dear. We're not going to leave you alone." Loretta's voice broke on the last sentence. Frankie said she'd be happy to help them find a place to stay.

"Maybe we can meet at the sheriff's department?" Frankie indicated, handing Loretta a piece of paper with the department address, along with her cell phone number. Loretta nodded wordlessly as she took the information, partly relieved, partly wary as to how the rest of this day would unfold.

Inside the SUV, Frankie handed Glenda a fresh travel mug of hot tea she prepared while Glenda packed, and some snacks she fished out of her tote bag from her last gas station stop. "You must be hungry. It's not much, but better than an empty stomach," she said, offering her a banana and peanut butter crackers. Glenda accepted them gratefully, peeling back the banana while telling Frankie as much as she could, beginning with why she began doubting Rawlins' identity.

"Dave was actually the first person to suspect Rawlins. He told me months ago to be careful around him. Later, before I left, he told me I should stop counseling with him. By that time, I already had… but I was also already pregnant, so I wasn't sure what to do." Glenda took another bite of banana and sip of tea. Glenda told Frankie she discovered the pregnancy in October and shortly thereafter, she found a computer file at Conway Quality Digital Printing Services, with Rawlins name on it and the fake documents it contained about him. Frankie was happy she didn't have to tell Glenda that she already knew this, having heard it from her sister, Kristine. She was afraid Glenda might feel betrayed by her sister.

"Deep Lakes is small; I knew Rawlins was counseling several church women and I knew their marriages had fallen apart. It didn't take me long to assume he was sleeping with more women besides me. In September, while I was working with Missy Geller at the church craft sale, she said something about all of us being part of his 'special angels' or something like that. It made me sick. I quit seeing him without any explanation." Glenda closed her eyes for several moments before continuing.

Frankie watched the light dimming in the sky, announcing the imminent twilight of washed-out slate gray, just before the blackness settled upon them. She couldn't believe how much had happened in one day, and how much more there was to come. Frankie wondered if Glenda knew about the million-dollar personal liability policy Rawlins had purchased through her husband's agency. But guessed she didn't since there appeared to be little communication between her and Dave, and she left town shortly afterwards. She chuckled inwardly for a moment, thinking of the audacity of Rawlins to buy a policy from a man who was not only the church council president, but whose wife he was having an affair with! Frankie asked Glenda where she went after the accident in the ice shanty, unable to conceive what she would have done in the same situation.

"It all felt like a dream, a nightmare, in slow motion. I knew I had to run after I checked his pulse, with all the blood, there was no way he could survive. I panicked. There were so many thoughts running through my head, stay or go, call for help..." Glenda admitted her senses were heightened and, realizing she had walked through blood, leaving a boot print behind on the ice, she had to obliterate it. Using her black woolen scarf, the best she could do was smear the bloody print, then she wiped the bottom of her boots onto the scarf and walked as fast as possible to her car. Frankie replayed that information through her legal mind, the one that had worked for several years at a law firm. The fact Glenda had attempted to conceal the incident was not going to be favorable to her. It made her look guilty, in fact, and she hoped Glenda would hire a seasoned attorney other than her sister. Frankie guessed that Glenda barely missed running into Tim and Troy Larson, who discovered the body. If she had, that would have changed everything - maybe for the better, Frankie concluded.

"I drove out of town and called my sister from my car. I must have been hysterical, and my head was pounding. She told me to go home, to my parents, I mean. She thought I'd be safer out of state than with her in Milwaukee." Yes, Frankie, thought, home is the safest place to be, with people who love you, who will take care of you, at least if you're as lucky as Frankie knew she was. Glenda said she couldn't remember calling her parents, but knew she must have because they were at the door waiting for her, waiting to help her in any way possible. She had a head wound that needed tending, but first Loretta helped her daughter change into the fresh clothes she'd found at a local thrift shop, after cleaning the wound as best she could. Meanwhile, Glenda's father made a fire from a brush pile that included her coat, scarf, boots, and blood-stained clothing. Donning a used winter coat, Loretta took Glenda to the local hospital with a story that she had fallen on the ice near the farm, smacking her head on the door of the shed. Of course, Glenda's injuries corroborated a fall on ice and a head injury caused by a wooden beam, so their story wasn't suspect. The diagnosis was a concussion; Glenda was very lucky she'd made it from Deep Lakes to the Dubuque farm without passing out. Frankie could hear her old bosses at Dickens and Probst piecing a defense together for Glenda, using the concussion to explain her actions in concealing the accident and fleeing the scene.

It appeared to be a reasonable and airtight story, except, as Glenda related it, Frankie could tell she was tortured by the deception. "I knew it was wrong, a horrible lie, and a terrifying secret to keep. I just couldn't decide how to go about making it right. And I betrayed the man I love!" Glenda's voice caught in her throat and tears began to fall. Frankie reached over to console the woman.

"Of course, you must have thought you loved Pastor Rawlins . . ." but Frankie was cut off quickly by Glenda's retort.

"Not him. Dave! I've always loved Dave." Frankie smiled at Glenda with warmth and certainty.

"Then somehow, this is all going to work itself out. It won't be simple, and it will take time and patience, but I truly believe it will work out, Glenda."

Now spent from her confession, Glenda was dozing as Frankie turned off the interstate onto Highway 76 East, which would lead into Deep Lakes in about ten minutes. The SUV clock indicated it was almost 8 p.m. An almost full moon lit up the darkness, revealing a clear sky with just a few gray wisps of clouds. Frankie's mind was on full alert as the drive was coming to a close and so was the Rawlins case, but she knew the highway was a high-volume deer trek, so she kept her eyes peeled to the right and left, looking for telltale glowing eyes. She hoped the deer had eaten dinner and bedded down for the night, but the moonlight was just as helpful to them as it was to humans for navigating purposes, guiding the whitetails into stubbled fields to scavenge any morsels from their paltry winter food supply. Francine saw a small herd in one empty expanse to her left, and she transmitted a mental message for them to stay put as she drove on.

Entering an all but empty town, she made a right turn onto Kilbourn, wondering if the bare streets meant her wine shop was having a slow night. She realized she hadn't talked to Carmen to let her know what was going on, and instantly felt a stab of guilt. She also imagined her mother was wondering why Frankie hadn't made a single appearance in the shop today. "I'll call them both as soon I can," she said aloud, stirring Glenda in the process.

"Hmm, what did you say?" she asked. Frankie was glad Glenda had slept a little - she would need all the strength she could muster to get through the interrogation about to take place.

"We're here, Glenda," Frankie patted her arm and squeezed her hand. Glenda tensed immediately, communicating a little shudder of fear through her body. "Hey, just tell the sheriff what you told me. You'll do fine. I know Alonzo. He really lives up to his name. He is a good man." Frankie parked right up front since the only vehicles in the lot belonged to Deep Lakes officers.

Helping Glenda from the car so she could walk her arm-in-arm through the door, Frankie rang the night bell as the Dispatcher answered, "Can I help you?"

"Sheriff Goodman is expecting us. This is Francine Champagne and Glenda Kilpatrick." The door made a loud echoing buzz, admitting the two women into the entrance where they laid their belongings on a conveyor belt for inspection and walked through the metal detector. Frankie didn't know the young man on duty, assuming he was an academy recruit, hired on the cheap to get some experience before moving onto a full-time gig.

"Ok. You're clear. Take the elevator to the second floor. Office will be down the hall at the end." The dispatcher yawned as he finished his sentence, confirming the usual slow pace of winter with little night time activity or excitement. Frankie smiled inwardly. "If only he knew what was happening here..." she thought.

The elevator doors opened onto a darkened hallway leading to the one lighted room at the end of it - the Sheriff's Department offices. Opening the main door, Frankie was startled to see not only the presence of Officer Shirley Lazaar, but the grim-faced figure of Attorney Kristine Duedenhoffer. She immediately surmised that Loretta had phoned Kristine, probably even before the SUV left the farm driveway, informing her of the latest, urging her to book it to Deep Lakes asap. And, truth be told, Francine felt relieved that Glenda would have legal representation with her as her formal statement was taken. Glenda rushed into the arms of her sister as fresh tears flowed. Kristine hugged her, then pushed her back to arm's length, still holding onto her hands, looking levelly into her sister's face.

"It's going to be okay. I'm here and I'll help you through this." Then, turning a serious face toward Frankie, Kristine commented, "Ms. Champagne. I understand you're responsible for this." Frankie felt like a school girl in the principal's office. She wasn't sure how to respond to the - what was it - accusation?

She mustered the courage to look into Kristine's eyes, "I suppose I am," she said, simply. Kristine nodded at her; Frankie wanted to believe it was a look of understanding, but perhaps not.

Alonzo emerged from his office, introduced himself to Glenda, and ushered the two women into a side office - probably the interrogation room Frankie decided, hoping she would never have to be in that room, on the hot seat. Shirley Lazaar followed behind, two water bottles in hand. After the door closed, Alonzo turned to Frankie, speaking quietly but sternly.

"I don't know how you got so deep into this, Frankie and, truthfully, I don't know if I should be furious with you or what." Alonzo was stumbling over his words, his right hand massaging his neck, an obvious location of some severe tension. Frankie supposed she was responsible for some of that tension and felt bad.

"Lon, I was following my leads, leads I put together so I could write a story…," she began but figured she sounded feeble in the midst of a possible homicide investigation. Alonzo scowled.

"Just wait here. This is going to take a while." Frankie was about to ask if she could go home and come back later - she wanted a shower, something to eat, and wasn't she going to check into hotels for the Duedenhoffers?

But a couple of purposeful strides brought Alonzo to the interrogation room and a closed door was all that remained between Frankie and whatever was happening in that room. She shuddered to think of how frightened Glenda must feel along with how much tribulation she had gone through at the hands of Rawlins, or should she say, Scott Bradley?

Feeling vulnerable herself, Frankie pulled out her cell phone to make a long-overdue call to Carmen, who answered with urgency after just a couple of seconds.

"Where are you, Frankie? I've tried calling you." Oops.

"I must have been out of range. Sorry. I'm okay, Carmen. I'm back in town," Frankie swallowed hard on the next words. "I'm at the sheriff's office - with Glenda Kilpatrick."

A thunderstruck Carmen gasped, "What? Hold on. I'll be there in a few minutes." Carmen explained it was a slow night at the shop, so the baking was ready for tomorrow. Adam and Frankie's mother could handle the clean up and closing. Her mother!

"Carmen, you can't tell my mother anything - not right now. You're going to have to make up a reason to leave. Please, please don't let her know. I'll talk to her soon." Carmen promised, and Frankie was sure she did her best, but 20 minutes later, Peggy Champagne breezed through the sheriff's office door, Carmen on her tail. Frankie jumped up, looking around her mother to glare at Carmen. Carmen shrugged.

"You know I have a terrible poker face, Frankie. I can't lie to people, especially your mother." Peggy embraced Frankie hard, then pulled back to scold her.

"What in the name of Wonder Bread is going on here, Francine?" Peggy Champagne made it her policy never to invoke God or Heaven except in prayer, so she continually came up with new "what in the name ofs" as the occasion called for it.

Frankie sighed, sitting back down. "I can't tell you too much, Mom. I'm in enough trouble as it is." Peggy was indignant.

"What do you mean, you're in trouble? I can't believe you've done anything *that* bad." Frankie laughed, uncertain whether her mother was defending her or not. She gave Peggy and Carmen a brief synopsis of the day, starting with the appointment in Milwaukee that led her to Iowa and Glenda's story. She kept the details to the bare minimum, but both Peggy and Carmen expressed surprise, shock, and even admiration at Frankie's discoveries. "Oh, goodness Dear, you must be starving and tired. Here, I brought you something from the shop." Peggy produced a container with a chunk of Mama Mia quiche - a suitable substitute for the pizza Frankie was suddenly craving. In a white bakery bag were four Paczkis, a fork and a knife. Carmen held out a large travel mug with a latte inside.

"You two are simply awesome," Frankie said, taking a big bite of quiche and drink of latte. "You know, you don't have to stay with me. I have no idea how long I'm going to be here." Frankie was overcome by a sudden overpowering urge to cry. "On second thought…," she began.

The department door opened again, revealing Glenda's parents, looking worn with worry. Introductions were made, and Frankie explained that Glenda and Kristine were behind the closed door across the room. The Duedenhoffers sat down in the hard-wooden chairs next to Frankie's mother. Frankie rose, found more water bottles after seeing where Shirley Lazaar had retrieved them, and handed them out to the line-up.

"You might as well take off your coats," she said to Glenda's parents. "We're going to be here awhile, I imagine." Then she remembered offering to help them find a place to stay. "Where are you staying?" The Duedenhoffers looked at each other, both shrugging their shoulders and slumping from weariness. It was Peggy who sprang into action; no surprise to Frankie since her mother was born for the role of hostess and problem solver.

"Oh, let me make a reservation for you. There are a couple of chains on 404 but I think the nicest place in town is the old Hotel Divine. I know the owners and I'm sure this time of year, it will be easy to get a room." The Duedenhoffers were grateful to allow someone to take over this small decision, having too many pressing matters to think about at the moment. Frankie wondered if they were at all concerned that they might be facing charges for their roles in covering up the accident.

Several minutes later, Peggy returned from the hallway where she'd made a call to Mike and Lori Hansen, owners of Hotel Divine on nearby Doty Street. "There are two rooms waiting for you. You just have to ring the bell when you get there." She handed the hotel address to Glenda's father along with a rudimentary drawing of a map to get there. When Frankie arched a brow at her mother, raising her hands in expectation of additional information, Peggy continued, looking smugly at Frankie, as if her daughter would have thought she couldn't handle the situation discreetly. "I told the Hansens we had unexpected guests and it might be awhile before they arrived." Frankie smiled in her direction. She should have known her mother would be able to create a convincing story. They all sat in silence after that, watching the closed interrogation room door expectantly as the wall clock ticked loudly, measuring the minutes much slower than normal.

When the door finally opened, Alonzo wasn't certain whom he should question first, finally settling for Mrs. Duedenhoffer, while Shirley Lazaar ushered Mr. Duedenhoffer into another office to take his statement. Alonzo told Frankie to go home but, "Don't leave town. I'll call you tomorrow morning." He gave her a small smile, but could that be on account of Frankie's mother, she wondered. No matter, Frankie was ready to go home and go to bed, thankful the day was over. She studied Glenda and Kristine. Both were obviously drained; Glenda's face was blotchy from crying, but Kristine looked steady enough. Frankie was satisfied Kristine would be a rock of support for Glenda, so Frankie's work was done for the day, except for one small bit of business.

"Ms. Duedenhoffer," she spoke to Kristine, "I hope you can forgive me. I didn't mean to hurt Glenda or deceive you." Kristine shook Frankie's hand firmly.

"I think you did our family a favor, in the long run. At least, I hope so."

Despite the long day, the barrage of information Frankie heard, and the hundreds of miles she'd traveled, sleep would not come. Frankie found an adrenaline rush that flooded her thoughts, making her head throb. The knowledge that Friday was on the horizon, bringing with it a deadline for an article that must be filed with *Point Press*, kept nagging Frankie's overstuffed brain, until she finally gave up. Turning on the bedroom lamp, she grabbed her charging cell phone then padded to the kitchen, opened her laptop, and carried it over to the living room sofa. How could she write a fair article without hurting the Duedenhoffers and the Kilpatricks? Only now did she realize that reporters cannot please everyone involved in a story, that being a reporter came with distinct consequences, many of which were unpleasant. More than anything, Frankie wanted to do the story justice, wanted the truth revealed without emotion or bias, what a tightrope she was walking. Only now it dawned on Frankie how difficult Alonzo's job must be, using only the available laws in place to seek justice when a crime was committed, no matter how he felt about the victim or the perpetrator. Just like Alonzo, Frankie had a job to do as a member of the press, regardless of her own personal feelings or judgment. Reviewing her notes as she wrote, slowly the article came pouring out onto the screen.

Trying to think objectively as she believed a reporter must, Frankie had to admit that Glenda and the other congregation women were at least partly responsible for their own decisions and actions. Still, a man like Scott Bradley, preying upon vulnerable people, people with emotional problems, people who were trusting - just made her blood boil! And he had a local accomplice in Milton Conway, a businessman whom citizens of Deep Lakes trusted and supported! She felt her dander rise once more. She would have liked to leave Glenda's name out of the article but knew she couldn't. Soon, the whole town would know the facts anyway, or some concocted version of the facts. Soon, Whitman County officers would release all the information to the press and Abe Arnold would pounce on it, hungry to serve it up in his newspaper to an astonished community. But, Frankie would already have scooped Abe and *The Watch*, publishing it in a larger regional paper, where so many more people would read every word. *Her* words. Frankie felt the weight of responsibility on her shoulders. She needed to make the story right, truthful, and fair. The next few hours, devoid of sleep and running on her quest for veracity, Frankie carefully selected facts and details to reveal to the public, using precise language and voice. By the time she was satisfied with the article, dawn was two hours away. She slept on top of the closed laptop.

Chapter 16

Even the most delicious gravy has some lumps
stuck to the bottom of the kettle.
– JAR

At 6 a.m., Frankie awoke to a text notification from her phone wedged somewhere in the sofa cushions. Already a half hour later than she hoped to wake up, she frowned, then giggled at Carmen's message: "Wake up: I can hear your alarm clock going off all the way downstairs!" So, Carmen was at her post in the Bubble and Bake kitchen, thank goodness. Frankie replied a thank you and notice she was heading to the shower, something she intended to do last night. First, however, she called Glenda Kilpatrick, knowing she would likely wake her up.

Next, she tapped in a call to Alonzo's cell phone. "Yup," came the abrupt answer, sounding irritated and probably tired. She figured Alonzo likely had about as much sleep as Frankie. Getting straight to the point, Frankie spoke forcefully.

"I wrote an article on the Rawlins case for *Point Press* last night. My editor needs it today." Alonzo was terse.

"What do you want from me? I'm not ready to

comment right now - still wrapping up loose ends."
Frankie softened her stance.

"Maybe I just want to know it won't ruin our
friendship if I submit the article," adding, "When are you
going to release information to the press?" Silence on the
other end - she hoped Alonzo hadn't dozed off.

"I might call a press conference later today. Depends.
You know, you can't publish Glenda's story word-for-
word. In case of a trial." Trial? Frankie hoped Glenda
wouldn't have to go on trial.

"I already spoke to Glenda, so I know you're not
formally holding her. You really think this will go to trial?"
Alonzo couldn't be sure, notifying Frankie that Glenda
was not formally charged with a crime - yet. Frankie
knew enough from her former life as a legal assistant to
expect that Glenda would be charged with some form of
obstruction and tampering with evidence, but it was a safe
bet she wouldn't be charged with intentional homicide or
even manslaughter. She was even willing to place a heavy
bet that a plea deal would be reached. She was certain the
Duedenhoffers and the Kilpatricks would want this to
end as quietly as possible.

"I have to send this article to my editor. If she wants
to wait for the press conference, that's her call to make. I
can promise you that the article is objective, just the facts,
Alonzo." Alonzo's grunt on the other end of the phone
didn't ease the tension, and Frankie found herself getting
hot under the collar at his lack of faith in her ability to be

objective. "Besides, my editor is experienced. She'll know if anything's out of line." It appeared Alonzo didn't have much faith in her editor either.

"Yeah, well, that doesn't mean she won't print it anyway. You know how the press can be - a nice juicy story is hard to resist." Again, the heat rose from Frankie's neck to her jawline, creating a twitch. Alonzo didn't even know Magda Guzman. She didn't appreciate the stereotype that all journalists were shady.

"Well anyway Alonzo, I cleared the story with Glenda. I have her permission and her lawyer's permission to go to press with what I have." Frankie didn't like it that she sounded smug - it wasn't supposed to be like this between friends.

"Then why did you even call me, Frankie?" Alonzo snapped, but sounded defeated at the same time.

Frankie's answer was honest and easy: "Because I respect you, that's why."

Twenty minutes later, Frankie was working on Paczkis in the kitchen with Jovie, Tess, and Carmen when Magda called, congratulating her on the article and the information she was able to obtain.

"Truth is, I didn't think you could do it. So, I'm sorry for jumping to conclusions about you. The article is good. Just going to check on a couple of legal and ethical policies. I may have to tweak it but I'm not making any major changes. You were careful, and I appreciate it, Francine." Frankie beamed at the comments. She felt like she scored a major victory - her first real piece of investigative reporting and, she couldn't help herself, she'd scooped Abe Arnold! For once, Frankie felt that being a woman was a definite advantage in a field dominated by men, because her information could only be obtained by gaining the trust of women - Glenda, Coral Anders, Kristine, and even Shirley Lazaar. This morning Glenda had essentially said those words to Frankie on the phone, giving Frankie peace of mind as she'd received Glenda's blessing on the article, despite it meaning a public display of the terrible ordeal. As soon as the case concluded, Frankie intended to write a follow-up in-depth piece on the matter, and hoped Magda would be receptive to it. Being objective was important, but writing something substantive mattered to Frankie, too. An hour later, Magda called to confirm the story would run in the Saturday edition, and again in the Sunday paper, following the official press conference, so long as Frankie could send an updated version sometime today or Saturday depending on the press conference date. Frankie said she would.

By 9 a.m., most of the bakery case was empty and just a few lingering customers were seated at tables in the shop. The door jangled as Frankie was wiping down an empty table, balancing a couple plates and coffee mugs. She raised her head to see none other than Barty Gouge and Rance Musgrove, the Shar-Pei and the Muskrat, from *The Whitman Watch*. Frankie wondered with suspicion why Abe had sent in his lap dogs. Did he already know about Glenda Kilpatrick? Had he spoken to Alonzo? Did he get official word of the upcoming press conference?

Both reporters were painted with expressions of beggars coming for table scraps, rousing Frankie's suspicions further. "How can I help you? Barty. Rance." Frankie nodded cordially at each man. Barty was clearly invested in the bakery case, swallowing hard each time his mouth-watering gaze met a pastry on display below the glass. It was Rance who took charge of their apparent mission to Bubble and Bake. He spoke, his voice cracking on a couple of words.

"Abe wanted us to pick up your latest feature article." Rance took a deep breath before adding a definitive "Please." Frankie decided to play dumb.

"What article are you talking about? I don't think I have anything new to offer the paper," she piled on a little syrup with a smile at Rance. Rance looked at Barty, clearly hoping for an assist, but Barty was flirting heavily now with a row of Paczkis, his face almost pressed against the bakery case. Was that a little dribble of drool on his chin? Rance cleared his throat, squinting and blinking, looking at a fixed spot on the shop's floor.

"Abe said you brought something in a couple days ago. He didn't think he had room for it, but he changed his mind. He definitely wants to print it today for the weekend edition." Again, Rance seemed to gulp for air, then added an emphasized, "Please." Frankie wanted to burst into laughter, thinking how diligently Abe must have been in his instructions. Figuring Rance, at least, had squirmed enough, she held up her index finger.

"Just a minute. I'll go get a copy - it's upstairs though." Then, with a curious glance at Barty, Frankie asked loudly, "Barty! Did you want something from the bakery case?" Barty jumped, roused from his bakery stupor with Frankie's booming question. He straightened up then, trying unsuccessfully to smooth out the wrinkles in his khakis, using the toe of one shoe to balance on one leg as he slid his foot across his pant leg, almost falling directly into the bakery case. Frankie thought she couldn't take much more of the Barty and Rance show. "I'll be right back," she said, escaping up the backstairs, but not before asking Carmen if she could please get some bakery for "*The Watch's* finest reporters." Carmen was taken aback, suppressed a laugh, and headed out front. A few minutes later, Frankie produced the article about the upcoming Wine Pairing Event and ushered the two reporters out the door. Only then did she laugh out loud, still bewildered about Abe's change of heart.

Alonzo and Shirley Lazaar held a press conference on the Rawlins case just before 5 p.m. Friday, after taking Glenda into custody earlier in the day. She was released on bond and instructed to remain in Deep Lakes, pending charges of obstruction of a police investigation, tampering with evidence, and fleeing the scene of an accident. However, those charges never came to light as the story of Rawlins' fraud and crime spree circulated, revealing his true character. The facts only bolstered Glenda's statement of a struggle that ended in self-defense, which proved to be the most accurate rendition of the event. Rawlins' accomplice, Milton Conway, turned out to be a first cousin to Scott Bradley and although there was no proof, he had likely helped him out of past scrapes with the law. Conway was charged with falsifying documents, and collaborating with and harboring a known fugitive, a case that would be tied up for a while as an ongoing investigation. Deemed a flight risk, Conway was denied bail, leaving his wife, Judy, to run the printing business. Frankie wondered if Judy would stand by her man or send him packing once the dust settled.

Long before Glenda's fate was determined, Frankie attended the Valentine Jubilee, which she hoped might bring her brother, Nick, and Jovie Luedtke together. They enjoyed one another's company, but Frankie didn't think Jovie was Nick's type. At least Jovie got out of the house and her mother's tight grasp for the evening. Frankie was surprised to see Garrett Iverson at the Jubilee dinner, accompanied by a pretty, and much younger woman. To her dismay and disbelief, she felt an old wound opening within her heart - how vulnerable she truly was when it came to relationships, even potential ones, she decided. Fortunately, Garrett and his companion approached Frankie's table where he introduced the lovely woman as his daughter, Amanda - probably around the same age as Sophie, Frankie guessed. Sometime later, Alonzo confided that Garrett was interested in the identity of Frankie's date, too, thoroughly relieved to discover that Nick was Frankie's brother. Well, maybe the potential relationship still had possibilities, Frankie mused.

The Valentine Jubilee event was highly successful, helping First Congregational to recoup some much-needed funds after Scott Bradley cleaned the church's coffers, something Dave Kilpatrick suspected, then attempted to track so he could have the "pastor" investigated by church officials. Especially after Rawlins/Bradley purchased the personal liability policy, Dave was on the fast track to find out reasons the pastor would require said policy. It became obvious after Bradley's death, and incidents of his phony counseling with women, that he thought the policy would protect him from eventual lawsuits. Interestingly, Dave had requested a meeting with Rawlins/Bradley the same day Glenda did, preparing to confront him about the church's missing money, but that meeting had been pushed off until later by Rawlins once Glenda had also contacted him to meet as a matter of urgency. Yet a third member of the Kilpatricks - namely Nan - had decided to pay a surprise visit to the pastor at the church that same morning, to give him a piece of her mind for his interference in her son's marriage, and it was her angry reaction at finding him absent that Frankie witnessed as she pulled into the church driveway that day. January 29th was indeed a day of convergence; no matter how you sliced it, Rawlins was going to be facing a Kilpatrick. His past was clearly catching up with him, sealing his fate.

Officer Pflug had been sent to Missouri after the discovery of Scott Bradley's former boss. Clayton Kirkpatrick had been fired from the Jefferson City Savings and Loan after his underling, Bradley, had swindled the bank's customers. Kirkpatrick had a viable motive for murder, but, he was clean with an ironclad alibi. Officer Pflug's time in Missouri was for naught, except for the discovery of Bradley's former girlfriend and toddler son – the mystery woman who was calling Patsy Long at the church, trying to get child support money out of Rawlins. It turned out the girlfriend had threatened to expose the phony pastor, but she too, had an alibi, never having set foot in Wisconsin.

Frankie wondered if Scott Bradley had a life insurance policy that might help support his toddler son, knowing the personal liability policy probably wouldn't pay. Meanwhile, Pflug's wild goose chase didn't sit well with his ego when he returned to find the case was wrapping up, thanks to Francine Champagne. Frankie was specific in omitting Pflug from her news article, only referring to the sheriff and investigating officer, Shirley Lazaar, by name. Pflug was still en route from Missouri causing him to miss the press conference.

Frankie spent much of February trying to patch up her friendship with Alonzo, complete her shop's inventory, and pull off a glorious Wine Pairing Event. By the end of the month, she had happily located a good home for Brambles, with none other than Helen Thursten, a woman who was decidedly a cat person and who could be just as independent and dismissive as the average feline.

Frankie's conversations with Alonzo began uncertainly, but progressed as Alonzo grudgingly accepted Frankie as a part-time reporter, an acceptance that came with a solid warning to operate within the boundaries of the law, and not to interfere with investigations. She only promised to do her best as the occasion arose. Meanwhile, her wandering mind entertained the notion that perhaps Jovie Luedtke would make a suitable girlfriend for Alonzo. Hmm. The fireflies began tap dancing, talking at the same time in her ear, clearly onboard with the notion.

Glenda's return to Deep Lakes was highlighted by a chance at reconciliation with Dave, although there would be much to work through in the forgiveness department. Frankie was pleased to find out she had judged Dave correctly as a man who wanted to be a father, and would be. Within a couple of months, the couple relocated to Eau Claire; an insurance agency opening offered them a chance to begin anew, and life in a new town allowed them to decide what secrets were worth keeping. A couple months after their move, Glenda gave birth to a daughter, an event openly celebrated by Nan and Roger Kilpatrick, who happily showed off photos of their grandchild at a church breakfast. Frankie made a point to congratulate Nan and Roger, handing them a large heavy cardboard box to take to Glenda on their next visit.

"I know Glenda's going to be happy to get this," Frankie said. Inside the box was a stunning round stained glass piece, featuring two bluebirds and a nest of babies that Frankie generously purchased at the Valentine Jubilee.

Spring was on the horizon, not just by calendar date, but by weather, when Frankie wrote her opinion column about the deception of a church congregation in a small, unsuspecting Wisconsin town. Both Carmen and Peggy applauded Frankie's reporting and encouraged her to continue her professional efforts, but Frankie decided her main ambition was to run a successful business and cultivate her vineyards with an occasional side of journalism. "I'm keeping my options open in all areas of life right now, but I'm passionate about Bubble and Bake and I love working with everyone there," Frankie confided to both women, who were happy to hear it. Still, Frankie wanted to put a final period on the January death that kept Deep Lakes in the deep freeze that winter.

Epilogue:
The Newspaper Article in *Point Press*

Deep Lakes Pastor is Wolf in Sheep's Clothing
By Francine Champagne

The small community of Deep Lakes in Central Wisconsin is a trusting one, a place where people know their neighbors and support one another. So how did this tightly woven community end up the site of both a mysterious death, and a web of deceit? Sadly, one of the town's own citizens, businessman Milton Conway, provided the so-called "Pastor Bradford Rawlins" the means to a devious end -with forged documents, enabling him to establish his residence in Deep Lakes as the new minister of First Congregational Church. Rawlins bled to death on January 29th when his ice auger struck his femoral artery during a struggle while he was ice fishing on Lake Loki. The death appears to be the result of an accident, but potentially could have been avoided if "Rawlins" had simply been an honest man.

Rawlins, also known as Scott Bradley, was a wanted man in the state of Missouri, where a bench warrant was outstanding for more than two years. Rawlins/Bradley, formerly employed by the Jefferson City Savings and Loan Association, was absconded with more than $150,000 of the bank's and customer's money skimmed from illegally drafted loans. Rawlins/Bradley preyed upon elderly and disabled S & L customers, then escaped Missouri with a new identity as a pastor to replace the beloved deceased minister of First Congregational Church in Deep Lakes, cleverly helped by Conway, his cousin.

During Rawlins/Bradley's two-year tenure there, the church began to suffer both financial and spiritual losses. Not only was Rawlins/Bradley skimming church funds, but his "counseling" techniques resulted in a number of broken marriages, along with a decline in membership. In particular, the phony minister used his charismatic power to charm many female members of the congregation, often convincing them to comply with his inappropriate wishes under the guise of ministry.

Attorney Kristine Duedenhoffer discovered Rawlins' real identity, investigating the minister on behalf of her sister, Glenda Kilpatrick, who was held in police custody connected to Rawlins' death. Kilpatrick, a lifelong Congregationalist, was one of several women counseled by Rawlins, and a victim of his treachery. Yet it is Kilpatrick who says she feels "tremendous shame" about the accident which caused Rawlins' death. Kilpatrick states she met Rawlins/Bradley January 29th on Lake Loki at his request, where she planned to confront him about his deception, but the imposter threatened her physically and a struggle ensued with the ice auger between them, resulting in the fatal injury.

Since the truth about Rawlins' identity became public, many members of the congregation have come forward with statements about his conduct while posing as the church pastor. Whitman County Officer Shirley Lazaar led the investigation following Rawlins' suspicious death, noting, "We are grateful to the women who came forward with their stories. Without them, we wouldn't have been able to piece this difficult case together as quickly and clearly as we did." Lazaar, a retired Milwaukee police officer, followed the maze of evidence that traversed through Wisconsin, Missouri, Iowa and beyond in just two weeks. The Rawlins/Bradley story continues to evolve as two other previous identities have come to light, including Rowan Bradford, a Nevada man who was suspected of illegal gambling activity while employed in an Elko casino, and Ronald Scott, a bank security guard in Billings, Montana, where he was wanted for his involvement in a robbery at the bank where he worked. A slippery grifter, Rawlins/Bradley always managed to avoid being caught, assuming a new identity in an unsuspecting community; however, in Deep Lakes, he met his match at last - perhaps portraying a pastor tipped the scales of justice against him.

The Deep Lakes community is a resilient one where kindness prevails over judgment and betrayal. Mayor Adele Lundgren says the healing process is ongoing.

"We are a connected community. Everyone here knows someone who was hurt by this imposter. But together, we will move forward and look to brighter days." Lundgren points to upcoming community events slated for spring, designed to promote unity. "We are proud to be hosting the "Outstanding Women" event in March, showcasing the many talented women in Deep Lakes." The event will take place in conjunction with International Women's Day on March 9-11, featuring workshops in a variety of professions and skills, musical performances, poetry and prose readings, and martial arts demonstrations led by Deep Lakes women. Other spring events are currently in the planning stages. Bottom line: all communities must promote a climate where women are empowered, not intimidated. Deep Lakes has been reminded of this doctrine in recent weeks, and paid a dreadful price in exchange. May all neighbors, near and far, bookmark this disheartening chapter in one small town and join forces to propagate that which is true and good for all.

Footnote: The unmistaken irony present in the demise of "Bradford Rawlins" is, of course, that his life ended on Lake Loki, named for the Norse trickster, who was also described in literature as a demonic force. That the imposter who sowed deception wherever he roosted, should succumb to his eventual downfall on this lake of all places, might be viewed as a fitting conclusion.

Acknowledgments

The content of this book would not have been possible without the life experiences I've enjoyed over the years. My dear dad, Alan Christensen, taught me almost all I know about gardening and instilled in me a life-long love of the natural world. Dad, I wish you were here to see how things turned out. My darling mom, Delilas Christensen, put my hands into cookie dough before I started school, probably to keep me from constantly pestering her. For this, I am grateful, because baking has been a therapeutic part of my life ever since. Both of my parents were hobby writers and encouraged their kids to explore all genres of reading and writing.

My three daughters taught me about enduring love, even in dark times, and gave me my best reasons to become a fierce woman. My husband, John, is the best publicity director anyone can have. Having self-published his own book, he has been my guru in navigating the publishing world and using technology to promote my craft.

I want to recognize both The University of Wisconsin Fruit Program and authors

Teryl R. Roper, Daniel L. Mahr, Patricia S. McManus, and Brian R. Smith for the informative booklet *Growing*

Grapes in Wisconsin. Both publications offer valuable advice to any stout-hearted Wisconsinites who want to try their hand at grape cultivation.

Since Frankie and I are both practitioners of hygge (pronounced hoo-ga in many circles), I must recommend the book I found helpful in cultivating hygge in my home, *The Little Book of Hygge, Danish Secrets to Happy Living*, by Meik Wiking. You certainly don't have to be Danish to understand the feeling of contentment that comes from sharing experiences with the people you love the most.

I also need to thank my early editors: Mom, Jen, Kay, Jill, and Angie - best guinea pigs ever and they work for free. That's real love.

Thank you to Ten16 Press for taking a chance on a new author, especially my creative team: Shannon, Kaitlyn, and Tom.

Finally, if you're reading this, I acknowledge you for taking a chance on a first-time author, who wrote this book because Frankie and other characters wouldn't allow me to sleep at night until I gave them a home on the page. Writing is a wonderful experience, but like all experiences in life, it only becomes genuine when shared.

Recipes

Frankie's Springtime Quiche

Use a 10-inch pie plate and your favorite single pie crust recipe, unbaked (Do not feel the least bit guilty if you buy a premade crust!). Roll out the crust and line your pie plate, pinching around the top to flute. Prick the bottom and sides with a fork - don't go crazy, just prick to allow crust to breathe.

Place the following in order in the unbaked crust:
Saute in a little oil:

 ½ cup diced onion

 1 cup chopped asparagus

 1 ½ tsp Herbs de Provence

 1 tsp French Four Spice

 1-2 cloves minced Garlic

 A sprinkle of Salt

Saute until softened over medium heat. Let cool a few minutes, layer onto crust.

Add on top of veggies:

 8 slices crumbled cooked Bacon

 2 cups shredded Sharp Cheddar Cheese

Over the top of this pour: 5 beaten eggs combined with 1 ½ cups whole milk. Zest one Lemon over the top before baking

Bake at 415 for 15-20 minutes, then turn down the oven to 330 and bake until golden brown on top, or about 30 minutes. Rest for 10 minutes, then cut and chow down!

Butterhorns

Dough:
2 packages Yeast
¼ cup warm water (110 degrees)
2 cups warm whole milk (110 degrees)
½ - ¾ cup Butter, melted
½ cup sugar
1 egg, room temperature
1 tsp salt
6 cups Flour (you may not need all of it)

Dissolve yeast in warm water, let stand 5 min.

In large bowl, combine warm milk and butter. Stir together and allow to cool.

Add egg and sugar. Then stir in yeast. First add 3 cups of flour and mix in. (A Stand Mixer is great if you have one.)

Add more flour, a cup at a time. The dough should look like shiny satin and be soft, sticky.

Place dough in a greased bowl. Cover and refrigerate for 24 hours.

Punch down the dough. Divide it in half. Roll out

one of the halves on a floured board to a 12 inch circle. Brush circle with melted butter (maybe a tablespoon, then half of whatever filling you make). Cut the circle into 12 wedges (looks like pizza slices).

Begin at the wide end, roll up into a horn shape, pointed end will be on the bottom when you place them on your cookie sheet.

Place about 2 inches apart, cover with a towel. Let them rise for an hour. Bake at 350 for about 15 minutes. When cool, ice or glaze them as you wish.

Filling options:
CinnaNut filling
1 TB Melted Butter
½ cup Dark Brown Sugar
½ cup chopped Pecans
1 tsp Cinnamon
1 pinch Salt

Combine all above ingredients.
Spread onto rolled out wedges.

Peach filling
3 peaches, chopped into chunks
2 TB Brown Sugar
1 tsp cinnamon (if you want)
1 TB Arrowroot Powder
1 TB Lemon Juice

Combine Peach filling ingredients in a saucepan over medium heat.

Mixture will thicken as it heats. You can allow it to boil. Cool it before spreading on dough.

Dark Side Chocolate Cherry Muffins

*If you can't get Door County Wisconsin cherries,
you can substitute another tart cherry.*

1 ¾ cup All Purpose Unbleached Flour
½ tsp Baking Soda
1 TB Baking Powder
⅛ tsp Salt
¼ cup Butter, softened at room temp
¼ cup Butter, melted (you will bloom the cocoa in the melted butter)
¼ cup Cocoa
½ cup Brown Sugar (I like dark brown)
2 Eggs
1 cup of plain yogurt or sour cream, your choice
2 tsp vanilla extract or 1 tsp almond extract
½ cup whole milk
2 cups of Door County tart cherries (fresh - cut in half, or frozen - thawed and well-drained)

Add the cocoa to the melted butter and stir until smooth. Set aside. Combine flour, baking soda, powder, and salt in large bowl.

In another bowl, mix butter and brown sugar until creamy. Beat in eggs until well-mixed. Beat in butter/cocoa mixture. Add in yogurt or sour cream and extract until combined.

Stir the wet into the dry ingredients. Gently, fold in the cherries with a mixing spoon.

Fill muffin liners about ⅔ full. Top with mini chocolate chips, gently pressed into batter, and a sprinkle of coarse baking sugar or cinnamon sugar.

Bake at 350 for about 30 minutes (depending on your oven. Check for doneness with a toothpick. You don't want to overbake them.)

Snow Pea Soup with Coriander (A nod to Joy's Dad)

2-3 large Leeks (sliced)
2-3 cloves minced Garlic
¼ cup Butter
1 TB Flour
4-6 Green Onions (sliced)
4 cups Fresh Snow Peas or Sugar Snap Peas with edible pods (remove strings)
4-6 cups Chicken or Vegetable Stock (I like chicken)
1 TB Lemon Juice
1 TB Whole Coriander Seed (you can add more to your liking)

1- 2 tsp French Thyme
½ tsp Black Pepper
½ tsp Kosher Salt

Saute leeks in the butter until limp. Add minced garlic and saute for another 2 minutes. Add flour and cook another minute. Add the stock, green onions, spices and herbs. Bring to a boil, reduce heat and simmer for about 20 minutes or so.

Add in fresh peas in the pods and cook another 10 minutes. Add the lemon juice. Taste test to see if more spices are needed. Let this settle, keeping warm on low heat to blend the flavors.

If you are a veggie fan, you can experiment with other veggies, adding them in with the green onion. Carrots taste great and look pretty with the green peas. I've seen similar recipes in which the soup is pureed, but my dad would never puree a soup, so we ate it as written in the recipe.

Deep Dark Secrets
Book Club Discussion Questions

1. Do you know any communities like Deep Lakes?
2. What do you think of the setting for this novel?
3. What role does Winter play in the novel? How would the novel be different if it was set in another season or month?
4. Which character do you most identify with and why?
5. Which characters did you enjoy? Why?
6. Were there any characters you disliked? Why?
7. What makes Frankie an atypical protagonist?
8. What do you think drives/motivates Frankie in life? In her business? In her desire to investigate the murder?
9. What are some of Frankie's character flaws? How do her flaws help her or hurt her investigation?
10. Discuss characters Carmen and Alonzo. Are either of them a foil to Frankie's character?
11. Which characters do you see playing the role of antagonists? Discuss these characters and how they advance the plot.
12. Track the clues the author includes in the novel. Which ones did you find helpful? Were there any clues that led you astray?
13. Who did you see as suspects in the murder? Why?
14. Evaluate the quotes used at the beginning of each

chapter. Were the quotes meant to be clues? Did the quotes enhance the novel?

15. Did you solve the mystery before the end of the book? If so, when and how?

16. What do you think of the budding romance between Frankie and Garrett? How would you like to see their relationship proceed?

17. What do you foresee for Alonzo's future?

18. Which wine do you find most appealing? Why?

19. Which bakery item do you think you would buy at Bubble and Bake?

20. Since this book is the first in a Deep Lakes mystery series, what advice would you give the author? How would you rate the author's writing style?

21. What did you like most and least about this book?

Joy Ann Ribar is a Wisconsin native who embraces her Scandinavian roots - wine-tasting and food-munching from every culture. A semi-retired English educator, Joy teaches writing classes at Madison College. She earned a Journalism degree from UW-Madison and a Master's in Education from UW-Oshkosh. She and her husband, John, run a backyard buffet for winged creatures, plus the occasional furry critter. Someday, they plan to sell everything, buy an RV, and escape Wisconsin winters. See more at JoyRibar.com

Deep Lakes Mystery Series: Book 2

Spring has sprung in Deep Lakes, Wisconsin where plans for the Roots Festival are underway. The Mayor assigns Bubble and Bake owner, Frankie Champagne, the task of assisting the town's granite quarry heiress in creating a presentation for the festival. Frankie becomes close to the heiress, who takes pride in rededicating her family's park to the community. But things go awry when the heiress turns up dead, raising Frankie's suspicions, especially since a stranger in town has been meeting with the heiress, too. Frankie follows a number of trails uncovering motives of greed, revenge, heartbreak, and family loyalty. An extended visit from Frankie's and Carmen's aunts complicate Frankie's sleuthing as the aunts make mischief. Will the baker-vintner be able to dig deep to expose the roots of this mystery, or will she be struck sideways by a branch from her own family tree? Find out in *Deep Bitter Roots,* the second book in the *Deep Lakes Mystery Series,* coming soon.

9 781645 380344